"Johanna," he whispered as he woke me up the next morning. Or, that same day to be exact.

Having sex with Jack Schiller was very similar to playing poker with him. He was hard to read, it got competitive at times, and was altogether an incredibly exhilarating experience.

But I didn't get these delicious stubble burns all over my body when playing poker.

"Johanna," he whispered again, nudging me this time.

Two things went through my mind. One, I had a plane to catch today and I had absolutely no idea what time it was. And two—"How'd you know my name was Johanna?" I tried to keep the suspicion out of my voice, but had he investigated me in some way?

I had my back to him, his arm thrown over my waist, his legs entwined with mine. I felt his shrug along my back. "Ben and Saul call you Hannah. You introduce yourself and play poker as Anna. And Lorelei calls you Jo. I am a detective after all, Johanna" he said.

"Oh," I said, letting out a small sigh of relief. I was just about to ask about the time when he continued.

"Johanna Elizabeth Dawson. Born thirty-four years ago in Madison, Wisconsin to Albert and Evelyn Dawson. One older sister, two brothers, one older, one younger. Attended high school and college in Madison. Left college—"

"Hey," I said, turning to him. My outrage fell away as I took in his tousled hair, his well-used mouth, giving me a grin that made me press my body into his, all thought of his looking into my past gone.

Other Titles by Mara Jacobs

The Worth Series
(Contemporary Romance)
Worth The Weight
Worth The Drive
Worth The Fall
Worth The Effort
Totally Worth Christmas

Freshman Roommates Trilogy
(New Adult Romance)
In Too Deep
In Too Fast
In Too Hard (coming soon)

Anna Dawson's Vegas Series
(Mystery/Thriller)
Against The Odds
Against The Spread

Blackbird & Confessor Series
(Romantic Mystery)
Broken Wings

Countdown To A Kiss
(A New Year's Eve Anthology)

AGAINST THE ODDS

Anna Dawson's Vegas, Book One

MARA JACOBS

Published by Mara Jacobs
©Copyright 2012 Mara Jacobs

ISBN: 978-1-940993-99-7

All rights reserved. No part of this book may be reproduced in any form or by any electronic or mechanical means, including information storage and retrieval systems—except in the case of brief quotations embodied in critical articles or reviews—without permission in writing from the author at mara@marajacobs.com. This book is a work of fiction. The characters, events, and places portrayed in this book are products of the author's imagination and are either fictitious or are used fictitiously. Any similarity to real persons, living or dead, is purely coincidental and not intended by the author.

For more information on the author and her works, please see www.marajacobs.com

*To my father, Ted.
Who showed me how to play the hand
you're dealt with grace and class.*

One

GET IT TOGETHER, *I told myself.*

This isn't life or death. It's just college basketball. Nobody was going to die from what I was about to do.

And yet, if not death, it could be very...unpleasant if I failed. I could almost hear my foot screaming out from remembered pain.

I quietly practiced a street twang. I tried to conjure up all the female bad-asses I've seen in the movies but couldn't picture Lara Croft doing what I was about to.

Finally, I just let JoJo come out.

I adjusted the gold lamé tube top to show optimum cleavage for my very average bosom, hiked my mini skirt up, set the grocery bag I was holding on the carpet, looked up and down the empty hallway then pulled the thong wedgie out of my butt.

It's not like I hadn't done this before, but that thought didn't make it any easier. It only made me slightly sick to my stomach to find myself in this position again.

Enough with the self-pity, I only had myself to blame.

I took a deep breath and knocked on the hotel room door.

After a moment, the door opened and I came face-to-face, or face-to-chest, with a giant. I looked up at the man, boy, really, smacked my gum in a way that would have made my mother cringe, and said, "You Mr. Smith?"

"Hunh?" came the laconic reply. He reminded me of Lurch, a

baby-faced Lurch. "Mr. Smith. You him?" I repeated.

He looked down at me, then out into the hallway, as if someone there could give him the answer to his identity. "Hunh?" he grunted again.

"Who is it, Lurch?" came a voice from inside the room.

I mentally smiled to find I wasn't the only one to peg the giant with the nickname. And it hadn't even been in the team's media guide.

"Don't know," Lurch said to the voice behind him as he kept his eyes on me. Me and my cleavage.

The giant was brushed aside—not an easy task—and a much smaller, and much darker man took his place. Ebony and Ivory. Mutt and Jeff. The two were complete mismatches, but it only confirmed that I had the right room.

"I think I've got the wrong room," I said.

Lurch seemed to accept the mistake, nodded and turned back into the room. The other kid, however, was not quite ready to see his unexpected visitor leave. Probably pretty damn boring for these kids being cooped up in a hotel room with just text books to study and TV to watch.

"Whoa. Whoa. Whoa. Who you looking for darlin'?" His eyes roved over my body and I had to hold myself very still instead of smacking him one. "Mr. Smith? I could be Mr. Smith." He spoke with an urban slang to his voice.

South side of Chicago. Hell, I even knew who his eighth grade coach was. His mother and sister sang in the church choir and here he was trying to make time with some floozy who showed up at his hotel door.

But then he flashed a grin that spanned his whole face—surely that was way more teeth than a human head could possibly hold—and I forgave him for the leer.

I almost—almost—smiled back.

I hid my amusement and instead raised my brows and licked my lips. I looked him up and down, jutted my hip out at a hard angle and said, "You sure, sugar? You don't look like you could afford me." My voice sounded so foreign to myself and I waited to see if the kid would call me on it or if he would bite.

"Awww shit, baby, give me an hour and you'd be paying me."

Hook, line and sinker.

I snorted with laughter, turned to leave, and then pretended to see someone down the hall. My feigned look of fear alerted Mr. Smith who started to step into the hallway to take a look for himself. Before he could, I placed my hand on his chest, pushed him backward and followed him into the room, shutting the door behind me.

"Wasss up?" Mr. Smith said with a drawl.

"Just give me a minute, sugar, 'kay?"

"Somebody out there?"

I nodded. "Yeah, security."

"Hotel security?" Mr. Smith asked.

"Oh shit," Lurch said behind us.

I brushed past Mr. Smith, walked further into the room, and set my grocery bag on the desk. I took a quick glance around the room. Duffel bags, gym shorts, and tee shirts were strewn all over. And all adorned with Central Iowa Wild Hogs logos. Definitely the right room.

"No problems, honey," I said to the nervous Lurch. "Let me just make a quick call, wait for security to scram and I'll be out of your hair."

Lurch breathed a sigh of relief while Mr. Smith grunted his disapproval. "No need to be hasty. Stick around. Make sure the coast is good and clear."

I turned around and looked at Mr. Smith. I gave him a pitying smile. "Don't get your hopes up sweetie, I didn't sign on for a party of three."

"Lurch here was just leaving, weren't you, Lurch?" He gave Lurch a hopeful look.

"Hunh?" Lurch said, looking from Mr. Smith to me.

I chuckled. "You don't wanna throw your poor roommate out

in the cold, honey. That's not neighborly."

The black young man waved a hand of dismissal at his sidekick. "Aw man, he can go crash with any one of the guys. We already had bed check, nobody will know."

I made a show of looking around the room, pretending to notice the athletic gear for the first time. "You on some kind of team or something?"

Both male chests puffed out but it was Mr. Smith that answered. "We're the Central Iowa Hogs, defending conference champs. Final Four."

And I could list both their stats for the last three seasons. But I swallowed my pride, looked back and forth between them, put a bored look on my face and said, "That's basketball, right?"

The chests deflated. "Yeah," Lurch said and then turned and sat on one of the two beds, pulling an open text book that had been lying on the bed onto his lap. His eyes, however, stayed on me. Or, more accurately, on my chest.

I pulled a cell phone from my large, bejeweled purse and punched speed dial. "Stu. What the fuck, man? You gave me the wrong damn room number," I said into the phone, careful to turn away from the men so they couldn't hear Stu's response. So they couldn't hear that there was no response.

No Stu. Just a dead phone.

"Yeah. Right. That's where I'm at, Stu. And there ain't no fucking Mr. Smith here." I shot Mr. Smith a warning look over my shoulder, correctly halting a smartass comeback. "You got a number?" Pause. "No number, Stu? That's fucking great." I turned back to the room, looked at the men staring at me. "I'm wasting valuable date time here watching two college kids get hard at the sight of a working girl in their room."

Lurch pulled his textbook higher up on his lap. Mr. Smith flashed me a toothy grin.

It was impossible not to like the kid. Which only made me feel shittier.

"Yeah, that's fucking right you owe me." I disconnected the unconnected phone and threw it into my god-awful purse. I reached into the grocery bag and pulled out a bottle of Jack Daniels and a six-pack of Coke. "Christ, I need a drink."

"All right. Let's get this party started," Mr. Smith said, walking toward me.

"Hey, Raymond, man, you better not," Lurch warned.

"That's right, Raymond, you better not. You got a game or something tomorrow?"

"Yeah, but man, we can beat Minnesota with one hand tied behind our backs."

"Really? But can you beat them with a hangover?"

"I've played with 'em before."

"Come on, Raymond," Lurch whined.

I grabbed three glasses from the vanity area, poured Coke in all three, opened the bottle of Jack and turned to Raymond. "You sure, sugar?" Raymond nodded. I turned back to the desk I used as a bar. I made sure neither man could see the glasses and then grabbed a small baggie from my purse and quickly dumped the contents into two of the three glasses, swirling them until the powder dissolved. I poured just a drop of the Jack into one of the glasses, then turned my body slightly so they could see, and made a show of pouring Jack into the third glass.

I took one of the glasses and handed it to Lurch. "This one's virgin, honey." Raymond snorted. "That's about right," he said. Lurch gave him a scowl.

I handed Raymond the glass with the Jack, took the Coke only glass myself. I raised my arm in a toast. "To the Somewhere Iowa... what did ya say you were?"

"The Hogs," Raymond and Lurch said simultaneously. Proudly. It was the most emotion Lurch had shown during the whole evening.

Never again, I told myself. Never again will I put myself in a position to snatch the pride from young kids who have nothing to do with my stupidity.

But I'd said that before, and yet here I was. Again.

"What's your name?" Lurch said. Raymond looked at him with surprise that Lurch would think of something so practical.

My hand went to my neck, but what I was looking for was gone. Idiot. I never wear it in these situations. I quickly dropped my hand. "You can call me JoJo," *I said, then took a long sip of my drink. I sat down in the desk chair and nodded for Raymond to sit, which he did on the other bed.* "Just give me a minute to finish my drink, boys and I'll be outta here. There's still a lot of night left for JoJo."

"You sure you don't want to stay?" *Raymond asked. I could almost see him mentally tallying how much cash he had in his wallet.*

"Can't, sugar. Just another minute to make sure the coast is clear and I'm a ghost. Like I never existed." *I took a large gulp of the drink and the guys followed suit. That's right, boys, follow the leader.*

Ten minutes later both were unconscious.

I took all three glasses, went to the bathroom and washed them thoroughly. Hanging on to the towel, I wiped them all down and put them back on the vanity, careful not to touch the now clean glass with my bare fingers.

Overkill, probably, but why take chances.

I slung the towel over my shoulder and returned to the desk. I picked up the bottle of Jack, the cans of Coke and placed them back in the grocery bag.

I looked back at the men sleeping. Boys, really. I walked over to them, brushed Lurch's hair off his forehead, lifted Raymond's feet up so he was in a more comfortable position. I pulled their bedspreads up over each of them.

I grabbed my purse and the grocery bag and walked to the door. I used the towel to open the door handle, then tossed it onto the vanity.

I took one last look around the room, only able to see the guys' feet from the angle of the doorway. Lurch was already snoring loudly. "Sorry, boys," *I whispered and walked out the door.*

Never again, I promised myself, knowing full well it was a promise I would probably end up breaking.

I took the stairwell down two floors. Opening the door a small crack, I looked down the hallway. Seeing it was empty, I entered the hall and quickly walked three doors down to my room. I took the key from the waistband of my skirt and entered the room.

I had the tacky clothes off in seconds, my face washed free of the garish makeup soon after. Pulling on blue jeans, a nondescript white blouse and brushing my hair out took all of five minutes. A quick ponytail and I looked like fresh-faced college co-ed.

I took another look in the mirror. A slightly older co-ed.

Okay. A world-weary woman well past her college days.

I yanked on my suede boots, zipped them up, pulled the jeans down and over. In the bathroom, I took the empty baggie from the purse and washed it out. Twice. Then I put it back in the grocery bag. I put the bag, the gaudy purse and the clothes I'd just taken off into a small carry-on bag, zipping it up tight. Putting on my leather jacket, I took a last look around the room, careful to make sure I left nothing behind. Satisfied, I grabbed a smaller, more demure purse from the desk, pulled up the handle on my carry-on and wheeled the bag behind me as I left the room.

Outside the hotel I politely declined the bell captain's offer of a cab and instead began walking down the block. As soon as I was out of sight from the hotel, I found the nearest public trashcan. I unzipped my bag, took the grocery bag out. I pulled the empty baggie out and one of the cans of Coke and shoved the grocery bag into the garbage. Then I continued on until the next trashcan where I deposited the baggie.

I crossed the busy street at the corner and approached a different motel. Here I allowed the bell captain to whistle down a cab for me for which I tipped him well but not so well that he'd look at me twice.

No need to be memorable.

On the cab ride I drank the Coke and tried not to look at all the snow piled up in downtown St. Paul.

I'd left snow behind years ago.

I arrived with plenty of time for my flight, even having time to pick up a Sporting News *at the newsstand. I had it mostly read by the time we boarded but I brought it with me in case I needed armor. I was in luck. I shared a row with a couple that was very into themselves and their upcoming vacation. Other than the initial hellos, I probably wouldn't have to speak to them at all.*

"First time going to Vegas?" the husband asked me.

I shook my head. "No," I said with a small smile then turned away, pretending to look out the window.

Not even close.

I sipped my drink as I watched the waning seconds of the game on one of the eight large screens at the Bellagio sports book.

My hand went to my neck, found my horseshoe pendant. I tapped it three times, then placed my hand back around my glass.

Raymond Joseph threw a lazy pass to his center but it was easily intercepted by a Minnesota player and taken the length of the court for a basket. The buzzer sounded, the game was over. I strained to hear the commentary of the announcers, lucky that this television was the one the crew had chosen as the audio for the room.

"Well, the Hogs pull it out, Steve, winning by twelve, but not a very impressive showing," one of the talking heads said to the other as college kids in the audience frantically waved behind them.

"Coach Wayne is going to be hot after this one, John. The Hogs came into this game heavily favored." Yeah, twenty-one and a half points favored. "And even though they won, it was one sloppy game."

"We heard reports during halftime that Raymond Joseph and David Pauls had both come down with a flu bug last night, and it sure showed in their play here this afternoon. Pauls only played five minutes in the first half. If Coach Wayne had another point guard that he could trust with the ball like Joseph, I'm sure he would have been on the bench as well."

"It just shows…" The announcer went on to talk about the team's depth—or lack of—and how that could be a factor come March. Nothing I didn't already know, so I tuned out. Besides, I knew that before my drink was empty I'd have company.

"Hey, Anna," he said and sat in the seat next to me.

"Hey, Paulie," I said, but stared straight ahead.

"Nice work," Paulie said, moving his elbow to touch mine. "Point guard *and* center, take no chances, hey?"

"Thanks," I said, taking a sip of my drink, careful to put my arm back down slightly away from his.

"Vince says to consider your debt paid."

"Thanks," I said again, my answer curt.

"Aw, come on, Anna. No harm done, they still won. Their record's still intact."

As if that was the point. I just nodded.

I could feel him looking at me, but I stared straight ahead, like I had money riding on one of the games. I didn't. I couldn't until I had my debt paid.

Finally seeing he wasn't getting anywhere—Paulie never got anywhere with me—he sighed and stood. He buttoned his expensive sportscoat over his gut, like that was going to hide it. He ran his hands through his thinning, well-oiled hair. He looked down at me and said, "Boy, you probably made a killing today, hey? We'll probably see you at a game tonight?"

"I didn't bet on the game," I told him.

"What do you mean?" he asked, puzzled.

I pointed to the big screen. "I didn't bet on the Iowa game."

"Why the hell not?" he said, almost mad. I suppose he was angry at my stupidity. In a way, so was I.

I took my eyes from the screens and looked up at him. "It would be wrong," I explained.

He looked at me hard, as if trying to figure me out. After nearly a full minute he tipped his head back and laughed. "Oh, that's rich, Anna." He walked away from me, chuckling. "Because it would be wrong," I heard him say in a soft, feminine voice; which sounded not at all like mine.

Not a great mimic, Paulie. A good enforcer, though.

This I knew first hand.

Two

THE ADRENALINE RUSH from watching the game—making sure I'd done my job; that I'd be around to watch more games—left my body and I was suddenly exhausted.

I got up from my seat at the book. I didn't have money on any of the games today. I'd been too distracted with my Minnesota trip to do my homework. I didn't make any sports bet without doing my homework.

Even that's not enough some times.

I waved to the guys seated at the counter where people made bets. They all waved back, a few, "see you tomorrow, Anna"s, thrown in.

These guys knew odds, and odds were good they'd see me again soon, if not tomorrow.

Yeah, probably tomorrow, now that I didn't have the debt to Vince hanging over my head.

I walked slowly past the poker room, scanning the few men standing in suits, looking to see if my friend Jeffrey was working.

Friend. Lover. Booty call. I'm not really sure what Jeffrey was to me. We slept together occasionally, but not enough that I knew his schedule. I caught Glenda's eye. She was one of the other poker room supervisors. I knew them all.

Jeffrey's the only one I sleep with.

Glenda's a tall, statuesque brunette who wears incredible

suits and styles her hair in very intricate buns and twists. I think I even glimpsed a snood once. Very put together.

She's actually much more Jeffrey's type—he's a bit of a clotheshorse and a little high maintenance when it comes to his looks—but he swears they've never messed around.

It should matter to me, but it doesn't.

The only thing that matters is going home and sleeping for twelve hours.

Eight hours later I sat in the Sourdough Café at Arizona Charlie's. I was the only woman at a table of six. And the only one under the age of sixty. I looked around the table at my male companions.

Make that under seventy.

The waitress, Grace, came over. Grace waited on us every morning. At the same table, near the back of the restaurant. She took each of the men's orders then turned to me. "You eatin' this morning, hon?" she asked. The men, previously talking amongst themselves, grew silent and looked toward me.

"I'll have the ham and eggs. Toast. And a side of pancakes."

She wrote it down and started to leave. The men let out collective groans. "And biscuits," I added. Grace waved that she'd heard me as she walked away.

"Oy," said one of the men, most likely Saul.

No, they weren't commenting on the size of my breakfast, though I'm sure I would be when I'd have to unbutton my jeans on the drive home.

"And," Ben said, like he was right in the middle of a sentence. "I had to wake her up this morning. And it looked like she'd been sleeping a while."

Not long enough.

Two of the men, Saul and Danny, looked at me with

compassion. Jimmy snorted. With glee or disgust, I'm not sure. Gus shrugged with a "whadda ya expect" attitude and sipped from his coffee. Only Ben, my Ben, had a look of concern on his kind, wrinkled face.

"How much?" Gus asked as he set his cup down, added more sugar. Gus adds nearly a packet of sugar with every sip he takes. By the end of breakfast he must be drinking coffeeade.

The other men looked amongst themselves. If I didn't answer soon, they'd start throwing out guesses, betting each other.

Just as Jimmy opened with "Ten thou—" I said, "I didn't play last night."

This isn't totally unheard of, but it is out of the norm. The men all looked at Ben, who studied me, then nodded. I guess if he believed me, they all did.

I could see why they were confused. When I play poker at night, I play late. I usually get something to eat after I'm done, or even sometimes while I'm playing. If I'm doing well, I get home just in time to take Ben to breakfast and am usually not hungry.

If I lose early, I'm home asleep when Ben comes looking for me, and usually famished when I wake up.

It's not a hard rule. Sometimes I lose on my last hand of the card game and walk in the door to a waiting Ben. But typically, if I order a big breakfast it's because I lost.

And when I lose, I lose big.

"We missed you at breakfast yesterday, Hannah, darling," Saul said with a question in his voice.

I looked at Ben. "Lorelei got you here okay, didn't she?" I asked, concerned that Lorelei had dropped the ball where Ben's ride was concerned. That wasn't like her, she ran our house like a top.

He put his hand on mine, squeezed, then took a sip of coffee. "Yes, dear, Lorelei was waiting in the kitchen for me, right on time."

I looked at the men as they all gave each other sheepish grins. Ben looked a little embarrassed.

I sighed. "You still didn't let her sit with you?" It wasn't really a question.

Ben looked more embarrassed. Saul and Danny evaded my gaze. Jimmy shrugged. Gus just gave an impish grin.

Gus was a looker in his day, and, according to Ben, a real ladies' man. He was still very handsome, a full head of thick wavy hair, turned a beautiful white. He still wore a suit every day, with a handkerchief in his front pocket. Most days the hankie matched his tie. His shoes were always immaculately shined. Ben told me once that Gus spread his shining business out, stopped at a different casino everyday, and tipped very well.

Ladies and shoe-shine men loved Gus. And I suspected everyone else who depended on tips for a living.

Which was pretty much everyone in Vegas.

"I would have thought you'd like a beautiful showgirl at your table," I said to them all.

"She don't fit in. She has no right at this table," Jimmy said.

"And I do?" I pointed out.

There seemed to be a silent agreement amongst the men that indeed I did. A rush of emotion washed over me. A sense of belonging. I tried very hard not to blush.

"You made your bones," Danny murmured.

I raised my brows at him. Making your bones in the old days meant you'd killed someone.

"Your gambling bones," Saul clarified.

If that meant winning—and losing—several fortunes, then I had indeed made my bones.

"So what did Lorelei do while you ate? Play slots?" Lorelei loved the nickel slot machines. Pennies if she could find them.

I never touched slot machines. The boys had told me early on to stay away from them. "For chumps," they'd said. And I'd listened.

They also said know when to walk away. I didn't always listen so well to that one.

"She ate, too. Man that girl can put away food."

Seeing as I paid for her grocery bill, I was just about to agree when Grace came with our food, needing another waitress to help her carry my order.

"How could you see what she ate?" I asked as I cleared enough space in front of me for all my food. There was plenty of space around me as Jimmy was the only one of the guys who ate a full breakfast each morning, the others got toast, or fruit, or oatmeal.

Most days, Ben and Saul shared a breakfast plate like an old married couple.

In some ways, they were. They'd grown up together in New York, came west together at eighteen. Their claim to fame was personally knowing Meyer Lansky.

Jimmy motioned to the next table. "She was right there. We could see every morsel. Damn, that woman must burn some calories dancing, the way she eats."

"You mean you made her sit at the table next to you all alone while you all sat here?"

They all looked at me and just shrugged. I tried not to laugh, to not even smile, so as not to encourage them. But then I looked at Ben, with his warm, mischievous, brown eyes and I started to laugh. "Very nice, gentlemen," I said when I'd regained my composure. "Very chivalrous. I thought you were old school."

"Old school meant women knew their place," Jimmy said with nonchalance as he buttered his biscuit. Jimmy was the only one of the group with no gray or white in his hair. It was still pitch black. I've stared at it for hours trying to tell if it was a dye job or a toupee, but I've come to the conclusion that the man was just blessed with a great head of hair. Too bad it was wasted on Jimmy, who couldn't have cared less.

All Jimmy cared about was the betting line and food.

If he weren't such a prick sometimes, he'd be my idol.

"I'm a woman," I said. "And you've just pointed out that this is my 'place'."

"Aw, honey, we don't think of you as a woman," Danny sweetly said, like it was a compliment.

In a way it was.

These five men had taught me everything I knew about gambling, and most probably about life itself.

Being considered an old man by them meant I'd arrived.

When the plates had been cleared, the men started pulling out newspapers, magazines, betting lines from various casinos, even notes on napkins.

This was my favorite part of the morning. I enjoyed their banter over breakfast, but by now I'd heard all their stories. It was their time. Time to reminisce, time to tell private jokes about people long since gone.

But when the papers came out, I perked up. I pulled out my own homework; this morning's paper, and the line for today's games I'd picked up at the Bellagio last night.

"Whoa. Whoa. Hold on everybody. I got show and tell today," Jimmy said. He reached under his chair and pulled out a brown envelope. He dumped it upside down and several copies of *Sports Illustrated* fell out.

The men all grabbed a copy as did I, and quickly flipped through it. "Is this the edition with the article about you guys?" I asked even though I knew it had to be, with Jimmy smiling like he was. He nodded.

"I thought it wasn't due out for a few days?" Ben said.

Jimmy shrugged. "I know a guy."

Yeah, Jimmy knew lots of guys. It was better not to ask any questions. No one did, they all just nodded and started flipping through the magazine.

"Page eighty-five," Jimmy said and the flipping continued.

I turned my copy to the correct page, and there were my boys. A group shot taken right here in the Sourdough Café. I'd been there. Had brought Ben and then disappeared while the writer interviewed them all. I'd watched from a corner booth as the photographer had snapped away. I'd been bursting with pride.

It was a three-page article about The Corporation. The five men who throughout the sixties, seventies and eighties had been the sports betting odds makers at five of the largest casinos in Vegas.

Back then there'd been a healthy competition between them all. When one would set odds that were way off, they'd give him shit. When one would be dead on, well, they'd still give him shit.

These men were responsible for making millionaires. And breaking them.

And all for modest salaries plus benefits.

I quickly read the article. The writer had really gotten the boys. Their pride in what they did. Their camaraderie. Their love for the old ways. His commentary on how odds are set now was written with a "the new way isn't always better" attitude.

Eighty percent of the casinos in Vegas get their odds from one company. The days when each casino had a man like Ben, or Saul heading a team of twenty that worked round the clock were over.

The article captured the sense of nostalgia that first appealed to me about the boys.

"Look, he even mentioned Black Sunday," Gus pointed out.

It was a famous story in odds maker history. Superbowl

Thirteen; Steelers vs. Cowboys. The Steelers opened at 2 1/2 point favorites. People bet it. Heavy. Pushing the odds to 4 1/2 points. That looked good to the Dallas fans (their Cowboys could lose, but by less than 4 1/2 points) and the money came in from the other side.

Then some really big money came in and bet Pittsburgh (it was rumored to be a big CEO at some steel company) at the last moment and almost turned the odds again, but it was too late to matter.

Pittsuburgh won by 4 points and everybody won.

"Except the poor schmuck from Pittsburgh that took the Steelers at four and a half," Saul was quoted in the article.

"And the odds makers," Gus had added.

The journalist wrote about the fall-out for the casinos after taking such a huge loss. Lots of odds makers lost their jobs. But the five men who would become known as The Corporation had survived.

By then, of course they were all aware of each other, but only Ben and Saul could be considered friends. And they were best friends. It wasn't until after they retired, some fifteen or twenty years ago, that they'd all begun meeting for breakfast each morning.

"This is a great article," I said, as I looked up. The men were all still reading except Gus, who had already finished and had flipped back to the first page, studying the group photo. I did as well, and then laughed as I read the caption. "They've got your nicknames in the caption. Did you guys tell him?"

They all shook their heads no as they turned back to the picture page. I watched as each man's face took on a different smile as they read their olden day's monikers. Jimmy the Wop's was a proud grin. Saul the Jew shook his head with a rueful smile. Gorgeous Gus ran his fingers through his beautiful hair, straightened his already straight tie. Danny the Mick broke out in an easy laugh. And Hyman Roth—Ben—sighed deeply. I figured he was secretly proud. His nickname, after the shrewd Jewish businessman, based on gangster Meyer Lansky, who brought casinos to Cuba in the second *Godfather* movie, was certainly the most creative.

The only one with a little imagination. I wouldn't have put it past Ben to have somehow started it himself.

"I wonder where that kid got all this?" Saul asked.

That "kid" journalist was about my age. "I give him credit for putting that in the caption," Gus said. "Not very politically correct."

"Fuck politically correct," Jimmy said what all the men were probably thinking.

And so was I. These men had worn those names with great pride back in the day. Just by watching their faces I could see how much being in the magazine meant to them. They'd all worked close to fifty years in the back rooms, breathing in smoke, taking calls from snitches all over the country that had hot tips about players, teams or coaches.

It was wonderful to see them out from the shadows, basking in a little limelight.

We never got around to today's games. I'd have to wing it on my own if I was going to place any bets this afternoon.

Not the first time, but I did like getting the boys' feedback. At least I had the ride home with Ben, I could pick his brain.

We left Arizona Charlie's. I walked slowly beside Ben, making sure the way was clear for his walker, but knowing better than to help him. I looked around at the clientele. Charlie's was well off the strip and as such catered more to locals than tourists. And much, much older.

You were more likely to see someone wheeling an oxygen tank than a baby stroller.

Old school. And that's how The Corporation liked it.

Ben was so engrossed in the magazine that I drove in silence. I made my way to Summerlin, into our swanky subdivision. When we got to the house, I was surprised to see several cars parked at the curb.

"You expecting people?" Ben asked when he noticed the cars.

"Nope. You?"

He shrugged. "Hannah, darling, anybody I would want to see, we just left."

I laughed. "Me too," I admitted. Ben just shook his head and rolled his eyes at me.

I got the walker from the backseat, helped Ben out of the car—the one allowance to his infirmity that he'd allow; getting out of my low sports car wasn't easy, even for me.

I put both Ben's and my copies of the magazine in my backpack with my betting materials, and walked slowly to the front door, wondering if Lorelei had decided to have an impromptu party.

At nine in the morning? Well, there were no clocks in Vegas.

I opened the door, waited for Ben to wheel his way in, then entered. We followed voices and walked to the living room. Lorelei was standing in the middle of the room, facing us, like she'd been waiting for our arrival.

Behind her, two men and one woman, none of whom I'd met before, sat on the couch and in chairs. They were all young, incredibly good looking with fantastic bodies.

Lorelei shook her flaming-red hair, squared her shoulders and delivered her line like only a frustrated actress-slash-model-slash-dancer-slash-waitress could.

"Anna, this is an intervention."

Ben sighed. I put my hands in my jeans pockets, tried to show nonchalance rather than my burgeoning anger as I

addressed Lorelei.
"What? Again?"

Three
❖

I'M THIRTY-FOUR YEARS OLD. That's a hundred and ninety in gambler years.

And right now I felt every one of them.

"Come on Lorelei, I thought we were done with these things. Where'd you find this crew?" I asked, pointing to the threesome in my living room eating my good bagels that I have shipped special for Ben from New York. There were coffee cups, juices. Lorelei had even made her famous egg casserole.

Darn, and I'd already had such a big breakfast.

"That's Mark, and Kenny and Tabby," she said pointing to the group. "They're in love."

I looked closely at the threesome as they continued to chow down. "Which ones?" I asked.

"Which ones what?"

"Which ones are in love?" Although knowing Lorelei, and Vegas for that matter, I guess it could have been all three. Or four counting Lorelei.

"All of them," she confirmed. She watched me as I again studied the dancers, then she burst out laughing. "The *show* Love, Jo." Ah, Love, the show at the Mirage. That made more sense. Although…

"Although…" Lorelei said, this time studying the dancers more closely herself.

"If you'll all excuse me," Ben started to walk down the hallway, but I put my foot down on his walker wheel.

"Oh no you don't, old man. If I have to sit through this crap, so do you."

He gave a resigned sigh, turned and went into the living room, seating himself next to Tabby. The three dancers looked at him in shock. They probably didn't see too many old people. They were likely constantly surrounded by young people with incredible bodies like themselves. Kenny, or Mark, eyed Ben's walker suspiciously, as if whatever ailed Ben might be contagious.

"We need you here for this Ben. You're the only person she'll listen to," Lorelei said.

"And she listens to me because I don't waste her time telling her nonsense," Ben replied.

I shot him a smile and he nodded his head toward me.

Lorelei ignored him, waved me to my seat; the guest of dishonor. She took a seat herself, pulled some papers from the coffee table, gave another hair flip and began to read. "Ten signs you are a compulsive gambler."

The three dancers looked up from their breakfasts. Apparently lured by the offer of free food, this was the first time they realized what they were here for. They looked from Ben to me, trying to figure out who was the compulsive gambler.

Truth was we probably both were.

Another truth was we both liked it that way.

"Number one. Is preoccupied with gambling, reliving gambling experiences, or thinking of ways to get money to gamble." She gave a dramatic pause, pointedly looking at me.

"Tabby," I said. "How often do you think about dancing?"

She looked at me. God, she couldn't have been more than twenty-two. "Dancing's all I think about," she said with such sincerity it nearly broke my heart.

I looked back at Lorelei, raised my brows, in a "whadda say to that!" way. It's a look I'd perfected at the poker tables.

She ignored me, returned to her papers. "Number two. Needs to gamble with a larger pot of money in order to achieve the desired level of excitement."

I thought about a couple of weeks ago. Betting five thousand on the Giants. As I'd walked away from the betting window I had this fear, this dread, that it wasn't enough, and had gone back to the window to double it.

"Kenny," I said, waiting to see which dancer would look at me. Ah, the blond. So the brunette was Mark. "What was your first job as a dancer?"

He smiled a warm grin. "At Miss Porter's school of dance. I helped her teach ballroom dancing to couples about to get married."

"And do you like dancing on the Las Vegas Strip, in one of its biggest shows, better?"

"Hell yes."

"You'd say it has raised the level of excitement? The bigger the show?"

"Right," he said quietly, looking toward Lorelei, contrite, probably wondering if she'd take away the food.

"Come on Jo," Lorelei scolded. "This is serious. I'm trying to help you."

"I know you think you are Lorelei. But replace the top of your list with the word professional instead of compulsive. It's my job. And I'm damn good at it. My gambling bought this house. The house that you live in rent-free, by the way."

"Do you want me to start paying rent?" she asked. "Because I—"

"No." I cut her off. "That wasn't our agreement." She started to come back with something but I held up my hand. I was on a roll. "Look in the driveway. My car? Gambling. Your car? Gambling. All the stuff you wanted for the gourmet kitchen? Gambling. My life—*your life*—is a very comfortable life thanks to gambling."

"Yes. Gambling has brought you a lot. But it also has you disappearing every few months, doing God knows what for people right out of a Scorsese movie. You can't say *that's* comfortable."

"Ben, help me out here," I pleaded.

"Hannah, maybe we should just let Lorelei finish. Go ahead, dear."

She looked at me. For permission? Yeah, right. I waved for her to continue.

Lorelei's lived with Ben and me for six years. Before her, Ben was able to run the household. But not so much lately, and I didn't want that kind of pressure on him.

I owned the house (though it was in Ben's name), had a car for Lorelei (also in Ben's name, as was my own) bought all the food and paid all the utilities. Or, I should say supplied all the money for those things.

That's where Lorelei came in. Whenever I won, I handed the money over to her. She paid all the bills with it, did all the grocery shopping, did most of the cooking when she wasn't working, and was my back-up for taking Ben places.

She also bought nice things for the house from my winnings. We had the latest electronic equipment, a huge in-home theater, an incredible state-of-the-art kitchen set-up. The works. It was her job to make sure the cash was spent. And that there was enough left—and I didn't want to know where—for the bills to be paid for at least two years.

That was my safety net. Two years. If I went more than that without being on the plus side then...well, I didn't know what, it hadn't happened yet.

There was never to be large sums of cash at the ready. It was all to be invested in things that weren't quickly—or at least easily—sold.

Responsibility and honesty were the only things I asked from her, and she had those in spades.

It was a good arrangement for everybody. Lorelei was a dancer, but on the waning end of that youth-oriented industry. She did mostly sub work, pick-up jobs. Took a bunch of dance classes to stay in shape. She kept odd hours, I kept odd hours, but between us there was usually one of us either here in the house or at least nearby and able to get to Ben if he needed us.

But a few times a year Lorelei got to feeling she should be doing more, and that usually translated to one of these faux interventions. Oh, it was real enough on her part, but it probably should have been a red flag of sorts when she could never find enough people that my "problem" had affected to populate one of these things.

I wasn't mad at her. I knew she meant well. But I'm always cranky for a few days after taking one of my "trips", and I was still feeling sleep deprived, so I was in no mood for her intervention this morning.

"Number three. Tries repeatedly to control, cut back, or stop gambling."

"No problem there," I said.

"No?"

"No. I've never tried to stop."

The two male dancers snorted at that, and Ben chuckled. Lorelei shot them all looks and they quieted. Ben winked at me.

"Number four. Becomes restless or irritable when attempting to scale back or stop gambling."

"Like I said, I don't try to stop, so I'm never irritable about it." She opened her mouth to continue but I cut her off. "I'll tell you what *does* make me irritable though."

She ignored me. "Number five. Gambles as a way to escape from family or work problems or to relieve a depressed or unhappy mood."

"Nah. I drink for that."

The boys laughed again, sat up, put their coffee cups down, and settled in to watch the show. Tabby kept right on with her breakfast. My God, dancers could eat.

Lorelei turned to the next page in her notes. Great, this was to be a multi-page intervention.

"Number six. After losing money, often returns another day to get even."

"I return everyday," I said. "It's my job." Nobody had any comment to that one. Lorelei seemed to take it as a small victory, but the men all just shrugged.

"Number seven. Lies to family members, therapists, colleagues or others to conceal the extent of the gambling habit."

I looked at Ben. "I have never lied to you."

"I know you haven't, Hannah, darling," Ben said, sympathy in his voice.

I looked at Lorelei. "I have never lied to you."

"Where were you two days ago?" she quietly said, no victory in her voice now.

I looked from her to Ben. The dancers, sensing a "moment", leaned forward. Tabby even put down her fork.

"I'm not going to tell you that," I said. "Because it's none of your business, and because I won't lie to you."

The moment was anti-climatic for the dancers whose attention returned to the table. Ben looked away when I tried to meet his eye. Lorelei held mine for a long time before returning to her notes.

"Number eight. Has jeopardized or lost a significant relationship, job, or educational or career opportunity because of the need to gamble."

"Nope," I said.

"No?" she prodded.

"The only job I've ever had—as an adult anyway—is gambling. And I've never lost that one."

"What about relationships?"

"What about them?"

"Most women your age are married, starting families."

"I could say the same thing back to you. And if you say you're married to "the dance", I'm going to come after you." I think that's exactly what she was about to say, because she shut her mouth pretty quickly.

"Besides," I said, thinking of Jeffrey. "My needs are met."

I thought of my parents back in Wisconsin. They'd just been out for a visit a couple of months ago. "I've got family."

I looked at Ben, smiled. "I've got lots of family." He smiled back, nodded his agreement.

"What about," she looked down at her notes, "educational opportunities? You said you left college one semester shy to come out here."

God, that seemed like a lifetime ago. It *was* a lifetime ago. "Yes, but I didn't lose that opportunity, I walked away from it. Big difference." At least it had felt like it at the time, now that decision process all seemed blurry to me.

"Number nine. Borrows money from friends, family, even strangers to pay off catastrophic debts from gambling."

"Have I ever borrowed any money from you?" I asked her, evading a direct answer to number nine.

"No."

"Ben?"

"No, Hannah, of course not."

Kenny cleared his throat. We all looked at him. "Oh. No. You haven't borrowed from me. But, like, hey, if you've got some to lend…"

"Shut up, Kenny," Lorelei said. Kenny shut up. Although I was thinking that breakfast alone might not be payment enough for this torture for these kids and that I should reimburse them. Except, hell, if I had to sit through it, so could they.

"Number ten."

"Finally."

"Drum roll please," Kenny said. Mark did the honors.

Lorelei ignored them both. "Number ten. Has committed

illegal acts like forgery, fraud, theft or embezzlement to finance a gambling habit."

Well, shit. Visions of Lurch and Mr. Smith sprawled across their hotel beds flooded over me. I made a sound of disgust, like how could Lorelei even dare to think I'd do something illegal.

I stood up, said, "We're done here," and walked out of the room.

Three nights later number ten was still zinging through my mind as I found myself in front of a municipal building on the west side of Vegas. Out of my territory, but that was good, less likely to run into anyone I knew.

That's why it's called Anonymous.

I believed everything I'd said to Lorelei. I'm a professional gambler. It's what I do, how I make a living.

And the thing is, drinkers can stop without losing their jobs. Druggies can stop without losing their jobs. But with me? It'd be like telling a professional wine taster they were an alcoholic and had to not only break the habit, but find an entirely different line of work.

I loved my job.

And yet…and yet here I found myself at midnight on a Wednesday night instead of in a poker room.

I looked at the notices on the front of the building. Gamblers Anonymous, room 214. Alcoholics Anonymous, room 334. Narcotics Anonymous, room 422. Different diseases, different floors. Man, I'll bet the doughnut and coffee industries made a killing at a place like this.

People filed into the building. I stood to the side, not moving, trying not to look the people in the eye. A few people came together, some couples, some just friends, I supposed. Or, what do you call them? Sponsors.

At quarter after, I still stood in front of the building, glued to my spot. The sidewalk was empty now, the people all inside. Taking a deep breath, I started to move toward the door when I heard someone walking up the steps behind me.

It was a man alone, dressed in khakis, a chambray work shirt and a leather jacket. His tie was loose around his neck and as he walked up the steps he took it off completely and stuffed it in his jacket pocket.

His walk up the stairs was slow, deliberate, and I knew just how he felt.

Dead man walking.

He had a cigarette in his hand and when he got to the door he noticed the no smoking indoors sign. He leaned along the metal railing on one side and took the smallest drag off his cigarette. Making it last.

I didn't even have the excuse of a cigarette, but I took my hand off the door handle and leaned back on the railing on the other side of the stairs.

He looked up, startled, like he hadn't noticed me until now, and that seemed to disturb him. He nodded at me. I nodded back.

I could pretend to be waiting for someone. Just hang out until he finished his cigarette and went in. I didn't have to let his presence drive me away.

Or in.

I watched him. He was reading the flyers on the front of the building and I thought I could get a good look at him without him noticing, but when he turned back to me I realized he'd known I was watching him all along.

I'd put him in his late thirties-early forties. His face was worn, lived in, but handsome. Not pretty at all, like Jeffrey, but his features were strong, and his eyes… he had the eyes of a gambler; weary, seeing everything, evaluating odds, chances, risk, all in a second. They were brown and soft and reminded me of Ben's.

I was just about to ask him if he was a gambler, when he said, "Which one for you?"

"Huh?"

He pointed to the three notices I'd seen earlier. "Booze, bets or blow?" he summed up our choices from tonight's menu.

I laughed, nervous energy expelling from my body, grateful for the outlet. "Bets," I said.

He looked at me again, harder this time, as if my answer had surprised him. This was Vegas, it shouldn't have.

"You?" I asked.

"Bourbon," he answered, sticking with the alliteration.

I nodded, looked closer at him too. For signs, I guess. It was too dark, even under the harsh light of the doorway, to see broken capillaries on his nose, or blood shot eyes. He wasn't jittery at all, no shakes. His hand, when he'd lift his cigarette to his mouth was steady. No nervous energy either. There was a calmness about him. I've known lots of drunks, and he didn't seem to fit. But I bet I didn't fit his idea of a gambling junkie either.

He looked at his cigarette butt as it spent its last breath. He seemed like he was willing the damn thing to come back to life, to give him more time.

I knew how he felt.

He stared at the cigarette for a long time, then looked at the building, staring into the window of the door like it was a crystal ball. Was his future in there?

Was mine?

He took a deep breath, just as I had moments ago before I reached for the door. But instead of heading for the door, he rubbed his cigarette in the overflowing ash can and leaned back against the railing, still facing me.

"Not going in?" he asked me.

I looked at the building, as if it could answer for me. When it didn't, I turned back to him and said, "That has yet to be determined."

He nodded, understanding. There was something so familiar about him to me.

Or was I just seeing myself in him?

He reached into the pocket of his jacket and pulled out a pack of cigarettes. He pulled one out, stared at it for a long time, then tossed it and the pack into the garbage can.

"Quitting all your vices in one night," I said. "Is that wise?"

"Honey, those aren't even the tip of the iceberg."

I laughed, then quickly quieted, not wanting those people inside that were pouring their hearts out to hear us.

And suddenly not wanting to hear them—in any form—either.

"I think I'm gonna let my iceberg float for a little while longer," I said, lifting away from the railing, stepping from the building toward the stairs back down to the street.

He smiled. And man, did a smile do wonders to that serious, troubled, haunted face.

"Atta girl," he said. "Show 'em who's boss."

I put up my dukes in an imaginary fight toward the building. Even took a swing.

He chuckled, low and throaty.

I started down the steps, he trailed behind me. When we got to the bottom, he put his hand lightly on my arm, just enough to get my attention, then took it away.

"Would it seem totally inappropriate if I asked if you wanted to get a drink?"

"Only if we can have it in a casino," I joked.

He chuckled again—a great sound. Then he looked at me, the smile leaving his face. He studied me for a moment, just long enough for me to want to see if my hair needed fixing or if I had something in my teeth.

"No. Really, would you like—" But he was interrupted by

his cell phone which he looked at and then frowned.

I surreptitiously looked to see if he wore a wedding band, that maybe it was a wife calling. No band. No tan line of a band. But he could be the kind of guy who doesn't wear one. Or it could just be a girlfriend calling. It was well after midnight by now, so it was probably some kind of booty call situation.

"Shit," he murmured, putting the phone back in his pocket without answering it.

I felt a pang of regret that surprised me.

"Good luck," I said and started walking away, toward my car, opposite from the direction he had appeared from.

"Huh?"

I nodded toward the building. "With your icebergs." I walked backward a few steps, not wanting to take my eyes off of him. He seemed reluctant to leave too.

"You too," he said so softly I almost didn't hear him. I turned and walked to the end of the block. When I turned, he was still there, not watching me, but instead turned to stare at the building which neither of us had entered.

He stood under a street light and the pain that wafted over his face was brief, but I caught it, and it made me hold my breath. Then he turned and walked away, into the darkness of the night.

Four
❖❖

I BROUGHT MY HAND UP TO MY NECKLACE, but instead of playing with it as I had intermittently for the last three hours, I quickly dropped it back to the table. I slid my chips to the middle of the table. "All in."

Come on, kid, bite. I saw his eyes flash to my necklace, then to the pot, thinking, wondering.

Yeah, that's right, I'd been fiddling with my necklace when I had cards. So, what did it mean when I didn't? I had garbage? Bluffing?

He sat across the table from me, right in my line of vision, which meant I was in his. He eyed me for several moments, but my face gave nothing away, nor did he expect it to. He knew who I was. I'd seen him before, too. Even in cash games in a casino as big as the Bellagio you were bound to run into the same players once in a while if you played often enough. And I did.

This kid had been here frequently since last fall, probably the day after he'd turned twenty-one.

He looked down at his hands. He made the tiniest movement, just a twitch at the corner of his mouth, and then quickly got it in check. But I'd seen it.

He wanted to smile. He thought he'd read me, that I'd given him a tell by not touching my necklace.

Ever since John Malkovich broke his Oreo in *Rounders*, a tell to Matt Damon who bet the farm and won the game, Vegas was full of kids thinking they could figure out someone's tell and take them down.

This kid was a good player, but he hadn't learned to read a trap yet.

I had him.

"Call," he said, as I knew he would, and pushed his stack in. I bit my lower lip, a show for the kid. It didn't matter now, he was in, but I thought I'd let the drama play out a bit longer.

The other players already had, or now dropped out, leaving me playing heads up with the kid whose chip stack was just about equal to mine. The two highest stacks at the table.

The other players didn't know whether to be happy that one of the leaders was going to be gone, or pissed that one of us would have the majority of the chips at the table.

The dealer counted out both our stacks, threw back one chip to me after making them even. So, at least if I lost I wasn't going to be out of the game. Not that I could do anything with one chip. And this was a cash game, not a tournament, so in theory the kid could just pull out his wallet and buy more chips, as could I.

Except I didn't have any more money in my wallet. And I needed a big win tonight. There was a college basketball game tomorrow morning that I wanted to bet. Needed to bet.

Had to bet.

Lorelei's intervention floated through my head, but quickly flew out when the dealer nodded for us to both flip over our hands.

The poor kid almost shit a brick when he saw my pocket aces. He limply turned over a queen and a ten. He looked at me questioningly. I wasn't going to gloat—not my style. But the kid could be a really good player if he learned some of the finer points. I subtly moved my hand back to my necklace. Put it in front of it, took it away, put it back, like a magic trick—now you see it now you don't.

The kid watched me, his brows furrowing. I saw the moment he got it, what I'd done, how I'd led him for three hours and then—when I had the aces—suckered him in with a false tell.

To the kid's credit he didn't say a word, nor gave away anything to the other players. He simply nodded to me, a tip of his hat if you will. I gave a small nod back. He'd know I'd tipped him off on how he'd failed not for my benefit, but for his.

He did, I could see that, as he lowered his head, thinking back over the game, mentally counting all the times I'd done the necklace fumble, a small smile of appreciation on his young face.

The dealer laid down the flop and it was my turn to shit a brick.

A queen, a ten and a nine.

Groans from the other players, and a gasp of surprise from the kid. Suddenly we had a game. And it didn't look good for me.

The kid stood up, which was usually the move of the player with the likelihood of losing, but that move never sat well with me. I stayed in my seat; as if I had no doubt I'd be there for several more hours.

The turn card was a queen. Kid had a full boat.

And it looked like I'd be leaving the chair considerably sooner.

I could still take him if the river card was an ace. I'd have a boat too, mine ace-high to his queens.

The dealer flipped over a ten. It was definitely the kid's night.

"Gentlemen, good luck to you," I said to the table in general as I got up to leave. I handed the dealer my one remaining chip—a nice tip for him, and he thanked me.

The kid came around to me as I gathered up my jacket. "Would you be pissed if I said I'm sorry?" he said sticking out his hand for me to shake.

I took it. "Never apologize for a win, kid." I gave him a smile, showing him there were no hard feelings. There wasn't room in poker for hard feelings, not if you were coming back the next day.

And the next.

"Yeah, but the way you played me," he said to me, quietly, so the others wouldn't hear. "That was a thing of beauty, then to take a bad beat, it almost doesn't seem right."

I shrugged. "That's why it's called gambling." I started to walk away, but he stopped me with a hand to my sleeve.

"My name's Jason, by the way," he said.

"Anna."

"Yeah, I know, I've seen you on TV. You're the Black Widow," he said, referring to the nickname some television announcer had given me early in my career due to the black suits I wore when I was at a final table. "I think you're amazing."

"Thanks," I said. What could you say to that, really? The little shit had knocked me out of a game I really needed to win and turns out he was a member of my fan club.

"Are you going to get into another game now?" he asked.

Not here, not with an empty wallet. There were games—in other places—to get into with no money, but I wasn't going to lead the kid down that path. "Nah," I said, "I'm going home to lick my wounds."

He got this apologetic look on his face. "I'm just kidding, Jason. You got me. And, you'll never fall for a false tell again, or at least not so quickly."

"Why did you tip me off to what you'd done?" he asked.

I shrugged. "Some very good players helped me along the way. I'm just returning the favor. Hopefully, you will too, someday."

"Thanks," he said, moving toward me, wanting to continue the conversation, but I turned and headed toward the back of the room.

"See ya around, Jason," I said lifting my hand in a reverse wave.

I could feel his eyes on my back. Kid should have been back at the game, taking the rest of the players down with his intimidating pot, not watching me.

I beelined for Jeffrey, who was working at the high desk area with a couple of the other poker room supervisors.

"Hey, Anna, you out?" he said as I approached.

"Kiss me," I said.

He knew the drill. I'd had him show me some PDA before for the benefit of anybody with ideas. Not that Jason had any ideas beyond knocking out a pro from a game, but why not send that message home.

Jeffrey didn't miss a beat, he wrapped his arms around me, gave me a hug, and then, just to show we weren't just long-lost cousins, he planted a wet, sloppy kiss on me.

I started to giggle but he only whispered, "You asked for it," and continued on.

When he pulled away I watched as his eyes went over my head to the direction I'd come from. "The kid?" he asked with just a bit too much disbelief in my opinion. Jason, as I suspected, must have been watching me. Watching us.

"What? I can't attract a twenty-one-year old?"

Jeffrey straightened his tie, which in no way had gotten askew from our kiss, looked at me and grinned, "I'm not touching that one."

"Smart man."

"I'm done in an hour, why don't you wait for me in the book?"

I nodded, and headed away after I'd said hi to the other poker room guys. I settled in at the book room. It was late, so no games were on, but ESPN and its sister-stations were on the televisions, so I watched the scores, calculated the point spreads, read the stats of the players, committing it all to memory. Well, not all to memory. I got up, went to the side of the room where all the odds sheets were, grabbed one not looking at what it was for, a pen from the box next to the sheets and went back to my chair ready to write down more stats as they came up.

I was about to flip the paper over to write on the back when I noticed that I'd grabbed the lines for tomorrow's college hoops games. They must have just been put out.

Shit. There it was, jumping out at me. Central Iowa at Northwestern. CIU was a twenty-five point favorite which is a hell of a lot of points. Especially for a win on the road. But Raymond Joseph had been playing with a vengeance since his embarrassing showing at Minnesota three weeks ago. And he was from Chicago, so he'd want to show off for his hometown friends.

I had to bet that game.

But my wallet was empty.

I turned away from the paper, up to the board. Amidst all the brightly colored lights that listed all the games and point spreads across the entire side wall of the book room, the CIU game seemed to burn brighter, as if it was almost flashing at me.

Yeah, I know, I silently told it. Iowa's going to win by thirty. Raymod Joseph's going to have the game of his life. I felt it.

I *knew* it.

My stomach clenched, I knew what I was going to do.

I gathered my things and headed back to the poker room, which conveniently sat right beside the sports book. I went through a side entrance to avoid Jason's table and found Jeffrey where I'd left him not ten minutes before.

He didn't seem all that surprised to see me coming. "Taking a rain check?" he asked when I got to him.

I smiled. "Yeah. You mind?"

He shrugged. "Would it matter if I said yes?"

I struggled for an answer, but he let me off the hook. "Don't answer that. I don't really want to know."

I gave him a quick kiss and headed away. "Anna," he called after me. I turned. "Next time I'm going to tell you to wait for me at the bar."

I smiled. "Next time I will," I answered.

But we both knew it wasn't true.

As soon as I was out of sight of the poker room I grabbed my cell phone and dialed. I should have this number in my speed dial, but Lorelei always sets my phones up for me when she buys me new ones and I didn't give her this number to enter.

We don't do cell phone contracts. No sense having another monthly bill that might need to be shuffled in a lean period. We buy the pay as you go ones and when I hit, Lorelei buys a bunch of phone cards.

Besides, I know this number by heart.

"Yo," the man picked up on the first ring.

"Paulie. It's Anna."

"Hey, Anna," his voice softened.

"Where's the game tonight?" I asked as I pulled the pen and paper I'd written stats on in the bookroom out of my jacket pocket.

"Caesar's," he said. I did a yooie, heading away from the parking deck and back toward the casino, to the walkway that led to Caesar's Palace. "Room fortythree-twentytwo."

I wrote it down. I'd played in too many different hotel rooms to imagine I could remember a different number every night.

"There room for one more?" I asked Paulie.

"There's always room for you, Anna," he said. It should have been sweet, but there was just enough come-on in his voice to make it oily.

Kind of like Paulie himself.

On my walk to Caesar's, I pulled a stack of hotel key cards from one of the pockets in my cargo pants. I didn't carry a purse when I was gambling. Between the pockets of my leather jacket (which became denim in warmer months), and multi-pocketed pants, I usually had enough room for my keys, cell phone, ID and money. Paper and pen could be found at every book room. Anything else just got in the way.

I flipped through the key cards until I found one from Caesar's and put the rest away, buttoning the pocket.

I moved quickly through the casino toward the hotel elevator banks. I flashed my key card to the security guard, the one that stood by the elevators and made sure only registered guests got by.

I tried not to make eye contact with those guys—I don't want them remembering me. Or questioning why I seem to be a hotel guest for one night, never have any luggage, and come back every ten days or so.

Of course, with the amount of people they see go through, it probably wasn't a problem, but I kept my head down just the same.

When I got to the room number Paulie gave me I knocked. When he opened the door I saw that it was a suite. I wasn't surprised. Vince had come a long way since I'd first met him. Back then he'd been running back room games in…well, back rooms.

Back rooms of restaurants, stores, whatever. But since he moved his floating operation to hotel suites his clientele had noticeably improved.

So, why were there ten guys up here playing poker when there were perfectly good poker tables only a few floors below? And those came with scantily-clad cocktail waitresses.

First of all, you knew if you played in one of Vince's games you were playing with real players. Not yahoo tourists who'd watched *The World Series of Poker* on ESPN and figured they'd give it a try on their next vacation.

Now, in theory, being at a table with bad players is a good thing in poker. It isn't like that in black jack where a bad player could take the dealer's bust card and the whole table loses.

But for those of us who truly loved the game, you wanted to play with good players. Great players. To know you took down a good player brought so much more satisfaction than bringing down a table full of tourists.

And more money.

Also, when you play at a cash game at a casino, you lose a little of each pot to "the rake"—the percentage that the house takes out of each pot. That's how the casinos make money on poker, because, of course, the dealer never wins as they do in black jack or other games. Instead, a percentage of each pot is taken in for the house. The rest to the winner.

These games tended to bring out the "whales", big spenders, big stakes, basically the biggest fish in the sea. Yeah, I know a whale is not technically a fish, but I didn't make up the term. There are high-roller poker rooms in each casino, and most times the whales played there, but sometimes they wanted even more privacy than those little enclaves afforded them.

Maybe they shouldn't be seen in a casino? I've played across from some politicians, a couple of NBA players and a high-profile college football coach, none of whom would want it known they were playing high-stakes poker in a casino.

The other reason people played Vince's games was the reason I was here tonight.

I stepped past Paulie, nodding hello, and over to a desk area where Carla, Vince's bookkeeper, was set up.

Carla was a pretty woman with what she would tell you—and often did—twenty extra pounds. She had dark hair that had just started showing streaks of gray, that she wore in a severe bob. In her late forties, she'd been working for Vince since I'd come on the scene.

"Hey, Carla," I said.

She looked up from her *People* magazine. "Hey, Anna. You playing tonight?"

You would think that would be obvious, but I guess I could have been there to pay off a debt or something. "Yeah," I answered.

"Cash or marker?" she asked.

"What's the starting stake?"

"Twenty," she said.

I pretended to think about it. Like any second I'd pull out twenty thousand dollars from one of my pockets. I saw Carla exchange a look with Paulie and knew I wasn't fooling anybody.

"Marker," I said.

Carla wrote it down in her ledger book. She flipped the book around and pointed for me to sign. I did. Not legal of course, but definitely binding.

She handed me a stack of chips, and just like that; with interest, I was in debt to Vince for twenty-four thousand dollars. If I didn't pay him back in one week, it would be thirty.

And I got the friends and family interest rate.

But I didn't think about owing Vince after tonight. I never did. I'd win more that 24K, pay Carla, stop by the book and bet the CIU game and if there was any left, I'd give it to Lorelei to stash.

Every time I stepped into this room—or one in any hotel just like it, I knew...*I knew*... I would win.

Why else would I bother?

Two hours later the plan was right on track. Just a couple more hands and I'd pay Carla, bet the game, have some for Lorelei and maybe even have time for a quick nap before taking Ben to breakfast.

I had Mr. Chow on the hook and he knew it.

I'd played with him before. Good player. Excellent player. But I'd had the cards tonight. And now I was two or three hands away from taking his entire stack. He or I had already cleaned out three other players. The other four were still in but limping. Mr. Chow was the big fish tonight and I was going to land him.

He raised my bet, as I knew he would. I hadn't bet much, just feeling him out. I had cards, but I thought he might too. I was just about to re-raise, but only slightly, when a cell phone went off.

All the men checked their jackets, pockets, all shaking their head as the phone continued to ring. Finally everyone in the room turned their eyes to me, looks of surprise on the faces of guys I regularly played with.

Not that a cell phone going off was that unusual, although these players—serious players—talked a lot less on phones than the guys in the casinos. But there were still plenty of plans made—and broken—on phones as the night wore on.

What was so unusual was that it was *my* phone. Nobody ever called me, and certainly not at this time of night.

Ben. As quickly as that thought processed, sheer terror shot through me. I reached for my phone, stumbling on the button of my cargo pants pocket. A quick look at the caller ID confirmed my fears.

"Ben?" I answered. Mr. Chow pointed to my cards, I held up my finger—"one second" style.

"Hannah, darling, come home. I need you," Ben said, his soft voice barely audible.

"Ben? Are you okay?" Stupid. Would he be calling me at three a.m. if he were okay? Would he even be up? Truth was I didn't know a lot about Ben's nocturnal habits, that was more Lorelei's shift than mine.

"No. I need you to come home," Ben answered.

"Do you need an ambulance? Is Lorelei there? What's happened?"

"I don't need an ambulance. Lorelei is here but she can't help." He paused, taking a deep breath. "I need *you*, Hannah. Please come home."

"I'm on my way," I said and hung up, already rising from my chair.

I reached for my chips and only then realized I was still in the middle of a hand. I looked at Mr. Chow. He probably had cards. I knew that. That's why I'd been betting small on this hand.

I should just fold, concede this hand to him and cash out. I looked at my stack. I could easily pay Carla and have some left over. Probably not as much as I'd wanted to have to bet on the basketball game, but depending on what was going on at home, I probably wouldn't get a chance to bet it anyway.

I picked up my cards, ready to toss them in…and then I stopped, my hand frozen. Call it the devil on your shoulder. Call it deep-seeded demons. Call it whatever they do in any twelve-step program.

I called it a "hummer".

No, not that kind.

And right then the hummer ran through me like a locomotive.

When it snuck up on you like that; in a hand of poker, or watching somebody hit a three point shot as the buzzer ran out to make the spread. Well, there's no feeling like it in the world. Part dread, part elation, and all exhilarating.

It was better than chocolate. Better than sex.

Better than chocolate-covered sex.

But also that feeling you get during a scary movie right before the starlet has her head chopped off.

I set my cards back down. Pushed my stack to the center of the table and declared, "All in." The hum rushed through me, making my stomach clench with anxiety. Dollar signs dancing in front of my eyes.

The hum lasted only a second until Mr. Chow nearly broke his arm pushing his chips in to call me.

And I knew I'd been the fish tonight.

He turned over pocket aces to my queens. I knew there'd be no miracles and there weren't. I motioned to the dealer to hurry up and he did, but I didn't need to stick around.

I shook Mr. Chow's hand, nodded goodnight to everyone and started to leave the room. I turned back, went to Paulie and Carla. "Something's up at home. Tell Vince I may need a couple of days to make arrangements."

Carla nodded, a look of empathy on her face. "Sure, hon, we'll tell him. Hope everything's okay."

Paulie had a look of suspicion—who could blame him. People probably gave him sob stories everyday about their debts. I had myself years ago, before I'd learned it wouldn't get me anywhere.

But on closer inspection, the suspicion gave way to curiosity. I had never tried this tactic with him. And I sure as heck never walked away from a game when I was winning.

I shrugged. He nodded. I walked out of the room and to the elevators. Then walked—and ran at times—as quickly as I could back to the parking deck at the Bellagio.

Five
❖❖

I SQUEALED OUT OF THE PARKING DECK. Cursed the pedestrians that walked across the no walking flashing light. Made my turn as soon as I could and once off the strip, headed to Summerlin. I let my mind wander.

Ben was eighty-two years old. I knew he wouldn't live forever. But I never really allowed myself to think of life without him.

Other than his hip, and arthritis in his other bones and joints, he was in good health. His mind was sharp as a tack.

If he'd been hurt—really hurt—he wouldn't have been able to call me. It would have been Lorelei on the phone.

Making the call I've been dreading since the day I'd met Ben.

Ten Years Ago

"Excuse me, are you watching that?" the old man in the wheelchair next to mine asked.

"What? Hunh?" I answered, coming out of my self-pity and pain killer-induced trance.

"Are you watching that?" he said again, pointing to the television. I looked at the screen, which apparently I'd been watching, though for the life of me I couldn't say what was on. Some kind of detective show.

"No," I said. "Help yourself," I added, leaning down to the coffee table in front of me to get the remote for him. I felt a twinge of pain race up my side and I sat back in my chair quickly, breathing hard. I started forward again, more gently this time, but he laid his hand on my arm.

"I'll get it, dear." Ashamed that a man so old—in a wheelchair no less—was more agile than myself in this state, I sat back in my chair and looked away. I moved to cross my arms across my chest—the universal body language symbol for stay away from me—but even that hurt.

I prayed that the nurse would come soon to tell me they were ready for me in physical therapy so I wouldn't have to make small talk with this old man.

I'd be here for a few hours every day enduring PT for the next few weeks, but my thoughts were on what I was going to do after that.

How I'd survive.

The man took the remote and changed the channels and a basketball game came on the television. "Ahhh," the man said, a sigh almost.

I looked at him, to see if he was in pain—that would give me an excuse to call for a nurse and hopefully get taken out of the waiting room/lounge area and into my session. Or at least take the old man into his.

But he wasn't in pain. His look was almost euphoric as he watched the game.

The game was just ending. "Your team win?" I asked.

He shrugged. "Yes. No. Both," he said. He looked at me with a little smile on his face, a bit of a twinkle in his brown eyes. He reminded me of some old actor. Lee Strasberg, that's his name. With his small stature, and his tuft of white hair standing up on all ends. Dead ringer.

"Both?"

He gave a small chuckle and pulled a small pad of paper

from the side pocket of his chair. Not as big as those steno pads reporter use. The kind that fit in the pocket of a man's shirt. He flipped back a couple of pages and then laid the pad on my wheelchair arm. I looked down, read out loud, "Stanford by five. Over/under one thirty-seven and a half." I looked up at him, not getting it. "So?"

He pointed to the television. I looked at it as the final score of the game flashed. Stanford seventy-one, Arizona sixty-six. I quickly did the math. "Was this game taped or something?"

He smiled widely. "No."

"I don't get it. How did you know that?" Before I even let him respond I added, "Who do you like in tomorrow's games?"

He laughed, hard, then winced and placed his hand on his waist. I grimaced, knowing his pain. "I'm sorry," I said, but he was already waving it off.

He stuck his hand across himself to me, withered and wrinkled, but still a strong grip when I took it. "I'm Ben," he said.

"Johanna," I said. "But everyone calls me Anna."

"A pleasure to meet you, Hannah, but I'm sorry for the circumstances," he said, indicating our shared convalescence.

I was just about to correct him and tell him my name was Anna, but I let it go. It sounded nice coming from him, with a tiny hint of New York and Yiddish accent.

Besides, after today, I'd probably never see him again.

"How much you in for?" Ben asked me three days later. We'd met in the lounge everyday before and after our PT sessions. Watching television, playing cards, talking. Sometimes just sitting.

I was in no hurry to get home, that's for sure.

I could pretend to misunderstand him, but I didn't want to insult his intelligence. Or mine. "Twenty-five," I answered.

"To Vince Santini?"

If I hadn't been surprised that he'd figured out *what* put me in the hospital, I was dumbfounded to realize he also knew the *who*. Well, not exactly the who. Vince didn't do his own dirty work; as I'd found out a week earlier.

I nodded. "How could you possibly know that?"

He pointed to my arms, bare to the short sleeves of my tee-shirt. I'd worn long sleeves at first, but was so warm during PT that I finally gave up on vanity. Besides, I'd figured people would think I was in a car accident, or at the very least, had an abusive boyfriend.

Even that wouldn't be as shameful as what had put me here.

"Classic Santini. No bruises that you can see. And always the broken foot," Ben said.

I looked down at my mangled foot. "Yeah, that's a real bitch."

"Vince thinks of himself as different. Above the fray. He'd never do something as cliché as broken thumbs or a kneecap."

I snorted. "Great. I had to find a loan shark with originality."

"Paulie do it?"

I nodded again, seeing Paulie's face as he hit me again and again. The only saving grace was that I think it actually pained him to do it.

Not as much as it hurt me, though.

There was no judgment from Ben as he asked these questions. No pity either. Which made me wonder. I pointed to his wheelchair. "Not you too?"

He chuckled. "No, Hannah, not me. I was too close to the odds to know the house always wins in the long run. In my younger days I liked to play the ponies a little, but…"

He didn't finish, so I did. "But you were never stupid enough to get mixed up with a man like Vince?" My self-disgust was evident in my voice.

"Oh, I was stupid enough—and young enough," he added,

pointedly looking at me, and I felt a teensy bit better. "To get mixed up in trouble, but it was never with people like Vince."

I wanted to ask more, but before I could, he asked, "How long have you been in Vegas?"

"Three years."

"And how old are you?"

"Twenty-four."

"Ahh," he said, his little head bobbing as if figuring out something. "How long after you turned twenty-one were you on that bus coming from," his eyes narrowed at me, "Minnesota?"

"Wisconsin," I said. He seemed pleased he'd gotten so close, but disappointed not to have been dead on.

An odds maker till the end.

"Two weeks after my birthday," I admitted.

"School?"

I sighed. "A term shy of graduation." He was the only person I'd told out here that I'd quit school early to come here and gamble.

His eyes grew wide. "And your parents?"

"Didn't take it very well," I summed up. No need to tell him about my mother's tears and my father's threats.

"You got the gambling bug, when?"

"My father taught us kids to play poker and we'd have family games. But I had a boyfriend in college who played in a regular game. That's where I really learned to play."

He thought about that for a minute, nodding, then said, "And you…did you… follow a boy out here?"

I nodded. He seemed disappointed until I smiled and said, "The Jack of Hearts."

He laughed, deep and crackly. "Well, he's about as likely to break your heart as any of them, I suppose."

"He has at that," I admitted.

"Any good runs in there?"

"I've made about three quarters of a million in poker since

I've been out here," I said with pride.

"And you've lost how much?"

I smiled. "About three quarters of a million and twenty five thousand."

"And how do you live? What kind of house?"

I didn't really want to tell him, but I knew he'd see through any sugarcoating. Besides, he'd seen me take a cab away from the hospital each day. Ben had different men pick him up.

"I share an apartment with four other people. Two gambling addicts. Two drug addicts."

"Not a good way to live," he said, though he didn't need to.

"No," I said, though I didn't need to.

He put his hand on mine, careful to avoid the bruises on my arm. "Hannah, dear, why don't you come by Arizona Charlie's for breakfast tomorrow morning. Before you have to be here. I have some friends I'd like you to meet."

The next morning I met The Corporation, and had breakfast at the Sourdough Café before PT. I continued the ritual for the next week. They had the same table everyday, and, it appeared, the same no-nonsense waitress.

After hospital food, and then the sparse pickings at my apartment, the breakfast was great, but being a fly on the wall and listening to these old timers talk about odds and gambling was even better.

The day before my last PT session, I was on my way to the workout room, happy to be on crutches instead of in a wheelchair, when Paulie caught up to me in the hallway.

"Hey, Anna, how you feeling?"

I started to shrink away from him but stopped. He seemed almost hurt. "Anna, it was nothing personal. You know that, right? Just business."

"Yeah, I know that." And I did, intellectually. But my gut

didn't.

And what gambler didn't rely more on their gut than their intellect?

"'Cause I really like you, Anna," He said. "I think that we—"

"What's up Paulie? Why are you here?" I said, cutting him off. I did not want to know where he was going.

"I'm here to make arrangements for payment."

"Oh, you mean bruises, pissing blood and two weeks of PT didn't wipe the slate clean?"

"Aww, Anna, c'mon. Don't be that way."

"Listen, Paulie. To pay back Vince I have to play poker. And to be able to do that I need to be able to move around. Which is why I'm in physical therapy. Besides the twenty-five K I owe Vince," I held up a hand as Paulie made to interrupt me. "I know, I know. It's not twenty-five any more. Interest. But, besides that, I now have one hell of a huge hospital bill—thanks to you—to add to that tab."

His face turned to stone. "Then quit, Anna. Play enough to pay Vince, pay your bills and quit. Go to college. Get a regular job. Find a guy and settle down. Do anything but gamble."

A wave of panic washed through me. "I…I…"

The stone turned to disgust. "No. Of course not. You won't quit. Not until you've totally destroyed yourself." He ran his hands across his face, let out a deep breath. "And I'm the scumbag, right? I'm the low-life muscle for a loan-shark."

I was just about to say his name when I heard someone else say, "Paulie? I thought that was you. Could I have a word with you for a moment?'

Paulie whirled around, and I hobbled to the side to see Ben sitting in his chair a few feet down the hall, the boys standing behind him.

"Ben?" Paulie said. "Ben Lowenstein? What are you doing here?" He seemed to realize exactly what Ben was doing in the hospital—the wheelchair was probably a big clue. "I mean, what happened? Are you okay?"

"Broken hip," Ben said. "And I'll be fine. Thank you. Today is my last physical therapy session."

I hadn't known that, but I was glad. Though I knew the boys in The Corporation would bring him, I didn't like the thought of Ben here each day without me.

I didn't like the thought of me in that rat hole apartment without him to talk to daily, either.

"Gentlemen," Paulie said, nodding at the boys. They nodded back. None stepped forward to shake his hand or pat him on the back I noticed.

"Paulie, do you have a minute? There's something I'd like to discuss with you. You don't mind, do you Hannah, darling?"

Paulie looked back at me, probably wondering who had my name wrong, himself or Ben. Or, more likely, wondering how I knew Ben so well that he'd be calling me darling.

"Physical Therapy bonding," I said to Paulie, who thought that over then nodded.

"Sure thing," Paulie said and started toward Ben. I put my crutches in position and swung-walked a few steps before Saul said, "You stay out here with us, dear. Ben would like some privacy, I think."

"Oh, sure. Okay," I said, feeling guilty that I'd assumed Ben wanted to talk with me as well.

Paulie and Ben went back into the lounge and I showed the boys how well I could do on my crutches. Saul was telling me not to overdo it. Gus had found the prettiest nurse on the floor and was chatting her up. Danny just sat in a chair and smiled, silently encouraging me.

"Is that as fast as you can go?" Jimmy said, earning a scowl from Saul and the bird from me.

After about ten minutes, Paulie came from the lounge, and walked quickly by us all. "See you around, Anna," he said as he passed me.

"See ya, Paulie," I said, not stupid enough to remind him we hadn't worked out any payment arrangements yet. He'd find me when he remembered, of that I was sure.

"Why don't you go in now," Saul said to me.

I started moving toward the room but stopped. "Aren't you guys coming?"

"In a minute," Saul said.

I looked at them all, but couldn't read them. They'd been around gambling far too long not to have developed good poker faces.

"What's going on?" I asked Ben when I entered the lounge.

"I just paid Paulie off," Ben said.

"What? But you said you never got involved with loan sharks?"

"It wasn't my debt I paid," he said quietly.

I felt my legs, already weak, go out from under me. I reached for a chair, slid down onto it. "Oh, Ben. You didn't."

He nodded. "I did. And now I'm going to tell you how you're going to pay me back."

And so I moved in with Ben in his tiny ranch house in Henderson, ostensibly to take care of him, though it was mostly the other way around for the first few years. He—and the boys—taught me how to handle my winnings, how to set up safety nets, how to ride out the losses.

And I listened and learned. And won. And won some more. We moved to a bigger place, and then five years after that we moved to the house—a sprawling one-story due to Ben's hip—in Summerlin.

And now I was walking into that house, scared to death of what awaited me.

♠ ♥ ♦ ♣

"Oh Hannah, darling, I'm so glad you're here. It's awful. Just awful." Ben was rushing toward me—or as much as he could rush with his walker. I could tell there was a man behind him, but Ben blocked my view. Lorelei was sitting at the table in the dining room crying.

At least they were both okay.

"He," Ben said, nodding his head over his shoulder. "Wanted me to go with him, but I said I had to wait for you. I need you to go with me."

"Of course, Ben. I'll take you. Where do we need to go?"

"To the morgue. Danny's dead."

Sweet, good-natured Danny. Relief that Ben was all right waged with grief over the loss of one of the best people I'd ever met.

Danny was the first member of The Corporation to die.

I always thought it would be Jimmy the way he ate. But no, he was too mean to die young. Not that late seventies-early eighties could be considered young.

I heard Lorelei sniffle at the table. She poked her head out of her Kleenex, shook her head at me, said, "Oh, Jo," and put her head back into the hands, sniffling some more.

I looked back to Ben who had such a look of pain on his face that it scared me. "Okay. We'll go together. I'm so sorry, Ben."

"Oh Hannah, it's so awful," he said, his voice catching, his hand, cold, grasping mine.

I wasn't surprised Ben would be upset about one of the boys passing—so was I. But there was a desperation to him that scared me.

"It's okay, Ben. Danny lived a great life, he—"

"I don't think you understand Miss," said the voice behind Ben. "Mr. Lowenstien's upset because—" his words were cut off when he rounded Ben and saw me.

Just as what I was about to say died on my lips.

It was the guy. The good-looking guy at the AA meeting. Or NA. Or GA. The one who stood on the stoop with me and didn't go in.

Not that I did either.

He wore the same leather jacket. Another chambray shirt with chinos. This time the tie was on instead of shoved in his jacket pocket. But he looked as disheveled and weary as he had that night.

Of course it was three a.m. and he was apparently on duty.

So, that phone call that cut off us possibly getting a drink probably wasn't a booty call.

More likely a body call.

"You. You're the—" I said rudely pointing at him only—thankfully—to be interrupted by Ben.

"Detective. That's right, Hannah. He's the one who told me about Danny."

The moment where we stared at each other, then silently decided not to out each other passed and the man stepped toward me.

"Detective Jack Schiller. I'm sorry to be the bearer of bad news. But Danny O'Hern was murdered tonight."

Six

❖

"THE DETECTIVE WANTS ME to go with him to the morgue, Hannah. To identify the body. But I told him no. 'I will wait for my Hannah', I said."

I stepped to Ben, placed my hand over his cold one on top of his walker. "That's fine Ben. That's good. I can take you to the…I can take you."

"Actually, I'll need to take Mr. Lowenstein, Ms…?"

"Dawson," I said. "Anna Dawson."

The time for shaking hands had passed, so he just nodded and went on, "But you're welcome to ride along with us. I know Mr. Lowenstein wants your company."

Ben's face went from despair to panic mode, which scared me. I'd never seen him like this—he was my rock.

"Why don't I follow you in my car, then I can drive Ben home when he's…done." I looked to see if that was acceptable to Ben. A silent, tiny nod of his head told me it was.

"I'd be happy to bring you both home afterward," the detective, the bourbon drinker, Jack Schiller, said. Though it was three a.m. and he had a weary, lived-in face, no emotion sparked on his craggy, handsome features. All business.

Murder. What a business.

And I thought gambling was stressful.

But with Ben pale-faced and shaking and Lorelei sobbing

in the dining room, and our poor Danny lying in a morgue somewhere, I sought out Detective Schiller's stoicism like a drowning man searching for a life raft. I took a deep breath, determined to be the calming force for Ben that he'd been so many times for me. I'd feel my pain for Danny's death later.

"No. I'll follow you, Detective," I said to him.

He nodded. "We're going to the city morgue in Henderson, it's on Palamino Street. In case we get separated. Do you know where that is?"

I nodded. "We lived in Henderson for awhile."

"We?" he asked.

I pointed to Ben. "Ben and I. Before Lorelei"

The detective looked to Lorelei and back to Ben and me, probably trying to figure out the dynamic.

Sugar daddy? Charity case? Trophy girlfriend? Trophy girlfriends?

His eyes narrowed on me, probably factoring in my standing in front of the municipal building, unwilling—unable—to go in. I offered up nothing.

A mystery he couldn't solve—at least not now. He seemed to mentally file it all away, shrugged, and said, "Let's go, then."

"Ben, do you want Lorelei to call anybody while we're gone?" I asked. "The boys?"

"The boys? Your sons, Mr. Lowenstein? Or maybe Mr. O'Hern's?"

"Hannah means my friends, Detective."

"Ben and Danny. They're—were—very close, as were three other men. They meet every morning for breakfast," I explained. A thought occurred to me. "Why is it Ben that you came to get? Why not any other one of the group?"

"Mr. Lowenstein's name was found on Mr. O'Hern's person."

Mr. O'Hern's person. Danny's body. Sweet, soft-spoken Danny. Gone from us.

Taken from us.

Ben thought for a minute, nodded. "Yes, maybe that would be best. I'd rather tell them myself, but I don't want them hearing it on the news or something like that. Maybe Lorelei—if you wouldn't mind, dear." Lorelei, as loyal to Ben as I was, wiped her nose, gave Ben a tremulous smile and nodded. "Of course, Ben. Should I wait for a while, or would it be all right to wake them?"

Ben looked to the wall clock. "Start with Jimmy. He'll be up. Then Saul. Leave Gus for last."

Lorelei nodded. "And should I tell them you won't be at breakfast?"

Ben straightened his hunched, aged body, refastened his grip on his walker. "No. I'll be there. I may be late, but tell them I'll be there."

The detective walked with Ben out the door. I hung back. "Lor, you have any plans for tomorrow? Today, I mean?

Lorelei got up from the table, crossed into the foyer, grabbed a pen and pad from the little table there and said, "Nothing that can't wait. What do you need done?"

"I'm not sure. Maybe some groceries? I have no idea what they'll be doing in way of a funeral, but we'd probably better stock up in case we have people over."

She nodded. "Ben would like that. I'll get some stuff and make some calls to have something lined up in case we host a gathering or something after visitation or the funeral. Or even just to have the boys over." She wrote down a few things on her pad.

"That would be good." I looked around the house, spotless as usual, no thanks to me. Lorelei oversaw all of that. Yes, we had a housekeeper who came in twice a week, but Lorelei oversaw the housekeeper.

I walked over to her, hugged her, which surprised her for a moment, then she fiercely hugged me back. "Thanks, Lor, for everything," I said.

I'm a tall woman, but statuesque Lorelei towered over me. She kissed the top of my head. "Thank *you*, Jo. I don't know what I would have done, where I'd be without you."

"Ditto," I said, and pulled away.

"And I don't know what either of us would have done without Ben," she added, though she didn't need to.

"Ditto," I said again, though I didn't need to.

The drive to Henderson was long and dark. And lonely.

I kept thinking of Ben and Jack Schiller in the other car. Was Ben okay? Was Detective Schiller asking Ben about Danny? It would probably be good for Ben to tell him stories of Danny. Or would it be too soon?

I was interrupted from my thoughts by my cell phone. Two times in one night. Not a good sign.

"Jo," Lorelei said when I answered. "I can't get a hold of them. No answer."

"Which one?"

"All of them. None of them."

"Did you try their cell phones?"

"I only have cell numbers for Gus and Jimmy, not Saul. Nothing."

"I don't think Saul has a cell," I said. I knew Ben didn't and those two were pretty similar about technology and their general distaste of it.

Pretty similar about most things.

"This is really weird," Lorelei said. "I mean, what are all those old coots doing out so late—or so early. Unless…"

"Unless what?" I asked cautiously. I thought I could see where Lorelei was headed, even though I didn't want to.

"Unless they were with Danny. Or something bad happened to them, too."

"Oh, man, Lor, don't even go there."

"Right. You're right. I'm just spooked that's all."

"Right."

"Except…"

"Yeah," I said. "Call me if you hear anything," I said.

"You too."

"I will," I said and hung up, my foot pressing a little harder on the gas.

I missed the last light so I was well behind the detective and Ben when I got to the morgue's parking lot. There were several cars, but I didn't know if that was usual or not for this time of night.

Could have been a slow night in Vegas for all I knew.

There was a receptionist at the front desk. He looked up, no emotion on his face at all. I suppose he was used to everything in this job.

"I'm with Detective Schiller and—" I didn't even need to finish; he pointed down the hall to the left. It's not like he would have known Ben's name anyway.

"Third door on the right," he said.

"Thanks."

I walked to the door, opened it slowly. I wasn't sure if I'd be walking into the room with the body. If Ben would be in there, needing me, or needing a moment alone.

But the door led to another hallway, which was empty except for Jack Schiller standing in front of one of several doors.

"Ms. Dawson, we're in here."

I walked toward him. "It's Anna," I said, and he nodded, but didn't correct himself. He held the door open for me. I took a deep breath, let it out, and walked across the threshold, expecting the worse.

But found only Ben sitting at a table in a small room. There was a coffee pot on a sideboard along the wall and another man was standing there pouring a cup. "Cream? Sugar?" he asked Ben over his shoulder.

"Black," both Ben and I said at the same time. The man didn't turn to me; he must have heard the detective in the hall addressing me. But Ben looked up, relief rushing across his face, his hand reaching for me.

I went and sat in the seat next to him, clasping his cold hand in mine. The other man sat Ben's coffee down in front of him. "Coffee?" he asked me.

"No, thank you."

"Ms. Dawson, this is my partner, Detective Frank Botz."

He leaned across the table and held out his hand. "Ma'am," he said.

The "ma'am" made me feel ancient, even though he had to be in his fifties. He had thinning hair and a bit of a gut that pulled his shirt slightly at the buttons. There was a stain on his Betty Boop tie that looked like mustard.

His eyes were kind, his small smile of greeting was warm, and his face was lined at his eyes and the corner of his mouth like he laughed a lot.

"Detective," I said, shaking his hand with my free one—Ben still clung to my left.

"We've had a change in plans," Jack Schiller said.

"Oh?" I said, trying to sound calm, but all I could think of was Lorelei's phone call about the boys. Did Ben now have to identify four bodies?

Ben's hand tightened on mine. Was he wondering the same thing? I squeezed his hand, trying to send strength. Or maybe trying to receive it.

"We don't need you to identify the body any longer, sir. But you're welcome to view it if you'd like."

Ben looked to me. "Do you want to, Ben?" I asked quietly.

He thought for a moment then softly nodded. "Yes. Yes, I want to see my friend. I need to see my Danny."

I nodded, understanding. "Why don't you need Ben

anymore?" I asked the detectives.

"Somebody else was able to make a positive ID," Detective Botz said.

Just as Ben and I both asked, "Who?" Detective Schiller asked, "How long have you known Mr. O'Hern, Mr. Lowenstein?"

He didn't seem to acknowledge our question, just waited for Ben's answer.

"I've known Danny O'Hern for over forty years," Ben said with something like pride in his voice. "A kinder, sweeter man you'd never meet."

Detective Schiller took a seat at the table, directly across from Ben and to my right. Detective Botz went back to the wall and leaned against the sideboard. He pulled a notebook out of his suit pocket.

In my foggy mind I found it odd and slightly amusing that he used the same kind of notebook Ben did—all the boys did—to make book.

He wrote something in it, then folded his arms across his chest and looked at Detective Schiller, giving him just the slightest of nods. Detective Schiller turned back to us.

Something about their movements seemed so practiced, as if they'd done this over and over.

Suddenly a shiver of fear went through me. These were homicide detectives and this was some kind of make-shift interrogation room.

"Why are you—" But again, before I could get my question answered—or even asked this time—Detective Schiller said, "Is that a bit of New York accent I detect, Mr. Lowenstein?"

"Bronx," Ben said, pride definitely in his voice now.

"Did you know Mr. O'Hern in New York?"

"No. No. I didn't meet Danny until I was out here. I've been here for over sixty years, but I guess I still have a bit of the old neighborhood in me."

"Nothing wrong with that," Detective Botz said, heavy on an accent of his own which I hadn't noticed until now.

"Philly?" Ben said to the man who chuckled.

"That's right. Good ear. You spend much time in Philly, Mr. Lowenstein? Or Pennsylvania at all?"

"No. None. I just have an ear for accents. And around here, sooner or later you hear all of them."

"Mr. O'Hern? He was from the East Coast, too, originally?" Detective Schiller asked, drawing Ben's attention back to him. Out of the corner of my eye I saw Detective Botz write something in his notebook, and my concern level went up.

"Danny? No, Danny's family came over from Ireland when he was just a baby. They settled in Chicago. Danny came out here when he was in his twenties." Ben's voice turned soft, wistful as he continued. "Danny only had an accent when he wanted to."

I smiled, thinking of sweet Danny and his lilting brogue that came out every now and then. For a joke. Or a toast.

Or to call me his "wee one".

Ben took his hand from mine, pushed his chair back and said, "I think I'm ready to see him, now."

Detective Schiller motioned for Ben to stay sitting, which he did. "Just a couple more questions." His voice held just enough authority in it to edge my concern to unease. "Do you know of anybody who would want to hurt Mr. O'Hern?"

"Danny? No. No," Ben said quickly, shaking his head.

"Detective," I said, "Danny O'Hern was the sweetest, most mild-mannered man you'd ever want to meet. No way would anyone want to hurt him. This—whatever it is that happened—had to have been random."

"You mean to say he lived in Vegas for over sixty years, worked in the gambling industry where the odds he set made people millionaires and others paupers and he didn't have one enemy?"

I narrowed my eyes at Jack Schiller. He obviously knew a

hell of a lot more about Danny than he'd let on.

He flicked a glance at me, and started to ask another question, but this time I interrupted him. "Is Ben allowed to see Danny or not?"

He didn't seem ready to give in. I pushed away from the table, rose from my chair, nodded at Ben to do the same.

Ben looked to both men, questioningly.

Detective Schiller let out a loud, disgruntled sigh as Detective Botz pushed away from the wall. "Yeah, you can see him now," Detective Schiller said.

We walked out into the hallway. Ben and I stood in the center of the hall, waiting for the detectives to lead the way. But instead, they each went to one of the other doors and gave a quick knock. Detective Botz then went to yet another door and gave a short rap with his knuckles. They stood back against the wall, waiting.

Ben looked at me, I shrugged in return. When all three doors opened, I got the willies, not sure what to expect.

Out stepped three uniformed police officers. They each stepped aside from their respective doorways, and motioned for the inhabitants to come out.

One by one, from three different rooms, stepped Saul, Gus and Jimmy.

Ben gasped. I took a step backward.

They looked amongst themselves. It was obvious the other three had been told about Danny, their grief plain on their faces. It was also obvious that like me—and probably Ben—they'd been wondering about the fate of the others.

The relief on each of their faces was heartbreaking.

Saul stepped to Ben's side, around his walker and hugged him fiercely. Gus came along side and patted them both on the back, leaving his hand there, as if to reassure himself that his friends—the ones in this hallway if not the other one in the building—were okay.

And Jimmy…well…Jimmy wasn't going to get within a hundred yards of a group hug, but I caught his eye. He just nodded to me. I nodded back.

But I knew what he felt.

"Gentlemen. This way," Detective Botz said, leading the men down the hallway to a swinging door. To Danny.

The boys fell in line behind him. Walking slowly, at Ben's pace. Two by two. Saul and Ben followed by Gus and Jimmy.

The police officers followed. As Detective Schiller passed me, I put my hand on his chest. "Hang on," I said, not looking at him, my eyes following the boys' progress. The detective waited.

When the boys and the officers had gone through the doors I turned to Detective Jack Schiller.

"Okay, Bourbon," I said. He snorted, then lifted his lip—not quite a smile, not quite a sneer—at my nickname for him. He raised a brow at me, challenging me.

Never one to back down from a challenge, I put my hands on my hips, raised my chin and asked, "What the fuck is going on?"

Seven

❖❖

TWO HOURS LATER the four remaining members of The Corporation and I were sitting at the Sourdough Café, though no one was eating. Danny's empty chair mocked us all.

Jack Schiller had merely laughed at my demand for information, further infuriating me. He'd followed the boys into the room with Danny's body and I'd waited out in the hall, giving Lorelei a quick call to let her know the rest of the boys were okay and accounted for. The boys had come out by themselves, and I'd never gotten the chance to talk to the detectives—either one of them.

Grace, our regular waitress, was beside herself when Saul told her about Danny. It was a good thing nobody wanted any food; it was all she could manage just to keep the coffee coming.

And we drank a hell of a lot of coffee. Not that anybody was sleepy. But the caffeine helped to stave off the numbness felt over Danny's death.

"So," I started, not wanting to broach the subject, but knowing it had to be done. "What are we going to do about a funeral? Do you want me to call Lorelei and have her come down here? She'd help us plan anything you want to do."

All four of them looked at me like I was crazy. Finally Saul put a soft hand on my arm. "Moira will do that, Anna."

Moira. Danny's wife. I'd met her a few times, and of course

she'd be the one who would handle the arrangements. It's just…I guess…I thought of myself and The Corporation as Danny's family.

I certainly thought of them as mine.

"Oh. Right. Of course. Moira. And his daughters," I said, realizing that others were yet to be devastated by this news.

"Yes, the girls, though they're grown of course and long gone. Kids of their own."

"Tina lives in Laughlin," Gus mentioned.

The others nodded. "I think Lisa is still in Florida," Ben said. "Of course, she'll come."

"Moira might like to have you do something, Anna," Jimmy said. "Maybe after the funeral? Some kind of wake or something?"

We all looked at him, but he only shrugged. "She'll have family with her. Their house ain't that big, not after they sold the bigger one when the girls left." He gave me a pointed look, but I wasn't sure what he was getting at.

"Of course we can do that. I'll let Lor know, and…" I looked at the men, "Should I contact Moira and offer, or should one - "

Jimmy raised a hand, stopping me. "I'll mention it to her. I'm going to stop by her place after I leave here and see if she needs anything until the girls can get here."

We were all stunned into silence, then Saul said, "That's very nice of you, Jimmy."

Jimmy only shrugged once again, gave me another look which I still wasn't deciphering, and drank from his cup of coffee.

"Detective Botz said he would be going to let Moira know as we were leaving," Saul said.

"Botz. Was that the older guy or the young one?" Gus asked.

"Older one," Jimmy and I both said at the same time.

"Oh. Then it was the other one that brought me in," Gus

said.

"Schiller," Jimmy and I both said, again simultaneously. He raised an eyebrow at me, but I looked at Saul. "Did Detective Schiller come and get you?"

He shook his head; his huge glasses seemed to take up even more space on his face than usual, as if the news of Danny's death had diminished him physically. "Detective Botz came and got me. It seems as if forever ago." He looked at his watch. "It *was* forever ago. They kept me waiting for so long. You don't know the thoughts that went through my head." He raised his hands in a gesture of surrender, then let them fall to his lap.

"That's what they wanted," Jimmy said.

"Why do you say that, Jimmy?" Ben asked.

Jimmy hailed Grace and ordered breakfast—apparently he'd gotten over the grief-induced inability to eat. He turned back to the group, all anxious for his answer. "Botz picked up two of us, Schiller the other two, right?" The men all nodded, I leaned forward in my seat, setting my coffee cup down.

Jimmy can be as full of shit as any gambler, but he'd been around, and seen a lot of stuff go down, and we all knew it.

"They could have sent patrolmen around to get us. Hell, they could have called us down."

We looked amongst ourselves, no one really knowing where Jimmy was going with this.

"They was lookin' for reactions. Trying to see what we'd do when we heard the news that Danny was dead."

Still nobody said anything, so Jimmy continued. "And we now know we weren't really needed to identify the body. And I don't believe the cock and bull story they told me about finding my name on Danny's body."

"That's what they told me, too," Ben said, as I nodded in agreement. Gus and Saul did as well.

"They came and got us, told us the news, then had us sitting there for Christ knows how long…letting us stew about Danny.

Not knowing if the other three were dead too."

"That's right," Saul said, in an almost accusing tone. Accusing of whom, I didn't know.

"It took so long to get me there because I made them wait for Hannah to come home," Ben said.

Jimmy shrugged. "I don't know about that, but I was there a helluva long time before they rapped on the door and led me out into the hall…only to see the three of you."

"Me too," Saul said. "And what was that all about, anyway? Getting us all in the hall like that?"

"Reactions," Jimmy said, and this time everyone began to slowly nod their heads, finally getting Jimmy's drift.

"We're all suspects," he said.

Gus scoffed at that. Ben waved his hands in dismissal. Saul said something in Yiddish that I hadn't picked up from Ben.

But a different feeling came over the table, and we all drifted to silence, watching Jimmy eat, finishing our coffee.

Thinking.

If I ever saw him again, I was going to rip Jack Schiller a new one for the looks that passed between those four men in the next half hour.

At first it was nothing, then an occasional glance at each other. And at some point, the looks had turned to questions.

Did one of them kill Danny?

"So Ben," I said on the drive home.

"Yes?" His voice was quiet, tired. No wonder, it was now eight in the morning. I hadn't been to bed and I wasn't sure if Ben had either. If he had, he'd been awakened by Jack Schiller in the wee hours.

It wasn't unusual for me to be coming home at eight in the morning, but I knew this night had taken a toll on Ben.

Would take an even harder toll in the upcoming days.

"Danny and Moira were married for how long?"

"Fifty-two years," he answered, a small trace of pride in his voice.

"And Saul? He was only married to Rachael, right, for, like forever?"

"Twenty years," Ben said, his face still to the window.

"That's all? The way he talks about her I thought it was longer."

"It was as long as she had."

Right, the love of Saul's life had died and he'd never gotten over it.

"And Gus? Was it two wives or three?"

Ben turned forward, a tiny smile on his face. "Gus has been married four times. Gus and women…" he put his hands up as if to explain, then threw them down into his lap. "Oy," he summed up.

"When was the last one?"

"Oh, fifteen, twenty-years ago. Long before you and I met."

"And Jimmy? He never talks about his personal life. Or at least not when I'm around."

"Mmmm, Jimmy," Ben said. I waited. "Jimmy and his wife split up when Jimmy's son was a little boy. His gambling did them in," he said, looking at me pointedly.

I kept my eyes on the road, not answering.

"His wife took the boy back east, remarried."

"Did Jimmy see his son very often?" I'd never heard Jimmy mention seeing his son in the ten years I'd known him.

Ben shook his head. "No. They tried at first, but Elaine didn't want Jimmy's 'bad habits' influencing little James. They'd fight. It was a mess."

"When was the last time he saw him?"

He thought about it. "Nearly forty years ago, I guess."

"That's so sad," I said, feeling sorry for Jimmy. As much as

I could feel sorry for Jimmy.

"Yes, Hannah. Gambling. Addiction of any kind…there's no place for it when you're raising children. You always put it first, when it should be the child."

"I'm not raising children, Ben. Unless you count you and Lorelei."

He let out a soft snort. "Not yet you're not. But there'll come a day, mark my words."

At this point I doubted it, but I didn't argue with him. "Besides," I said, "gambling is my profession not my addiction."

He looked closely at me, his stare making me squirm. "Hannah, darling," he said quietly, "don't ever mistake me for Lorelei."

We rode the rest of the way in silence.

When we got home, I went around the front of my car to help Ben out. We do it every morning, and it's not an easy task, but this morning Ben huffed and grunted a little more than usual as he got out of the low seat. It took a good pull from me to get him upright. I put the walker in front of him and stepped away, knowing he wanted as little help as possible.

He got past the car door and before I could reach to shut it for him, he slammed it shut with a force I didn't know he had. "God damn car," he whispered under his breath as he shuffled up the sidewalk.

Lorelei was full of questions when we came in, but Ben only patted her arm, said he was tired and continued on to his room.

I told Lorelei what I knew, that Danny had been shot, execution style, in the back of the head and found in a parking lot. One rarely used and without any kind of security camera set-up. The police were unclear whether he'd been killed at the scene or if he'd been moved there after.

"Oh, come on," Lorelei said. "They can tell that stuff right away."

"I know. I thought the same thing. The boys seemed to buy it."

"Did you get anything out of him? That yummy detective that was here?"

Ah, so Lorelei had noticed Jack Schiller's…yumminess. Not the first adjective that came to mind when I thought of him—I'd use intense, shrewd, disturbing—but certainly not off the mark.

"No, not really. I tried, but by the time they offered up even that much the boys had just seen Danny's body and were in no condition to really think straight. And then they just wanted to get out of there.

"I need to get some sleep," I said and started to rise, but then fell back into the chair, a new thought invading my mind.

"Lor, how's the slush fund these days?" I asked, referring to the fund that Lorelei kept for the household. The fund built on my winnings.

"Good. Healthy as a matter of fact." She seemed to realize that I'd never asked her this question before. If it was getting low, she'd let me know and I'd take care of it. I never queried the amount. And I *never* asked for any money from the fund. It was a one-way fund as far as the family was concerned.

"Why?" she asked, with just a trace of suspicion in her voice.

I pulled the *Sports Illustrated* that sat on the table over to me. It was the one that had the article about The Corporation in it. Lorelei had bought twenty copies when it came out. I flipped through it until I came to the article. The picture of them all at the Sourdough brought stinging tears to my eyes. I flipped the magazine shut and turned back to Lorelei, hoping her suspicion had abated.

"Think it could spare thirty thousand?"

"Yeeeessss," she said in a question, her voice definitely suspicious now.

Feelings rushed through me. Guilt. Fear. I looked at Lorelei, her pretty face turning from suspicion to apprehension. She bit her lower lip waiting for my …request? Sob story? Outright lie?

Loyalty. And shame. Those were the emotions that won out. Mostly shame. "Could you take Ben shopping for a new car in the next few days?"

Relief washed over her face. "Yes. Of course."

I nodded. "Something big, that's easy for him to get in and out of. Make sure you have him test a couple of them out. He's not going to like it, but make him."

She was nodding, grabbing for her pad and pen, which always seemed to be just a reach away from Lorelei. "Right. Right. This is good. It'll take his mind off Danny."

I nodded, like that had been my plan all along. Who knows, maybe it had been.

She was writing furiously on the pad. "What about the Porsche? You want me to trade it in?"

I looked behind me, through the windows to my baby parked in the driveway, next to Lorelei's BMW. "Nah, not if the slush fund can swing it without it."

"It can. No problem." She wrote something else.

Another thought occurred to me, and I pulled my cell phone out of my cargo pants pocket, laid it on the table. "While you're at it. You're right, it's time to upgrade our phones. Go to town."

A look of bliss passed over her face. For a dancer by trade, Lorelei had an odd penchant for techno gizmos. Thank goodness someone in the household did or we'd still just have a toaster in the kitchen and be woken up each day by hand-wound alarm clocks.

"Iphones," she whispered with reverence.

"Really? That fancy? I won't know how to use it." And if I couldn't, Ben probably wouldn't be able to either.

She rushed on, not wanting to lose me. "I'll do everything. I'll totally set it up for you. It'll just take a couple of clicks for you to do anything."

"I don't know," I hedged. Technology kind of intimidated me. We had one family computer in our house growing up, and not even internet access until after I left for college. Which was just before every student had a cell phone and a laptop. I was out here by then, and those first few years either didn't have the time - because I was busy winning at cards—or the money—because I was losing—to buy all that stuff.

I still got all my scores from newspapers unless Lorelei got online and printed them out for me. I was the only poker player I knew that didn't play online.

Fifty-two playing cards had been working for hundreds of years—that was my kind of technology.

I could still learn all of that stuff, it wouldn't be hard, but I don't trust myself to not be online all day playing poker if I did.

Yeah, much better to be in a smoke-filled casino all day playing poker.

"And I'll set it up so with just one little click you'll be able to get scores," Lorelei pulled me back into the conversation.

Ah, Lorelei, a born saleswoman, which is probably why she still got an occasional dancing gig at the ripe old age—for dancers in Vegas—of forty.

"Okay. Iphones," I said and was instantly rewarded with a squeal of delight.

"You're more excited about a phone than a new car?" I asked. She just shrugged.

"Make sure mine is idiot-proof," I said. "And set up a separate ring tone for Ben and a separate one for you," I said, remembering my looking around stupidly when my phone had rung at the poker game earlier.

"And a separate one for Jeffrey?"

I shrugged. "Nah," I said. Lorelei shook her head with dismay. "He doesn't call much, we see each other at the Bellagio," I rationalized to her, but she wasn't buying it.

Neither was I.

I rose from the table, taking my phone with me. "I'm going to hang on to this one. Even after the new ones, so keep getting me a refill card every now and then, okay?" She nodded, lost in her Iphone victory. Good. I really didn't want her thinking too much about why I wanted a phone that wasn't traceable to any account or contract.

"I'm headed for bed. You need anything from me before I go?"

She shook her head. "Oh. Wait. The new car? You want that in Ben's name, right?"

I thought for a minute. "Put this one in yours, Lor."

"Really?" she said, obviously touched. That made me wish I'd done it sooner.

I really *had* to start thinking about things other than gambling.

"Okay. You sure you don't want to come with us?"

I shook my head. "Nope. Can't. I have to be somewhere later."

I thought of my eventual visit to see Vince today—empty handed. Yes, *definitely* time to think about things other than gambling.

I went to my room, pulled off my jacket. I turned on the television then went to draw the black-out blinds Lorelei had thoughtfully had installed when we'd moved into this place. I toed off my shoes, peeled off my socks, slipped off my cargo pants and crawled into bed, shirt, panties and bra still on.

My clothes held a strong aroma of smoke from the poker game and ammonia from the morgue. I peeled my shirt off and threw it across the room as if to rid myself of the last twelve hours.

Scores were running across the ticker on the television. I waited to see the one I wanted. The game I'd needed money to bet. The reason I went to the back room game in the first place.

With the time change, and it being an early game in the Midwest, I figured the game would be over by now.

Central Iowa eighty-three, Norhtwestern fifty-four. CIU easily covered the point spread. Raymond Joseph had a career-high game.

Just as I'd predicted. And I not only didn't clean up in that game, but was now into Vince for twenty-four k. Probably an eighty thousand dollar swing.

Not in my favor.

I turned the television off and pulled the comforter up over my head.

Eight
◆◆

"**YOU'VE GOT TWO WEEKS**," Vince said to me later that night.

When I woke up late in the afternoon, Lorelei and Ben were out, so I'd called Paulie to find out where—or if—I could find Vince. Vince Santini didn't have many face-to-face meetings; Paulie was his man of action. And meeting with Vince was never a good thing.

I was kind of surprised when Paulie'd called back five minutes later and said Vince would meet me at the gelato stand at the Bellagio.

Which was where we now sat, on the little wrought iron chairs in front, a cute café style table between us. Vince eating an ice, me having my morning coffee—at seven o'clock at night.

I nodded to him. "I'm going to need at least that," I said, hoping I didn't sound like a dead-beat gambler begging for time.

Which, of course, was exactly what I was.

"Yeah, I heard about Danny. That's not right. Killing an old man like that. What's happening in this world?"

Maybe he owed somebody money, I thought, but had the good sense not to say it out loud to Vince.

I was kidding, but maybe I wasn't that far off base. Maybe Danny was into somebody for big numbers. I wouldn't have thought it, but I didn't think the boys knew about my occasional "jobs" for Vince.

The one thing I've learned about life is you never really know anybody's money situation. You might think you do, but you'd probably be surprised. People lived beyond their means, people lived below.

I suppose Jack Schiller had already thought of that—Danny owing money. Gambling was probably at the root of a lot of homicides in Vegas. We'd probably find out if the investigation led anywhere.

Finding out things about someone that they'd never want you to know—the idea didn't appeal to me, but the idea of whoever had done that to Danny being out there, on the loose, was something I couldn't bear to think about.

"Yeah," I said to Vince. "It's horrible."

"How's Ben taking it? And the rest of The Corporation?"

"Not very well," I said, and Vince just nodded. "So, anyway…"

Vince put up a hand to stop me. "You get one week, no vig, for Danny and the boys. Next week the clock starts ticking."

I looked at him, flabbergasted. Vince never gave anybody interest-free time. I wouldn't be surprised if he had an hourly chart on his office wall. If he had an office.

But a whole week? Totally unheard of.

"What's the catch?"

"No catch," he said. I looked closely at him. Vince, on the surface, was not your stereotypical wise guy. Nice suits, but not at all flashy. He wore an expensive, but under-stated watch. His Italian heritage showed with his black hair that he wore perfectly trimmed and pushed back from his olive-complected face.

A nice face. A very handsome face. Until you owed it money.

But Vince, to my knowledge, wasn't connected to anyone; he ran his own show. With his own muscle. He respected the old ways, but embraced the way things were now.

He'd accomplished a lot in his nearly forty-five years.

And Vince loved books. He always had a different one with him, always non-fiction, and usually some massive tome with an impressive title with lots of colons in it.

Vince loved books about historical leaders. The greats—Washington, Jefferson, Churchill. And the not-so-greats—Hitler, Mussolini.

I suppose he was learning what worked, and what didn't. As a frequent customer, I hoped he was taking inspiration from the right leaders.

Lately, the books Vince had been reading were about DaVinci, Michaelangelo and other famous artists.

A real Renaissance man, my loan shark.

"No catch?" I repeated.

He shook his head. "I know you're going to be busy this week taking care of things, seeing to Ben. The clock starts a week from today. Regular rates."

I nodded my understanding. "Thanks, Vince. That's really generous of you."

He shrugged. "I have a lot of respect for The Corporation. And everybody loved Danny."

That was true. And also reminded me how small Vegas really was, for such a huge city.

"Vince, do you know if Danny…if he…"

"He didn't owe me, if that's what you want to know," Vince said, a little disappointment in his voice that I could—albeit it inadvertently—think that Vince would off Danny.

Though I know of at least two people who'd owed Vince, took a drive into the desert with Paulie and were never heard from again.

Maybe they were living in Barbados, but I doubted it.

"Maybe somebody else?"

"Not that I know of," he said.

"Would you tell me if you did?"

He thought on that for a couple of seconds. "Yes. I would."

"Fair enough," I said and started to rise. Vince put his hand on my arm keeping me in place.

"I'll ask around," he said.

"Thanks, that would be great."

"If I find anything out…you want Ben to know?"

"No," I said quickly. "Just me."

Vince nodded, agreeing with my decision. He took his hand off my arm, and not wanting to press my luck—still not believing the gift Vince had given me—I rose to leave.

I pushed in my chair, wincing at the scraping noise the iron made against the marble floor. "Thanks, again, Vince."

He nodded. "I know you're good for it, Anna," he said in a low, ominous voice, then took a bite of his ice.

My foot, where the bone had been smashed years ago, ached as I placed weight on it after sitting. It was an almost Pavlovian response to Vince's voice when it turned loan shark.

"Besides," Vince added, wiping his mouth with a napkin. "I know where you live."

I nodded, started to turn away but my step faltered as Vince said, "And *who* you live *with*."

"God, I forgot how much I hate wearing fucking ties," Jimmy said to me, tugging at said neckwear two days later at Danny's funeral.

We were standing in the anteroom of the church, watching the service through the windows. I'd gotten Ben situated with the rest of The Corporation in a pew and then retreated to safety behind the glass. Lorelei was sitting behind the boys, her hand rising to wipe the tears from her face every so often.

Yes, definitely safer back here.

Jimmy had escaped their row and snuck back to stand with

me during the most recent hymn.

"Didn't you have to wear one every day at the Stardust?" I asked, sympathizing. I was in my own private hell having to don panty hose and heels.

Usually the only thing that got heels on my feet was a final table television appearance.

"Yeah, and I hated it. The only part of my job I didn't love." He pulled at the wide, broadly-striped tie again. It looked like Jimmy hadn't bought a new tie since the day he'd retired over fifteen years ago.

Jimmy had set the odds at the Stardust for over thirty years. During his tenure, the Stardust was known as the best book in town. A fact that Jimmy basked in, and secretly irked the other members of The Corporation.

Ben said the day they imploded the Stardust, Jimmy had stood like a stone and watched. Then stood for another hour after everyone had left. Not saying a word the entire time.

He stood next to me now, dry-eyed. But there was a haunting in his eyes that I'd seen in Ben's earlier.

It was probably in the eyes of every member of The Corporation.

It was probably in mine.

I turned to Jimmy, brushed his hands aside and straightened his tie, slightly tightening it, careful not to catch one of his many jowls. I patted the tie in place over his barrel chest and he placed his hand over mine, held it there for just a fraction of a second then let it go.

Big time emotion for Jimmy.

The crowd rose again—joining in another Catholic ritual of some kind that I didn't know.

Jimmy and I both sighed at the same time.

"You in withdrawal yet?" he asked me.

"Yeah," I said.

"From the bets or the cards?"

I thought about it for a minute. "Bets."

He nodded his head knowingly.

"You too?" I asked. He nodded again. "Why do you suppose that is?"

He shrugged, that fabulous Jimmy shrug. "You're a gambling junkie."

"I don't mean that," I said, deciding not to address the accuracy of his label for me. "I mean, why do you suppose it's bets that I miss, and not so much poker."

"Cock squeeze," he said.

I looked around the anteroom, but nobody had joined us. Thank God. "What'd you say?"

"Cock squeeze," he repeated.

"That's what I thought. Dare I ask?"

He shrugged again. "That feeling you get. You know it, Anna. When you put down large change on a bet, knowing you're going to win. Watching the game. The clench in your gut when some pimply-faced kid misses a free throw. The adrenaline when some doofus off the bench hits one at the buzzer to be the hero."

"Oh. A hummer," I said, saying the word out loud for the first time. It'd always just been in my head, not thinking anyone else could understand.

Naïve of me.

"Hummer. Cock squeeze. Po-tay-to. Po-taht-toe."

I chuckled. "Yeah, so, why do you suppose I have more of a hummer from sports betting than poker? I'm *good* at poker. Really good. I make a very nice living at it."

He nodded, seemingly agreeing with my self-assessment. "It has nothing to do with skill. In poker, you have control. Sure, you play the cards your dealt, and lady luck can be as much a bitch in poker as anywhere else, but ultimately either you bet or you fold. Your call.

"But with sports, you got no control. The minute you

place that bet, it's all in the hands of someone else. Bunches of someone elses."

I nodded, understanding.

"Total cock squeeze," he summed up.

"Did he just call you a cock tease?" a warm, deep voice whispered in my ear.

I knew who it was even before Jack Schiller stepped from behind me and stood on my other side.

"Do I need to defend your honor?" he asked with a small smile on his weathered face.

"Not necessary," I said.

"Because you weren't offended, or because you have no honor?"

"Both," I said, staring straight ahead. I heard Jimmy give a small snort of laughter.

"Mr. Mancino, good to see you again, although I'm sorry for the circumstances." He stuck his arm across me, grazing the tip of my boobs, his hand out for Jimmy to shake.

I gave him a sideways look, but his eyes were on Jimmy. But…there was just a hint of some deviousness in his brown eyes.

Jimmy shook his hand. "Detective," he said in greeting, his tone cool. Which normally wouldn't mean anything, but it was cool even for Jimmy. "Any word yet on who done this to Danny?"

And just like that, any playfulness that I might have imagined on Jack's face was gone. Cop face was back. He shook his head. "No, sir, we're still looking into it."

Jimmy snorted at that and faced forward again. I stared at Jack Schiller while he studied Jimmy. "Mr. O'Hern owe anybody money that you know of, sir? Gambling debts unpaid?"

I turned my head to Jimmy, who stared straight ahead for a moment. "No."

"No, you know for sure, or none that you know of?"

"Both," Jimmy said.

Jack sighed, ran his hand over his face in a movement I was beginning to recognize. "Mr. Mancino, if you know anything that would help in our investigation, I think you owe it to Mr. O'Hern to—"

Jimmy turned toward Jack and me. He thrust his meaty hand out and pointed a finger at Jack. "You don't know the first thing about what I owe to Danny O'Hern, Detective. Don't think I don't know why you brought us all to the morgue separately the other night. Didn't let on the others were there till the end. You was watching us. Watching our reactions to the news. You like one of us for Danny's killing, don't you?"

I looked at Jack, but his face was unreadable.

If I've been around somebody for as long as I've been around Jack Schiller—granted, not a ton of time, but on three separate occasions now—I can usually read them pretty well.

Especially strangers. Believe or not, it's easier to read strangers than people you know really closely. With strangers it's a clean slate. Everything is noticeable. With those you know well, you bring your own feelings into it.

It's what makes me a good poker player. If I'd wanted to help people rather than win their money, I'd probably make a good shrink.

But I couldn't read Jack Schiller.

And that just made me want to all the more.

Jimmy gave up on an answer from Jack, gave my hand a squeeze—which startled me—and headed back into the main area of the church.

"Something I said?" Jack said as he watched Jimmy make his way down the aisle and settle in next to a surprised Lorelei. He hadn't wanted to disturb Ben on the aisle ahead of them.

"More like something you didn't," I said, trying to draw his eyes off of the boys.

"Such as?" he asked, but continued to watch the crowd

ahead of us.

"Like, 'don't worry, Jimmy, we don't think you or any of your friends could have had anything to do with hurting Danny'."

He gave a little snort. Turning his head slightly, he looked at me out of the corner of his brown eyes. "Good thing he didn't hold his breath."

The crowd was standing again, singing another hymn. I turned fully toward Jack. "You can't possibly believe that any of those sweet old men had anything to do with this?"

"Sweet? Jimmy Mancino, sweet?" He raised a brow at me. He had that down perfectly, the one brow raise. I'd practiced it in the mirror when I first started playing, practicing poker expressions. Intimidation tactics

I could never pull it off.

But what was probably intimidating to most—Jack's brow raise—had a different effect on me. One I chose to ignore while talking about the welfare of The Corporation.

"Jimmy *can* be sweet," I said, but didn't have much conviction in my voice. I decided to try a different tack. "What motive could they possibly have? They all loved Danny. Everybody loved Danny."

Jack turned back to the front, sighed. "That's what I'm finding out. Everybody loved Danny O'Hern."

"You sound disappointed."

He shrugged, and for the first time I noticed he was wearing a sports coat and tie instead of his usual leather jacket and tie. I looked down. Slacks instead of khakis. And nice loafers.

I liked the idea that he'd put some effort into this. For Danny.

"Everybody loving the victim just makes my job harder."

"You like it when everybody hates the victim?"

"Well, that's difficult too. Too many suspects."

"You didn't answer my question," I said.

"Which was? Sorry, I was so involved in the Danny O'Hern love fest."

I gave him my best scowl, but he either didn't see it or ignored it—the idea of either infuriating me. "What motive could one of the boys have for killing Danny?"

"The same motives for any murder—revenge or money."

"What about a crime of passion?"

He looked at me. "Same as revenge, only with a twist."

"What about just a random act of violence? That happens all the time. No motive other than needing a few bucks for a fix."

"There was nothing random about Danny O'Hern's murder."

"How do you know that?"

He looked around us, at the empty room. But apparently that wasn't secluded enough. He took my arm, just above the wrist and pulled me toward an empty hallway that led to offices.

Was I going to get some details? We'd all been going crazy the last few days with knowing—or not knowing—exactly what had happened to Danny that night.

"They knew exactly where to do it. What parking lot didn't have any kind of security system. That suggests somebody who knows Vegas."

"So, you think it was somebody who knew the town—that narrows it down," I said, the sarcasm dripping.

"Or somebody from out of town hiring local talent," Jack said. "Mr. O'Hern's car was not at the scene, so he was most likely brought there by the killer. If he was brought there against his will, we probably would have found some signs of struggle on his body; there weren't any."

The words brought a chill to me. "Jesus," I said. It couldn't have been any more real to me than Danny being in a coffin two rooms away, and yet, this made it seem so...scary.

"I guess...I mean... I got that he was dead, and that he'd been killed, but I guess..."

"You hadn't thought about someone actually putting the gun to the back of his head and pulling the trigger?"

A vision of sweet Danny with the muzzle of a gun to his head came to my mind and a shudder ran through me. I looked up at Jack. It wasn't too hard; he was only a couple of inches taller than me.

There was something close to compassion in his eyes. And also…measurement of some sort.

I took a deep breath, put my chin up, and nodded for him to go on.

He studied me for a second, then nodded, like I'd passed some kind of test.

"We're thinking he knew the killer. Was lulled into a false sense of security. Enough to get into a car with them, anyway."

"So, you really think it was a friend?" I said, disbelief in my voice.

"Spouses, friends and family come to mind the quickest in all homicides, yes. But…"

I clung to that but. "But?"

He raised a shoulder, a half shrug. "Think of all the people you'd get in a car with. More than just close friends and family, right? I mean, there are business associates, neighbors."

I thought of the car ride I took ten years ago with Paulie, the one that ended in a hospital stay. "Yes," I whispered.

He saw that I'd left him, that I was remembering something. He just didn't know it had nothing to do with Danny.

At least I thought it didn't.

One of the funeral directors peeked his head down the hallway. "There you are. Miss Dawson, we're ready for you."

I nodded, started to move past Jack. He stuck an arm out, stopping me. He leaned into me, but not touching. I could feel the heat, the intensity pouring out of him.

"What are you needed for, Miss Dawson?"

"Anna," I said, a little more breathily than intended. "I'm a pallbearer. A stand-in for Ben."

He nodded, but left his arm where it was, blocking me from the hallway. His other hand came up and went to my throat. He turned over my twisted pendant, patted it to my skin, much like the way I do when I'm watching a game or playing poker.

"Horseshoe. For luck," he said softly. It wasn't a question, so I said nothing. "Does it work?"

I thought of all the money I'd won over the last ten years. More money than my parents had made in their whole careers.

And then I remembered Vince; out there, probably cursing himself for giving me a week interest-free.

"Not often enough," I said.

He looked from the pendant to my eyes. "I hear that," he said and dropped his arm away from the wall, though he kept his hand on my necklace. On my skin.

"Will you tell me if you think of anything that might help in the case? So far, we've got nothing."

"Is that why you told me about Danny's death? So I would help?" The thought didn't really bother me; I just wanted to know up front what Jack's motives were.

Though something told me one never knew what Jack Schiller's true motives were.

He shrugged. "Does it matter?"

"Yes."

"From what I understand, you know Vegas well, know a lot of players. I just thought you might hear something from somebody that could shed some light on this."

Like Danny was a degenerate gambler? That he owed someone not-so-nice a lot of money? That the life he led outwardly to his friends and family was a sham?

Those thoughts ran through my mind so quickly that I didn't even stop to wonder how—or from whom—Jack had found out I was in a position to possibly know something.

"Will you tell me if you hear anything? Anything at all,"

he said.

If it would hurt Danny's reputation, or destroy his family, and not even help solve the case? I couldn't make that promise to him, and something told me not to lie to him. "I don't know," I said.

He looked away, took a breath, then looked back at me. "Fair enough," he said.

He pulled his hand away from my neck and as he did I noticed the slightest tremble in his hand.

The weakness pissed me off. Unfair, yes, but it did. I didn't want to think of Jack as human. I needed him to be more. I needed him to avenge Danny for us all.

As I brushed past him I said, "Need a drink?"

"Need a casino?" he zinged right back.

I studied him for a minute, recognizing a part of myself. Perhaps that's what had pissed me off.

"Desperately," I said softly, then turned to go bury my friend.

Nine

MY NEW PHONE RANG TWO DAYS LATER. "Dancing Queen" came on and I knew who it would be. I excused myself from the poker table. I hadn't been in a hand in half an hour anyway.

I'd been trying to build the small amount of funds I had available to me into something I could parlay into enough to pay Vince back, but hadn't had any luck. Hard to build something that big with just a few hundred dollars. And there was no way I could play at one of Vince's games on marker while I still owed him so much.

I'd tried different casinos, looking for bad players with big wallets, but no fish swam today.

"Hey, Lor," I said when I got to the small alcove that used to be used for payphones but was now only used by those needing to be heard on a cell. "You're the inaugural call." So wrapped up in my new gizmo that Lorelei had given me a crash course in yesterday, I'd forgotten that Lorelei rarely called me while I was playing cards. "What's wrong?" I quickly asked.

"Nothing. Nothing. Sorry," she said. "I didn't mean to scare you."

I exhaled, not realizing I'd been holding my breath. "That's okay. You didn't," I lied.

"Ben and I are car shopping," she said.

"Oh. That's right." I'd forgotten all about that. It seemed like years ago when I'd brought Ben home from the morgue. It'd only been a week. "Did you find anything?"

"That's why I'm calling. Is it okay if we go over thirty thousand? We both really love this Lexus SUV. It's exactly the perfect height for Ben to get in and out of. Not too high, but not low like our cars."

Her voice was so innocent, so blasé. And why shouldn't it be? We had a Porsche and a BMW 650i in the driveway. We bought expensive cars.

How was she to know what that money could do for me? That it could get me out of debt with Vince. That I wouldn't have had to spend the last two days grinding at the tables to try and prevent the re-emergence of JoJo onto the college basketball scene.

"Can the slush fund handle a Lexus?" I asked.

"Oh yeah," she said, and I cringed. God, I wish I hadn't known that.

"Lor…I,"

"Yes?"

I opened my mouth and then shut it. I couldn't. It would bring down an avalanche of shit. Lorelei would freak out. The interventions would ratchet up. She might even leave.

It would bring stress to the entire household on top of Danny's murder still being unsolved. And most of all, Ben would be disappointed in me.

I'd rather deal with Vince, Paulie and JoJo.

"I think a Lexus sounds great," I finally said.

There was a sound of relief and I vaguely wondered if perhaps her thought process had gone in the same direction as mine.

"Thanks, Jo. We'll see you later?"

I thought of my small stack at the table. "Yeah, I won't be too much longer."

A few hours later I pulled into my driveway the same time Lorelei and Ben did in a shiny gold Lexus. Lorelei's Beemer was already parked in the open garage.

I didn't even want to think about how Lorelei could pull off buying, registering, insuring the Lexus and getting both cars home in just a few hours.

The woman was a wonder and I didn't tell her enough how much I valued her.

I was just about to as we all gathered together to admire the new wheels, but a blue sedan pulled up to the curb and Jack Schiller stepped out.

A tiny zip went through me until I realized that it probably wasn't a good thing he was here. I looked into his back seat. Empty. I don't know what—or who—I expected to see.

The rest of The Corporation in handcuffs?

As if they'd even fit. Jimmy alone would take up most of the back seat.

"Detective Schiller," Ben said in greeting. He shook Jack's hand.

"Mr. Lowenstein. Ladies," Jack said, nodding to both Lorelei and me. I tried to read his face, but as usual, came up blank.

"Hello, Detective," Lorelei said. I just nodded, waiting.

Oh God, waiting for what?

"Mr. Lowenstein, I'm sorry to have to tell you this…"

Ben reached for me as I stepped to his side. Jack waited until I took Ben's hand.

"Who?" Ben said, bracing himself.

"Gus Morgan was shot a few hours ago."

Ten
❖❖

GUS WASN'T DEAD. At least not yet. We were taken to the hospital by Jack Schiller instead of the morgue this time.

This time. Funny how quickly you can come to expect the worse.

Expect there'd be more times.

Actually, *I* was taken by Jack Schiller. Lorelei and Ben followed in the Lexus. I don't know how that worked out, it seemed like I should drive Ben myself, but somehow he and Lorelei headed to the Lexus and Jack took my arm and led me to his car telling Lorelei which hospital we were going to.

"Was he found at the same place that Danny was? That parking lot?" I asked as he drove. His hands were strong and sure on the wheel and it made me feel better to look at them.

"No. He was at home. Coming home, actually. It happened in the walkway to his apartment from the carport."

Gus had moved into a ground-floor apartment after his last divorce saying he'd never buy another house only to see it end up as part of a settlement. Saul had said he should give up the wives before giving up houses, but Gus had only laughed.

He used the guest bedroom as a walk-in closet for all his beautiful suits and shoes. Arranged with loving care by color. I smiled to think of it, and then just as quickly my smile faded as I thought of Gus lying in a hospital. I tried to put on my poker face. Too bad I didn't have poker skin.

"How bad is he?" I asked.

"I'm not sure. Detective Botz is at the hospital with him. A couple of patrolmen are getting Saul and Jimmy. I came for you. For Ben. We're rounding up his friends, getting them to the hospital."

"His friends, or your suspects?"

He looked across at me, his eyes conveying something I couldn't quite read. Compassion? Pity? "This tends to put a different spin on things."

"So, The Corporation members are no longer suspects?" I asked. "Not that they ever should have been," I quickly added.

I looked over at him. We were at a red light and he turned fully to me. He reached out a hand; I think intending to touch me, but who knew with him. Instead he pulled his hand back and put it on the wheel.

I knew what he was going to say, and the dread made me cold.

"Suspects? No," he said. "Potential victims? Yes."

I remember reading once that when Jackie Kennedy was asked why she took her children to Greece she said, "They're killing Kennedys" about life in the United States.

I knew what she meant. *They* were killing The Corporation, and all I wanted to do was put Saul, Jimmy and Ben in the back of that big Lexus and drive. And drive. And drive.

But nobody was leaving the hospital waiting room until we had word on Gus.

He'd been in surgery for three hours. Jimmy, Saul, Ben, Lorelei, Jack, Detective Botz and I all sat in the various couches, loveseats and chairs. Lorelei and I took turns running for coffee. The detectives had left when we'd all first arrived—returning to

Gus' apartment. But they were back now and had grouped us all together, moving some of the furniture so that we could all see each other.

They pulled out their notebooks and we all shifted more upright in our seats.

"Any word?" Jack asked me.

"Still in surgery," I said, and he nodded. He checked his watch. I wanted to ask him if that was good or bad, that Gus had been in for so long, but I didn't know if I wanted to hear his answer.

"Gentlemen," Jack said, looking from Saul to Jimmy to Ben. "We have reason to believe that Danny O'Hern's murder and Gus Morgan's shooting are related."

Saul let out a soft moan. Ben grabbed for my hand. Jimmy snorted and said, "No shit," under his breath.

"The question is, why were they targeted, and can we assume that the three of you are also in danger?"

This time I grabbed Ben's hand.

"Why would anybody want to murder us?" Saul asked.

"Revenge or money," Jack and I said at the same time. Our eyes locked, he gave me a small nod of approval, and, yes, I admit it, a small thrill shot right through me.

"Money? None of us have any money to speak of. We did okay, but we were all working stiffs. Hell, Anna's probably got the most money out of all of us," Jimmy said.

Jack raised a brow at me. All I could think of was the debt to Vince hanging over my head and the ticking clock.

I just shrugged. "So, it must be revenge, then," I said.

"Revenge for what?" Ben asked. "We're just a bunch of retirees."

Detective Botz flipped back through his notebook. He wore a Yogi Bear tie today that clashed with his sports coat.

"That may be true, sir, but didn't all of you set the odds at various casinos for a lot of years?"

We all nodded. "And you probably caused some people to lose a lot of money," Detective Botz continued.

"And many to win a lot of money," Ben pointed out.

"Those people don't tend to seek revenge," Jack said.

"Why would someone seek revenge on the odds makers for a lost bet? Wouldn't they be more likely to try to kill the player that lost the game for him?" I asked.

"Unless it was for a lot of losses, a lot of different teams, over a lot of years," Detective Botz said.

"Then you'd just go after the guy at the casino you bet at, not every odds maker," Jimmy said. He didn't dismiss the idea of revenge for lost bets, I noticed, just wanted specifics on the logistics.

"Unless you blamed all the odds makers of the time? Thought they were in collusion or something?" Detective Botz offered up. The three men scoffed, insulted.

"It was a point of pride that the boys all set their own odds, Detective," I said gently. It seemed to pacify Jimmy, Ben and Saul.

"But, we haven't set odds for over twenty years. If this was revenge, why now?" Saul asked, anger and what I guessed was fear in his voice. He beat his hand on the coffee table in front of us. "Why now!"

The magazines that had been on the table fell to the floor from the impact. I bent over to pick them up, laying back on the table months old editions of *People*, *National Geographic* and *Sports Illustrated*.

My hand traced the letters on the SI cover, invoking a memory.

"Because he didn't know who you were until now," I said quietly, more to myself than the group.

But Saul, sitting on the other side of me from Ben heard me. "What, Hannah? What did you say?"

I held up the magazine. "The article about you guys. It finally gave him names."

"What article?" both detectives said at the same time. Jack snatched the magazine out of my hand.

"Not in that one. That one's ancient. But there was an article about The Corporation in *Sports Illustrated* about three weeks ago."

"What was in it?" Detective Botz said, putting his pen to paper, looking at me expectantly.

"Wait a sec," Lorelei said, her head half buried in her huge purse. "I think…yeah…no…" Her hand came out of the bag with the magazine attached. "I thought I still had a copy in there."

We all looked at her, dumbfounded.

"What?" she asked.

Jack reached for the magazine but I snatched it out of Lorelei's hands first. I quickly flipped to the article about the boys, scanning it quickly, looking for casino names.

"They don't mention which casinos you each specifically worked at. They don't even mention all of them."

"So?" Ben said.

"So," Detective Botz said. "Say somebody's been holding a grudge for twenty years and this lands on his lap and now he's got names and faces but not sure which one was his odds maker. He starts eliminating one by—" his voice cut off as he saw the expression change on our faces. He seemed to remember who he was surrounded by. "We'd like to take that magazine Miss Dawson," he said reaching out his hand.

I held my finger up for him to wait. I swore I heard a little snort out of Jack, but I kept scanning the article. "Seems to me there was mention of…yes…here it is. Hell, it's even in a pulled quote. That had to piss him off."

"Who?" Jack said as the others said, "What?"

I flipped the magazine to the page I had looked for, folding it over and then turned it around. I placed it on the coffee table and pointed down to the pulled quote box.

"Everybody won. Except the bookies. And the poor schmuck from Pittsburgh that bet the Steelers at four and a half," Jack read out loud. When he got to the word Pittsburgh he gave a very pointed look to his fellow detective. The others were looking down at the magazine and had missed it, but I caught it. Detective Botz wrote several things down in his notebook.

"Explain this," Jack said pointing to the magazine.

Saul launched into the story of odds making, point spreads, over under ratios.

Jack held up a hand. "Whoa. Whoa. I don't speak gambling." He looked at me. "Explain this to me in layman's terms."

"Superbowl Thirteen. Steelers and Cowboys. The point spread fluctuated so much because of first Steelers bets and then Cowboys bets that with the final score falling right in the middle, everybody ended up winning and the casinos lost millions."

"Except some schmuck from Pittsburgh," Jack said, pointing to the quote while Detective Botz wrote furiously in his notebook.

Jimmy took up the story for me. "Some big time money came in at the last minute betting on Pittsburgh. At each of the casinos." He waved his hands at Saul and Ben who nodded agreement. "But it was too late to make a difference on the spread, and he was the big loser. Besides the casinos. Word at the time was it was some hotshot CEO at one of them steel places in Pittsburgh. Old money, they said."

"And that money came in at each casino?" Jack asked.

"The five we worked at, yes," Ben said. "We talked about it at the time, after the shit had hit the fan. We'd all thought about changing the spread again late because of that amount of money. But none of us did. It was just so close to game time."

"So, this guy loses huge. Everybody else wins. He stews about it for thirty years and then this comes out." Jack summarized, lifting the magazine.

The two detectives looked at each other. Then Jack looked at me, almost expectantly.

Then I got it. "Revenge *and* money," I whispered and he nodded.

"*Mishegoss*," Ben murmured. It wasn't some of the Yiddish that I'd picked up over the years between Saul and Ben, but I context clued it out to totally fucked up.

"*Mishegoss*," I agreed quietly.

Just then the doctor entered the small waiting room. Lorelei, the detectives and I jumped to our feet. Jimmy, Ben and Saul remained seated, I suppose preparing for the worst.

"Mr. Morgan came through the surgery very well," the doctor said. There was a collective sigh of relief from us all. From the corner of my eye, I saw Ben reach for Saul and Jimmy's hands. "The bullet just missed his femoral artery," the doctor continued. "Another centimeter and he would have bled out before anybody could have gotten to him."

Saul cried out, his whole body sagging with relief. Ben put his arm around his life-long friend. Jimmy patted Saul's back. Lorelei reached for my hand and squeezed. I squeezed back.

"Doctor, when will we be able to question Mr. Morgan?"

"Not for quite some time, I'm afraid. He's going to be sedated for at least the next eight or nine hours."

The detectives nodded. The doctor started to leave after receiving the thanks and handshakes of everyone, then he turned back to the policemen. "I'm not sure he'll be able to tell you much though. The bullet entered from the back. And I'm no forensics expert, but it looks like he was shot at from quite a distance."

I noticed the look that passed between Jack and Detective Botz, and I remembered that Danny was shot point blank, execution style. It didn't seem to fit.

"Gentlemen, we're going to ask you to be very careful. We'll set up squad cars to patrol the area around each of your homes at regular intervals. We suggest you stay inside as much as possible. But please use extreme caution when not at home."

Ben and Saul nodded. I saw a flash of something cross Jimmy's face and knew he was thinking about how he'd place bets. That's probably what I'd be thinking about too if told it'd be in my best interest to be housebound.

"For how long?" Jimmy asked.

"Until we can find out who's behind your friend's death," Jack said, his voice forceful and commanding.

I expected Jimmy to tell Jack to fuck off, but Jimmy only looked at him for a few seconds and then nodded.

"If you'll excuse us," Detective Botz said and he and Jack left the room.

I looked at my boys, what remained of them, as they looked at each other. It reminded me of their glances at each other at the Sourdough the morning after Danny had been shot.

Only this time the looks weren't "could it be you?"

They were "who will be next?"

"I'll be right back," I said to the others and followed the cops out into the hallway. As soon as the door had fully shut I called out to them. They turned and waited for me to catch up.

"What's going on?" I said to Jack.

"We need to make some calls. Check some things out."

"What things?"

"I'm not at liberty to discuss the case," Jack said in his cop voice.

I raised my brows at him—I still couldn't pull off the one brow like him. He'd certainly seemed willing to discuss the case with me at Danny's funeral—when he thought I could help him.

I didn't say that though, figuring that would piss him off and possibly not set well with his partner. But I didn't need to say it; he could see it in my eyes.

"Miss Dawson, thank you for the information about this article," he said, holding up the magazine.

"Oh, come on," I said. "That seems like such a long shot. Unless there's something more?" I looked at them both. Nothing. I tried again. "Just what was your 'reason to believe' that made you make the connection between Danny and Gus?"

The two men looked at each other. There was a questioning look from Jack to his partner. Detective Botz finally shrugged and gave a small nod toward me.

"We think it's a very viable lead and one we're going to follow up on."

"Why?"

"A piece of Pittsburgh memorabilia was found at both crime scenes."

"What? Why don't we know that?"

"It's part of an ongoing investigation. We don't give out that kind of information. And certainly not to…"

"Potential suspects," I finished his thoughts and at least he had the good grace to seem a tiny bit embarrassed.

"At the time, yes. Besides, would it have made any difference?"

"Maybe," I said, though I couldn't really see how. Although… "If we'd known about the Steelers thing after Danny's death, maybe one of us would have connected it to the SI article."

"And we'd be exactly where we are now," Detective Botz

said.

"But maybe Gus wouldn't have been shot," I said, though I didn't need to, I could see they were both thinking the same thing.

If I looked at it logically, I really couldn't blame them. It was a piece of evidence and cops don't discuss evidence with outsiders, let alone possible suspects. But I didn't look at it logically. I couldn't with Danny dead and Gus in a surgery recovery room.

A memory from the night at the morgue came back to me. "You were hinting around that night about Danny being from Pennsylvania. You were trying to find some connection." Jack nodded.

"Detective Botz isn't even from Philly is he? He was just trying to get Ben on the Pennsylvania track." I said, anger building.

"Peoria," the detective admitted.

Okay, this was getting us nowhere. They'd followed procedure and Gus was shot. Might have been shot even if we'd made this connection earlier. We'd never know.

The thing to do now was concentrate on finding the big loser from Pittsburgh.

The men turned, headed away from me, most likely planning to do just that.

"Wait," I said, and they turned once again. "What Steelers piece was found at the scenes? Was it the same thing at both?"

They nodded. "It was a piece of cloth with the Steelers' logo on it. The crowd whips them around at the games."

I knew what they were. "The Terrible Towels," I whispered, turning around to go to my boys.

Eleven

"Jimmy, can you get me in to a back room game in Pittsburgh?"

"Yeah, sure, Anna."

"You're sure? Short notice? People who would know the players in town. Big rollers, Jimmy."

Jimmy shrugged. "I know a guy."

Of course he did.

We walked down the hallway of the hospital, Ben shuffling in his walker a ways ahead of us. Lorelei and Saul were staying for now. I'd bring back Ben later, after he'd rested for a bit, and we'd trade off with Lor and Saul.

Jimmy would come and go, I suspected. Probably after a quick trip to a book room.

I didn't blame him, the itch was eating me up too.

"When you wanna play?" he asked. Bless him, he didn't ask more than that, but he had to suspect what I was up to.

Part of what I was up to, anyway. "I need to check a couple of things first. Can I get back to you?" He nodded.

I thought of the four days left before my marker was due with Vince.

"It'll be soon," I added.

Lorelei was right—as usual—the Lexus SUV was just the perfect height for Ben to get in and out of comfortably.

When we got in the house it was just after nine at night. Ben headed right for his room. "I'm just going to take a quick nap and then we can head back."

"Sleep as long as you can," I said, knowing the long night ahead would wear on Ben if he insisted on staying at the hospital with Gus.

I peeked out of the window and was mollified, and slightly freaked, to see a patrol car parked just down the street.

I wondered if Jimmy had a tail heading to a casino with him. Something I should have checked on, but I'd been in too big of a hurry to get Ben home.

And, if I was honest, too big of a hurry to get out of the hospital. I hadn't been in one since the time I'd met Ben, and the thought of being back didn't sit real well with me, considering I could be back in soon as a patient.

I bypassed my room and went right to the home office Lorelei had set up for us. She'd even found one of those cool partner writing desks, she taking one side and me the other.

You could tell whose side was whose by just a quick glance. Lorelei's was neat, organized, nothing on top but her laptop, phone and one of her ever-present tablets.

Mine had odds sheets strewn all over. A seldom used laptop pushed to one side. Losing betting slips, and other receipts in a shoe box that would ultimately end up with my accountant. The cost of being a professional gambler.

It must kill Lorelei not to straighten my side, but she never did.

I really have to do something to show her how much she means to me. To Ben. To our little family. If I'd learned anything this past week it was you never knew when you'd lose the people you loved.

I quickly found what I was looking for. It was a mess, but I knew where everything was, as most slobs will tell you.

I searched through the entire NCAA basketball schedule that Lorelei had found online and printed out for me last fall until I found what I was looking for.

Pitt was at home this Sunday against Louisville.

Yes. All the stars were aligning.

I pulled out a bunch of my old editions of sports magazines, doing some quick research on both teams, although nothing was new to me. I do extensive research at the beginning of every season.

Every betting season.

I turned on my laptop. Navigating the thing like Lorelei had shown me—a thousand times it seemed—so that I could get on both Pitt and Louisville's websites and read any news on the teams that hadn't been in my research.

Louisville was leading the conference, trouncing most of their opponents by over twenty points. Pitt was in the middle of the pack.

Louisville, it seems, depended solely on the play of their big man in the middle. A seven footer, who was almost as wide as he was tall, accounted for eighty percent of the team's points throughout the season. They called him the next Shaq.

This was going to be easy.

I called Paulie to see if Vince would see me. Vince never discussed payment arrangements on the phone. Paulie said he'd call back. I took the phone with me to my bedroom, threw off my shoes, socks and pants and crawled in to bed.

It was Ben who woke me up before Paulie called back. "Hannah, darling, are you awake?" he said quietly.

"Ben? Are you okay?" I said, coming out of what was surprisingly a deep sleep complete with dreams about handsome men that just kept running and running, while I stood frozen in place.

"Can we go back to the hospital now, dear? Saul must be

awfully tired." I looked at the clock. One thirty in the morning. I checked my phone, seeing if I slept through Paulie's call, but I hadn't.

"Sure. Give me a few minutes to shower and throw on some clean clothes, okay."

"Of course, dear. I'll go put some coffee on," he said, leaving my room.

Paulie called as we entered the hospital a half hour later. I let Ben walk ahead of me, down the long corridor to the waiting room near Gus' room where the nurses told us Lorelei and Saul had moved.

"Can you meet Vince tonight?" Paulie said with no preamble when I answered.

"I need to get Ben situated here, then I can," I answered.

"Where are you?"

"The hospital. Gus was shot."

"Gus Morgan?"

"Yes. He was in surgery for a long time, but it looks good now."

There was silence on the phone, then, "You sure you want to do this tonight?"

"The clock's ticking on me," I said and waited for him to deny it, or to give me some words of encouragement, but he didn't.

"He'll be at the Bellagio, in the book room for the next hour."

"I'll be there," I said and hung up.

Saul and Lorelei looked beat, and had never even been able to see Gus, but everybody seemed to feel better that Gus had friends nearby.

I was trying to figure out the logistics of how to get to the

Bellagio without leaving Ben alone when Jimmy walked in. He'd showered and changed, and, I suspected, placed several bets and looked all the better for it.

"Can you stay here with Ben if I run out for an hour or so?" I asked him. He nodded, probably knowing where I was headed, if not for exactly the reasons he thought.

I walked over to Saul where he and Ben were huddled together. "Saul? How about if Lorelei takes you to stop by your house? You can pick up a few things and then come and stay with us?"

I expected him to balk. Saul was adamant about his independence. Much as I suspected Ben had been before his hip surgeries had made him somewhat dependant on people.

On me. And Lorelei.

I thought I'd have to talk him into it with reasons like the police would be better able to look after him and Ben if they were in the same place, but Saul surprised me. After giving it some thought, he turned to me and said, "Yes, Hannah, that's probably for the best."

I turned to Jimmy. "Don't even think about it," he said.

Well, that was probably for the best, too.

I smiled, patted Jimmy on the chest. "The offer stands." He clasped my hand and squeezed, then turned to the coffee pots against the wall.

I pulled Lorelei aside. "So, you'll take Saul in his car? I'll keep the Lexus?"

She nodded. "Is there anything else I should be doing? Should I go shopping for groceries? Are we looking at some kind of siege situation? Are we going to the mattresses?"

I looked at her and she shrugged. "Ben's always watching *The Godfather*. I guess some of it stuck."

I chuckled. "I don't think we're to that point." I looked around the sterile room. "Yet," I clarified.

"Do you know a service that can deliver whatever we need?"

She looked at me like I had insulted her. "Please."

Of course she did. Much as I had this town wired for gambling action, Lorelei had its domestic nooks and crannies down pat.

"Then order what we need in the morning and just stay close to Saul."

She nodded, started to go, but I touched her arm to stop her.

"Lor, can you get your hands on twenty thousand in cash by tomorrow afternoon?"

"Yeesssss," she said, a questioning look in her shrewd green Irish eyes.

"Do it. I'm going to fly to Pittsburgh. Jimmy can get me in a game there with people who might know who the big player who lost all the money is."

Her eyes grew wide. "Really? And you're going to just do that? Fly to Pittsburgh, spend your money to find out something that the cops could do with a few phone calls?"

"One, I don't plan on spending the money—that would mean I lost. Two, the cops may or may not be able to get a name with a phone call. It was a long time ago. The cops that are there now may not be in tune to the Pittsburgh gambling scene of thirty years ago."

"So why would you think that poker players would be?"

"Gamblers never forget," I said.

"Kind of like elephants," she said with just a touch of distaste in her voice.

"Kind of."

"But poker players might not know about sports gamblers," she pointed out.

"Odds are if you're a big money poker player you dabble with bets. Or maybe more than dabble," I added at her pointed look. "And a story like that would be legend status by now. If you were in the right circle."

"Gambling circles," she said.

"Yep."

She took a deep breath, let out a large sigh. "I can get the money. I'll have it in an envelope in your top desk drawer by the time you and Ben get home."

"Thanks, Lor," was all I said, though my mind was furiously racing wondering if she had that kind of money stashed somewhere in the house. And if so, how much more? Enough to get me out of Vince's debt?

A vision of me ransacking my own home flashed before me and the distaste was palpable. I added Ben or Lorelei walking into a tossed room and watching me to the vision, and the notion fizzled away.

"You don't have to do this, you know," she said. " You could just let the police handle it."

I thought of Ben and Saul and Jimmy. And poor Danny. And Gus most likely hooked to tubes and machines a few doors down. But I'm ashamed to admit I mostly thought of the Louisville / Pitt game and what that would mean.

"This is something I have to do."

"So, it's thirty thousand on Saturday," Vince confirmed. He sat at a horse race betting carrel in the Bellagio's sports book, a biography of Donatello sitting in front of him, a marked-up horse racing line-up sheet pushed to the back of the carrel. "Are you going to have the money or are you here to make other arrangements?"

"Other arrangements," I said. We both knew what that meant.

Vince nodded, then turned his chair away from the horse racing screen and toward the big digital board with all the sporting events and their odds on it.

"Sunday. Pitt / Louisville," I said and waited a moment. The game wasn't on the board yet, wouldn't be until late Saturday.

"What's your guess on the spread?" Vince asked me.

"Louisville giving ten," I said. I was happy to see Vince nodded, agreeing with my prediction. It helped that I lived with one of the best oddsmakers ever.

Louisville would be a ten-point favorite, much closer than any other games they'd played, but the odds makers would take into consideration Pitt's strong home court advantage at the Omni.

"Take Pitt and the points," I said.

Vince seldom questioned my picks, but this time he turned to me. "Are you sure? Louisville's been blowing out everybody."

"They won't on Sunday."

He ran his long, graceful fingers along the cover of his book, tracing the title much like I had traced the *Sports Illustrated* letters earlier tonight at the hospital. "I don't like Pitt only getting ten. You like something else on the board?"

I did, but that wouldn't get me to Pittsburgh to ask questions.

"Maybe. But that's the game I want to do. I want this over, my debt out from under me. I need to be with Ben."

"Paulie told me about Gus. How's he doing?"

"He's stable now."

"Good. Good. And the others? How are they doing?"

I thought of the boys and how I'd left them at the hospital. "They're a little freaked out."

"I would imagine. I never heard anything about Danny being in debt, by the way."

"They don't think that was the motive now."

"No, it seems like something else is in play, with Gus and all."

"Right. Which is why I need to be with Ben."

"But you won't be with him on Sunday?" he asked. His way

of making sure I was taking care of the Pitt game myself.

I didn't blame him. He was shelling out big money on a game. He wanted to make sure I wasn't farming it out. Not that I'd ever considered doing that.

I knew Jimmy, Lorelei and Ben suspected that my trips were not entirely above board, but to my knowledge Vince and I—and most likely Paulie—were the only two that knew for sure about JoJo.

That's how I intended it to stay.

"Okay. Your entire debt rides on Pitt getting ten points," he said and I let out a breath I hadn't known I'd held.

"Thank you," I said. I got up to leave, but he reached out to stop me.

"How do you feel about the over/under?"

"Take the under, but you can't hold me for that one."

"Agreed."

I walked away from Vince and out of the book room. My eyes automatically scanned the back of the poker room and landed on Jeffrey standing behind the desk.

I started to duck my head, not having the time, wanting to get back to the hospital, but his head came up at that moment and our eyes caught. I smiled and waved, but pointed out to the main floor, like I had to be going somewhere. He waved for me to come to him.

I turned and walked through the room, saying hello to some of the players I knew as I weaved around the tables. That kid who beat me the night Danny was killed—Jason—was there and he pointed to an empty seat at his table but I just gave him a small smile, shook my head, pointed to my watch and kept walking toward Jeffrey.

"How's Gus doing?" Jeffrey asked as I neared him. I noticed he didn't come out from behind the desk and I was glad. I thought if he tried to hug me, if I fell into Jeffrey's arms, I might never want to leave, and I needed to get back to Ben.

"How did you know?" I asked.

"Jimmy was here earlier. He told me what's been going on." There was accusation in his voice and it took me a minute to realize that keeping Jeffrey apprised was my job.

"Yeah, it's been pretty crazy. I'm sorry I haven't been in touch."

"I've been trying to call you."

"I got a new phone."

"And it didn't occur to you to give me the number?"

No, it hadn't, but instead of admitting it I said, "It's just been so busy with the arrangements for Danny and now Gus."

He studied me hard. He shook his head. "It just kind of makes my point for me, that's all."

"What point?" I asked, but I thought I knew where Jeffrey was going.

"That this is never going to be more than some late night screwing after we're done working. We're not even friends with benefits. Just fucking benefits."

I blinked, taken back by his harshness. Jeffrey was nothing if not smooth, couth. He reminded me of Gus in that way.

"Does it need to be more?" I said, a bit of hostility seeping through though I tried to temper it. "It never needed to be before," I added.

He looked down at the desk, and I read him like I would a tourist in from Des Moines playing his first hand of poker.

"Glenda," I said, and his head popped back up.

"Nothing's happened," he said quickly, not even questioning how I'd guessed. He knew how good of a player I was.

Glenda, one of the other poker room supervisors. The one who dressed as smartly as Jeffrey. I always thought they'd be great together, but the consolation of being right didn't sit all that well with me.

She wore snoods, for Christsake.

"But something's *going* to happen," I led for him.

He shrugged. "That's why I wanted to talk to you so badly. To see where you thought we were headed."

Ah, so we were at the fork in the road, Jeffrey and I. He wanted me to step up. And maybe I could someday. But not today.

And not for Jeffrey.

"Good luck with her, Jeffrey," I said, a gentleness in my voice. This, ultimately was my choice.

"Really? Anna, do you think…" But he didn't finish. He could read me pretty well, too.

"I'm not giving up the Bellagio," I said jokingly, although I was dead serious.

"No problem. I'll always be happy to see you here, you know that."

I did. "I'll see you around," I said and left before he could answer.

Ben and I headed home the next day at noon after Lorelei and Saul spelled us. They'd gotten Saul settled at our place and taken naps, then showered, ate and came back to the hospital.

Gus would be able to see visitors in a few hours, so I'd just get what I needed for Pittsburgh, let Ben get a quick nap and then drop him off at the hospital on my way to the airport.

In the drawer of my desk was a thick envelope full of hundred dollar bills. I put it aside to put in my money belt that I wore under my clothes when going through airports.

On top of the desk was a credit card in my name with a note from Lorelei. "For your flight and expenses. I reserved several flights, but wasn't sure which one you'd want. Just call this number and tell them and they'll cancel the others."

I usually paid in cash for all things when JoJo came out to play, not wanting a paper trail, but there was a legitimate reason

Anna Dawson was headed to Pittsburgh, so using the credit card would be fine.

I called the airlines, choosing the flight times I wanted, then headed to my room. I pushed away the hanging clothes in my closet, pulled out a suitcase, unzipped it and stared at JoJo's clothes.

I took a deep breath and started to pack.

Twelve
❖

This time I didn't even feel all that bad as I watched the drugged player lying across the hotel bed.

Oh, I was disgusted with myself for being in this position again, but the star center had been so arrogant, it'd been almost a pleasure to watch him totter and fall back onto the bed.

The bigger they are…

The whole thing had gone off like clockwork. JoJo had no trouble finding the room of Louisville's scoring machine. A quick call to the front desk asking to be patched to Richardson's room. A fake inquiry from room service to Karl Richardson himself got the room number.

I'd become JoJo in my own room at the Omni Hotel, two floors down. Gaining entrance had been even simpler than it had with Raymond Joseph and Lurch back in Minnesota. Richardson had even thought JoJo had been ordered for him—like he deserved it.

Who knew, maybe he got hookers from grateful alumni on a regular basis.

Maybe that's why he had no roommate.

Though after only a few minutes with him—and his ego—I imagined that a rare single room for a visiting team member was a prerequisite he demanded as his due.

The kid had none of the enthusiasm for his team that Raymond Joseph had displayed. No pride in his school. He was obviously just racking up points and stats so that his draft position would be one of the highest. No doubt he'd bolt for the NBA after this, his sophomore year.

There'd been a few anxious moments while trying to keep his grabby hands off of me until the drug kicked in, but I'd doubled the normal dose for the giant and was rewarded with quick effects.

I went over to the bed, made sure his breathing was steady. I started to straighten his legs and neck, then stopped myself. Let him wake up with one hell of a crick in his neck as well as the after-effects of the drug.

I gathered up my things, careful to eradicate any evidence of my time in the room. I poked my head out into the hallway, determined it was clear and hurried to the stairwell door.

Back in my room, I quickly showered and changed, left JoJo strewn across the floor, and headed back out into the night.

I really liked Pittsburgh. The working-class feel to parts appealed to my Midwest background. The stadium area was nicely laid out for a town that loved its teams.

Mount Washington sat over the city, as if its guardian. Beautiful homes sat at the top, and an apartment building was built into the side of the hill itself. Gondola-type cars that ran on a steep track up and down the hill were, I was told by my cab driver, the Inclines.

I wanted to take the Incline to the top of Mount Washington, it looked so cool and wasn't anything I'd ever ridden in before, but by the time I got to it, it had shut down for the night. Instead I continued on in the cab to the home of the poker game.

I'd been surprised when Jimmy told me that the game would be at a private home, used to Vince's games in hotel suites.

Apparently, it was the same five or six high rollers from the Pittsburgh area. A couple of guys came regularly from Philly.

They allowed guests, but it was typically on an invitation basis.

I didn't know what guy Jimmy knew to get me in, but the fact that he did, and that their monthly game was being played this week—the night before Pitt played at home—had me feeling extra lucky as I walked to the front door of the home.

Mansion was more like it, though it was very modern looking. Not at all stuffy. If I wasn't mistaken, it was the house I'd seen from the bottom of the Mount. The one that had a circular extension of all windows that jutted out over the side of the hill. I hoped I would be able to see that room, the view must be amazing.

My hand reached for my horseshoe pendant. I tapped it three times then rang the doorbell. The door opened immediately, as if someone had been standing at the door, waiting on me.

"Hello," I said to a small Asian man. "I'm Anna Dawson. I hope I'm not too late."

"They have started already," is all he said, then stood back from the door and waved me past him.

"Are you Mr. Stankowski?" I asked figuring the chances of that were pretty slim.

"No. I am Mr. Lee. I host these gatherings for Mr. Stankowski," he said as he took the lead, winding his way down a long hallway and into a large, beautifully furnished room. Opulent, yes, but still very livable. Warm colors. Great textures. Lorelei would have loved it.

Mr. Lee led me to a gorgeous dining room table at the far end of the room. From this view I could see where the men were playing cards.

It was in the circular, glass room that extended over the hill. The poker table was abnormally large, and was the exact angle of the room as though it had been specially made to fit.

I was really starting to like Mr. Stankowski. At least until he tried to win my money.

From here I could see eight players, five of them with their backs to me. I would make nine. I liked a table of nine or ten for a high stakes game best. It gave you more time than a smaller table to get the feel, find your pace.

And more people whose money you could win.

"How many chips do you wish to purchase, Ms. Dawson?" Mr. Lee asked.

I realized he had Carla's job, though without the *People* magazine.

"What did the others buy in with?" I asked.

He looked at me as though I asked for privileged information. He then looked me over from top to bottom, probably wondering how I'd found my way into these hallowed halls.

I liked Mr. Stankowski's taste in houses and décor, but not so much in his game-runners. I'd have to remember to tell Carla how much better she was than this guy.

Assuming Pitt covered the point spread tomorrow and I'd be allowed back into one of Vince's games.

Thinking of that slumbering giant back at the Omni, I smiled and said to snobby Mr. Lee, "I asked what the others bought in for."

He sniffed and grudgingly said, "Thirty thousand."

Shit. I hadn't brought enough. These were bigger fish than I'd thought. These guys weren't pros and they played monthly at these stakes?

There was some money to be made in Pennsylvania.

"I'll take twenty thousand in chips, please," I said. Mr. Lee didn't even try to hide his smirk and right then I vowed I'd watch that smirk slip away when I cashed out the majority of the chips by the end of the night.

I handed my money over to him, still in the envelope Lorelei had put in my desk drawer. He counted out nineteen-five in chips and put the other five hundred to the side.

The cut for Mr. Lee. Five hundred times nine players; a

forty-five hundred dollar night for answering the door, cashing chips and making sure everybody's drink glasses were filled. Plus whatever Mr. Stankowski paid him on the side.

Not a bad gig.

I looked down at the table and saw a waiter, filling drinks, asking the players if they'd like anything to eat.

Mr. Lee didn't even have to fill the drinks himself. Hell, even Carla closed her magazine, got off her ass and filled up my Diet Coke for me on occasion.

He put my chips in a tray, carried them himself—I was paying for some service after all, it seemed—and led me down the steps, across the sunken, sumptuous living room and to the circular alcove.

"Gentlemen," he said, and waited for the men to stop talking. Like he was announcing me at a ball, he said, "May I present Ms. Anna Dawson."

I'd decided to use my real name on the off chance that one of these players would recognize me as a pro. I didn't want them to think I was trying to put one over on them.

"Ms. Dawson," a robust man said as he got up from the table and headed toward me. "I'm Ralph Stankowski. Welcome to my home."

"Thank you. It's a beautiful home, Mr. Stankowski. I was admiring it from below. I'm afraid that's why I'm late, I'd wanted to take the Incline up, but didn't realize it shut down for the evenings."

"Damn, I wished I would have known that, I have a private key for one of them, I could have gotten you up here lickety-split." Probably in his early sixties, his face was as round as his body—not necessarily fat, but definitely round. His smile was genuine, as was his disappointment for me that I hadn't gotten to ride in his Incline.

I smiled at him, instantly liking the older man. But then, after the boys, I had a partiality for old men.

No, not in that way.

"Well, we'll be sure you get down the Mount in an Incline," he said, leading me to the empty seat.

"I might have to take you up on it, sir," I said. "You gentlemen don't look like the type to even leave the loser with cab fare."

The men all laughed and whatever uneasiness there might have been about a woman joining the group was gone. They knew I knew there'd be no concessions made to a woman at this table.

I wouldn't expect any.

"Mr. Stankowski, I—"

"Ralph. Ralph. Please call me Ralph," he said, taking my chips from Mr. Lee and putting them in front of the only empty seat at the table, then shooing Mr. Lee away with a bit of a scowl, raising my estimation of Ralph Stankowski.

"Ralph. I appreciate you letting me sit in on your game. It's nice to be able to play when I'm away from home."

"And where is home, exactly, Ms. Dawson?" the man directly to my right asked.

"Las Vegas," I said. "By way of Wisconsin," I added, hoping that at some point in the night it might bring up talk of the Packers and that could lead to talk of the Steelers.

But the men were much more fixated on the Las Vegas part of my heritage. One man even leaned forward. "Las Vegas? So you must play poker a lot?"

I liked Ralph enough that I was totally candid. "I'm a professional player."

There was some murmuring amongst them. I thought I heard a, "I thought that was her". I didn't know whether they'd take exception to my joining their game or not. Some private players like the idea of playing with a pro, beating a pro. It gave them bragging rights.

"Shuffle up and deal," the player on my right said, deciding my fate.

"Anna, let me introduce you to our regular players," Ralph said and did the introductions with six of the other players. All were men about Ralph's age, all had the look of money about them. Of course, they wouldn't be here if they couldn't afford it.

I paid close attention to the names, committing them to memory, so that I could pass them on to the authorities if I believed any of them to be the big loser from Superbowl Thirteen.

I wasn't expecting to get that lucky. I was just hoping that this circle of high rollers would have heard of the man who supposedly lost so much that year. Pittsburgh wasn't *that* large of a city.

Ralph finally got to the last player, one I hadn't noticed until now, and I realized keeping track of names wouldn't be necessary.

"And this is a new player too," Ralph said, almost suspiciously. "Danny Lowenstein." He waved his arm to indicate the man who sat in the seat that would be directly across from me.

The man stood, walked around the table and came to a stop directly in front of me. "Ms. Dawson, it's a pleasure to meet you. I'm a big fan of yours."

My poker face firmly in place, I stuck out my arm. "Thank you, Mr. Lowenstein," I said in a crisp voice as I shook hands with Jack Schiller.

Thirteen
❖❖

RIGHT AWAY I KNEW I COULDN'T WIN TONIGHT. Not because the players were that good, although a couple of them were.

No, I couldn't win because Jack and I were two new people at their table. If either one of us walked away a big winner they'd smell a scam. And they'd be right, but not for the reasons they'd think. But that didn't mean I had to lose, either.

Let Jack hold up that end. *Danny Lowenstein.* I didn't know whether to read his name choice as an homage or a bad omen for the night.

Once we were all seated, a waiter came around and took drink orders, a few players at a time. The man on Jack's right ordered bourbon, and when it was put down next to Jack I saw the hungry look he gave it.

"Coke," he said to the waiter. He looked across the table at me. I didn't know what he expected to see. Acknowledgement of his sacrifice? Censure? Applause?

He'd get none of them from me. I intended to totally block him out for the evening. I admit, I was miffed that he'd had the same idea I'd had about getting to know the high-rollers of Pittsburgh. Not relying on phone calls to Pittsburgh's finest—fine as they may be.

I should be proud that my instincts were dead on, but the

competitor in me was just plain irked.

Introductions done, drinks ordered, we settled in for some poker. The first hour was mostly silent as the players got the lay of the land. The regulars feeling out the new players. Jack and I testing the others in a couple of hands.

I think Jack bluffed a couple of times, but I wasn't sure—and that fact alone impressed me. And pissed me off even more.

I quickly concluded that these guys knew what they were doing. And I also got the feeling that once again there was more to Jack Schiller than I had guessed.

When everybody relaxed, and conversation started, it was taken up by the fact that a pro was amongst them. I answered the usual questions I do when playing with amateurs who might not have played with a pro before: What's the most I ever won at one time? How did I get started? What's the most I ever lost at one time? Is Phil Hellmuth really as big of an asshole as he appears?

I told a couple of good inside stories about players they would have seen on television. The men seemed to loosen up around me, and at about that time Jack won a large pot.

"So, Danny, where ya from?" Ralph asked Jack as most of the men's attention turned to him, the only unknown left at the table. The one pulling a good deal of their chips to his side of the table. "When my buddy called to get you a seat at our table he just said you were in investments and from Seattle."

"Portland," Jack said.

"Right, right, Portland," Ralph said. "My mistake."

But it wasn't a mistake. Ralph was trying to trip Jack up. Sure, there had to be more important crimes going on in Pittsburgh than a bunch of guys playing poker. But, this was an illegal game for a lot of money. Ralph was just trying to make sure he was on the up and up.

Jack had no intention of busting up the game, but that didn't mean he was who he said he was.

Suddenly, I was very grateful that I'd told Jimmy to have his "guy" stick to the truth about my identity. Keeping track of lies while playing poker—its own set of lies at times—was more than I could handle after a JoJo escapade.

"Although," Jack said as he folded his cards to my raise, not even throwing a glance my way. "I've been in Portland only a couple of years. I'm originally from the Bay area."

He said this with a hint of taunt in his voice, but I wasn't sure why.

"A Raiders fan," one of the other men—Herman somebody—asked. It wasn't a question, and there was evident disgust in his voice.

"Yes, sir," Jack said. "And proud of it." He smiled and I allowed myself to appreciate the sight. He smiled so seldom, and when he did…dangerous.

There were catcalls and boos across the table and then it hit me.

The Patriots were the archrival of the Steelers these days, but these guys were all older and back in the day, nobody hated each other more than the Steelers and the Raiders.

Jack was probably from the Bay area like Botz was from Philly, which is to say not at all. But discussion went to talk of old time Steelers with warp speed. Jack caught my eye, for just a fraction of a second, and raised a brow at me.

"I fold," I said, though I had a pretty good hand. Damn, I didn't need to be here at all, Jack was getting the job done all by himself. And I wouldn't even be able to walk away a big winner and rub my chips in Mr. Lee's face.

When faced with such turbulent emotions in a setting which demanded passiveness, I did what women have done since the beginning of time.

"Mind if I help myself, Ralph?" I asked motioning to the buffet table set up along one of the outer walls.

"Please, Anna, absolutely. We've got people who will bring

you whatever you want." He looked around for the waiter who'd just stepped out, and I was in just pissy enough of a mood that I hoped he'd give Mr. Lee hell about the staff not being there when needed.

I got out of my chair. "Thank you, but I need to stretch my legs a bit."

The spread was magnificent. It sure as hell beat whatever Carla ordered in for Vince's games.

One of the other men, Len, came over with me and we chatted a bit while I stuffed my face. When it looked like I was finishing up, he came close and said in a low voice. "You wanna get a couple of guys at the table riled up?"

"Maybe," I said noncommittally.

"Ask Chuck about him betting the Steelers in the Superbowl."

I almost dropped my plate, but my face never changed. "Which one's Chuck again?"

"The one in the green cardigan."

"You've all been very nice to allow me in your game. I'm hardly going to go out of my way to piss one of you off, Len," I said.

"Taking our money would piss us off more."

I laughed. And, I might have imagined it, but I swore Jack's back stiffened just the slightest at the sound. I looked beyond him, to the windows which now reflected the men back to me. His head was down slightly, looking at his chips, but there was just a tug of a smile at the corners of his mouth.

"Besides, it's nothing like that. It's just an old joke. Ancient," Len explained.

"We'll see."

Len shrugged. "Any advantage at the table, right?"

"I guess," I said, and headed back to my seat.

Talk of football was still going on. To the Steelers' chances next year, who they should take in the draft.

A couple of hands later I was in a hand which whittled its way down to Jack, Chuck and Ralph. I raised and all three of them stayed in. "So, Chuck, Len tells me you do some sports betting. Me too," I said.

"Really?" Chuck said, looking at Len suspiciously.

"He said you might be able to give me some advice. Who do you like for next year's Superbowl?"

The entire table erupted into laughter.

Well, not the entire table. Chuck, of course wasn't laughing. Nor was Jack, who wasn't supposed to be in on the joke anyway.

But the rumbling laugh I'd heard from Ralph throughout the night was missing. I looked over at him and he was smiling, laughing even, but no sound was coming from him.

"Call," Ralph said and pushed some chips into the pot.

There. Blatant as any tell. His hand clenched into a fist for just a second when he drew it back. It could have been because he was bluffing. Or because he had a good hand.

But somehow I sensed that wasn't it.

I looked across the table at Jack. He was staring straight at me, and though no brow was raised, no nod was given, I knew he was telling me he saw it too.

"Sorry, Chuck," I said. "Len said it'd be a good joke."

The other men laughed. Chuck shot Len a dirty look then folded his cards. Len was right, any advantage…

The flop came up and it gave me absolutely nothing, but I figured this was a good time to bluff, as I'd already bet high—they'd think I had good cards in my hands. I bet and turned to Ralph. He, Jack and I were the only ones left in the hand.

"No harm done," Ralph said. "It was a long time ago, Anna, but you know how old men love to rib each other."

"I do know about that, yes," I said, looking right at him.

He watched me for a long time, trying to read me. I let him watch, my face a study of composure, giving nothing away. He'd learn nothing from me.

At some point he seemed to realize that, looked at his cards once more and called. Jack called almost instantly and my eyes flew to his face. Nothing there to read.

The turn card came and I still had garbage. I bet high trying to chase them away. Ralph took even longer this time, nearly burning a hole in my forehead with his stare. Finally he threw in his cards, "I fold," he said, disgust in his voice. At me or himself, I wasn't sure, but I had a feeling I wouldn't be invited back to one of Mr. Stankowski's games anytime soon.

I didn't blame him.

"See, Ralph," Jack said as he watched me. "I think she's bluffing."

The other men all turned to me; I guessed so they could see what a pro looked like bluffing. Believe me, it isn't any different than what a pro with good cards looks like.

At least not this pro.

"You'll have to pay to know for sure," was all I said.

"Either you're bluffing or…" Jack looked at his cards again, he looked around at the other men and their stacks of chips—or maybe he was just looking at their drinks with longing. I didn't know what he was looking at, but it was beginning to bug the hell out of me, though not a thing in my demeanor changed.

"Either you're bluffing or…" Jack repeated. "Or. And this is probably it."

He looked me straight in the eye. "You're looking for a jack." The men looked down at the cards on the table, trying to figure out how a jack would help me.

It wouldn't.

"A jack won't do me any good," I said, to the astonishment of those around me. They'd kibitzed about their hands throughout the night, but I'd never mentioned anything about mine. No trash talk, not much talking at all.

Jack raised that damn brow at me. "Oh, I don't know. One, solid Jack can round out a lot of so-so hands."

I was trying to think of a witty comeback that involved solidness when he said, "I believe I *will* pay to see. Call." He pushed his bet in.

The river card was a jack, and the other players leaned forward in their seats. "All in," I said, putting the chips in quickly. The second I did I cursed my impulsiveness. It wasn't a bad play. He only guessed I was bluffing.

I was committed to the pot, as much as I'd already bet. Putting all my chips in was one way to *really* make him guess. And from the cards on the table, he couldn't have had too much of a hand. A pocket pair, probably. Nothing he'd feel real great about calling me with.

But somewhere deep inside I knew I wouldn't have made the same bet against anybody other than Jack Schiller. He'd goaded me into it, and that had never happened to me before.

But it was too late, the bed was made. The bet. The bet was made.

"Call," he said with no hesitation and turned over pocket jacks. The one on the table making three jacks.

Four too many at this table.

Fourteen
❖❖

The game broke up shortly after that. Only a couple more hands were played. Len ended up being the big winner. Jack, as far as I could tell, was up twenty thousand.

My twenty thousand.

Ralph was up and I was glad for that. He'd been a good host.

It was near six in the morning. Just a hint of sun was beginning to shine through the enormous windows of Ralph Stankowski's poker room. I'd stuck around even after I was out because Ralph had promised me a ride down the Mount in the Incline and I wanted to do that. Besides, it was less humiliating to leave when everyone else did than to have to have Mr. Lee call me a cab.

I was light twenty k but that wasn't totally out of the norm for me. I'd be out of debt tomorrow and would be able to recoup that at one of Vince's games next week. Or whenever I felt it was okay to leave Ben and Saul long enough to play.

And I had a couple of names. Chuck and Ralph were definitely at the top of the list as far as looking into Danny and Gus' shootings. Len offering up that information so easily had to put him on some kind of list too.

All in all, a pretty good night. Except for losing to Jack Schiller.

"Mind if I ride down in the Incline with you, Ms. Dawson?

I've never seen one before, either." Jack said in front of the group of men as we stood in the foyer.

"No," I said and started out the door.

Ralph walked with Jack and me about a half mile to the Incline station. "I didn't mean to cause this much trouble," I said.

Ralph waved my comment aside as nonsense. "It feels good to get out and get some fresh air after a night like that.

It did, and the crisp winter night felt refreshing, if not colder than my Vegas blood was used to. It reminded me of Wisconsin in the winter; when you'd breathe in deep and feel the insides of your nose freeze up.

My leather jacket wasn't really warm enough, but I didn't mind.

I walked ahead of Jack and Ralph, heard them talking but couldn't make out the words. I heard Ralph laugh, so I assumed Jack wasn't reading him his Miranda rights or anything.

We got to the Incline station. Depot. I don't know what they called it. I hadn't seen anything like it in the U.S.—though granted, my experience was limited to Wisconsin, Vegas and the cities that JoJo frequented.

Ralph opened the building with a key and after entering some numbers into a keypad. When we got into the building, he went to a control panel and inserted his key and pressed some more numbers into a different keypad.

A loud hum surrounded us and I saw the Incline car start its way up the hill along the metal monorail track.

"It'll take a few minutes for it to get up here," Ralph said.

"This is great," I said. "Thanks, Ralph."

He nodded. "Once I get you on the car and get it started, I'll call a cab company and have one meet you at the bottom of the hill, it's still too early for the regular traffic to be out."

"Thanks, I appreciate that," Jack said.

Ralph acknowledged the thanks. Then he put his hands

on his ample hips, looked at us both like we were misbehaving school children and said, "Do you appreciate it enough to tell me what the hell the two of you were doing at my game tonight?"

I looked at Jack. Let him field this one.

"No. I'm afraid not," Jack said, his cop face firmly in place.

Ralph tried to read him as if we were still playing poker. I could have told him not to bother. Jack's cop face was as unreadable as any pro poker player I've run across.

Ralph looked from one of us to the other, than back again. He sighed, rubbed his hands over his eyes. "I get two calls. Both from people I do a lot of business with. They both have someone they want to get in my next game. I say yes, because I respect and trust these people." He looked at me. "And fear them."

I figured that had to be Jimmy's "guy", but I said nothing. He'd probably scare me, too. Hell, Jimmy scared me sometimes.

"At least you only won each other's money, so I won't have to explain too much to the other players."

Jack nodded, like that had been our plan all along. Again, I said nothing. Jack winning my money had been nowhere in my plans.

The Incline car had reached the top of the hill and Ralph, sensing he'd get no more out of Jack, walked us to the loading area.

The car sat at a forty-five degree angle with the track, so that it jutted straight out. The car contained three rows of seats that sat two or three per row. The rows were at a slight angle, stadium style, so that each row could see the spectacular view.

We said our goodbyes, shook Ralph's hand and entered the car. I went to the front row and sat at the edge. Jack sat in the seat behind me. The car began its slow downward journey. I should have been enjoying the view—which really was spectacular.

I should have been talking to Jack about Chuck and Ralph and telling him about Len so easily giving up the information about Chuck and the Superbowl.

But instead, I continued to face forward and blurted out, "How'd you know I was bluffing that last hand? And I don't mean my needing a *jack*."

He leaned forward, his lips near my ear. "You have a tell," he whispered.

I turned my head slightly, not facing him, but I could see him out of the corner of my eye. "My necklace. I try to –"

"Not your necklace. I saw that fake tell coming a mile away, although you got that one guy to bite with it earlier."

I turned fully around now. "That's the only tell I have. And it's not a tell, it's a trap."

He nodded. "And it worked. Just not on me."

I studied him, trying to see if he was bluffing.

"I'm not bluffing. You have a tell."

"What?"

He snorted. "Yeah, right, like I'm going to tell you."

"We'll never play poker together again, you might as well tell me. As a thank you," I nearly cajoled. I'd watched hours of tape of myself playing making sure I never gave anything away that I didn't want to.

This guy thinks he can read me in one night?

"A thank you for what? And don't be so sure we won't… play again."

I ignored the second part of his statement, and went right for the first. "Thank me for getting information out of those guys. You've got Ralph Stankowski as a prime suspect now, with the names of two others to check out."

"And I have you to thank for that?" He didn't ask who the other name was. So he'd picked up that Len must have given me that Superbowl tip while we were at the buffet. It didn't surprise me.

"Come on. What tell?" I said, and was shocked to hear the small amount of whine in my voice.

He chuckled, shook his head. "Unh unh, no way," he said

then sat back in his seat. He looked outside, nodded. "You're missing the view."

I turned around in my seat, looked outside, barely seeing through my frustration. I took a deep breath. He had to be yanking my chain. No way did I have a tell, I'd worked too hard on it, for too long.

He didn't say another word the entire ride down, just let me review every move I'd made in the last six hours. And stew.

He knew how to play me in more than just poker.

A cab waited for us at the bottom. Apparently Ralph hadn't been too pissed to leave us to our own devices. That, or he was too afraid of whoever got us into the game.

"Where to?" the driver asked.

"The Om –" I started to give directions but Jack put his hand on my knee and squeezed.

"The Hilton," he said and the driver put the car in gear.

I looked at Jack and he gave just the slightest shake of his head. I stayed silent for the ride.

When we got to the Hilton, he took my hand and led me to the lobby bar which was just opening up with fresh coffee and some pastries.

"Bourbon. Neat," he said to the bartender. He looked at me and I shook my head. "Make it two," he added.

"Sir, the bar closed hours ago. We do have fresh coffee and some pastries if you—" the bartender stopped in mid-sentence as Jack slid a hundred dollar bill across the bar to him. "Two bourbons, neat," the bartender repeated and disappeared behind a swinging door. Taking the hundred with him.

Jack swiveled the barstool from the front to the side, facing me. "We have about four minutes—or however long it takes that kid to pour some drinks—before I'm officially off duty so…" He rubbed his hand across his face, looking as tired as I felt. "I'm not even going to ask you why—or how—you were at that game. Just what do you think right now?"

I was so taken aback that he wasn't going to chastise me that it took a second to put my practiced defenses to the side. "I think we need to look at Chuck. And Ralph," I said. "You saw his fist clench when Chuck was talking?"

Jack nodded. "What about Len?"

"Yeah, him too. It was just too easy. He *could* have been trying to get an advantage on a fellow player by busting his chops, and we *were* talking about the Steelers, but…"

"Yeah. But." Jack was looking beyond me, his wheels turning.

The bartender came back, setting two glasses down in front of us. At least Jack got a lot of drink for his money; the glasses were full to the top. "Thanks," was all Jack said and the bartender went down to the other end of the bar.

I pushed mine in front of Jack, but other than his original acknowledgement when the bartender set them down, he didn't seem to notice they were there.

Or, he was trying to ignore them.

"Anything else?" he asked.

I shrugged. "It could have been nothing. Chuck, Ralph and Len. It could have just been good friends ragging on each other about some small time bet they had with each other years ago."

"But you don't believe that?"

"No," I said quietly. "I think one of those guys was the big money that lost out in Superbowl Thirteen."

"And therefore has revenge as a motive to hurt The Corporation," he finished my thought.

"Yes."

He nodded. He took a deep breath, swiveled in his chair and looked down at the drinks in front of him.

The cop face melted before my eyes. His shoulders relaxed, tension I hadn't even noticed left his body. A look of reverence washed over his weary face as he lifted the first glass to his lips.

He took two small sips, savoring the liquid. His eyes closed, a look of near rapture on his face. It was so intimate I felt I should look away and yet I couldn't.

I knew this was the closest I'd come to seeing the real Jack Schiller. I couldn't tear my eyes from him.

He downed the entire glass on the next gulp like a shot, though the tumbler was nowhere near as small as a shot glass.

The look on his face was one I was sure was on mine when I stepped away from a betting desk after plunking down a large amount of money.

Euphoria. Glee. Then caution. And then a shimmer of self-loathing.

When that last came across Jack's face I stood to leave, not being able to bear the emotions it brought up in me.

I couldn't help him. I couldn't even help myself.

His eyes still closed, he reached out and put a gentle hand on my knee, urging me to sit back down, which I did.

He opened his eyes then, the brown seemed darker, more intense as he looked at me.

"I'm officially off duty. Let's talk about something else," he said.

No clock had struck the stroke of anything. It was quarter to seven in the morning, no shift was ending. Jack's shift was over when the bourbon flowed.

I admired his skewed moral code. Kind of like me not betting on a game JoJo was involved with.

The truth was I did not want to leave Jack Schiller tonight.

I nodded, making myself more comfortable in the barstool. "Like?" I asked.

He pushed the empty glass to the side, much like I try to distance myself from losing betting slips.

At least he didn't have to carry his empties home for tax purposes.

"Like," he said, taking a drink from the second glass. "Like why is it that I have this case and two other homicides on my desk at the moment and all I can seem to think of is you."

I blinked at him several times, not sure I'd heard him correctly.

I'm no dummy when it comes to reading people. I do it for a living. And I'd known Jack was attracted to me—had known it since that first night outside the municipal building that neither of us had entered.

But not in a million years would I have bet money on him coming out and admitting it.

I didn't know if the real Jack—vs. the cop Jack—was really that much different from the man I'd been dealing with these past couple of weeks, but I doubted it.

So, was it the bourbon that brought on this confession? Or the lure of a different town with a hotel bed just an elevator ride away?

I started to analyze it like I would a poker hand. What cards was he holding? Was it all a bluff? Was the rush of winning my money some type of warped foreplay for him?

Then he reached out, turned my pendant over, barely grazing my skin and placed his hand back on his khaki-covered knee, and suddenly I didn't care about his motives, I only cared about being with him.

"Looks like the horseshoe didn't work for you tonight," he said, with absolutely no gloat in his voice. He looked at me with those deep brown eyes.

"Oh, I don't know," I said softly, nearly whispering the words to myself. He leaned in as if to hear me better, though I knew he'd heard me. My lips came to his edge of his ear, much like he'd done to me in the Incline. "I might still get lucky."

He grabbed the second glass of bourbon taking it with him and we both rose and left the lobby, heading for the elevators.

Fifteen
❖❖

"JOHANNA," HE WHISPERED as he woke me up the next morning. Or, that same day to be exact.

Having sex with Jack Schiller was very similar to playing poker with him. He was hard to read, it got competitive at times, and was altogether an incredibly exhilarating experience.

But I didn't get these delicious stubble burns all over my body when playing poker.

"Johanna," he whispered again, nudging me this time.

Two things went through my mind. One, I had a plane to catch today and I had absolutely no idea what time it was. And two—"How'd you know my name was Johanna?" I tried to keep the suspicion out of my voice, but had he investigated me in some way?

I had my back to him, his arm thrown over my waist, his legs entwined with mine. I felt his shrug along my back. "Ben and Saul call you Hannah. You introduce yourself and play poker as Anna. And Lorelei calls you Jo. I am a detective after all, Johanna" he said.

"Oh," I said, letting out a small sigh of relief. I was just about to ask about the time when he continued.

"Johanna Elizabeth Dawson. Born thirty-four years ago in Madison, Wisconsin to Albert and Evelyn Dawson. One older sister, two brothers, one older, one younger. Attended high school and college in Madison. Left college—"

"Hey," I said, turning to him. My outrage fell away as I took in his tousled hair, his well-used mouth, giving me a grin that made me press my body into his, all thought of his looking into my past gone.

He shrugged again. "We did a background check on everyone connected with the case."

"I wasn't connected to the case and you know it," I said.

"You could have been," he hedged.

"If I was the least bit connected to this case; a witness, a suspect, a potential victim, you never would have slept with me."

"You wanna bet," he said. He started to lean in to kiss me, but I put my hand to his chest, stopping him.

I looked at him hard. "Yes. I *would* bet on that. I'd go all in on that."

He hung his head in an aww shucks kind of way.

"That's not necessarily a compliment. Sometimes you have to bend the rules to get the job done," I said.

"I know that. And at times I have. But if I start breaking *my own* rules, what hope is there?"

I had two simple rules; I never bet on a game JoJo was involved with, and JoJo never involved a player - at least knowingly—in her plans. They were innocent victims, not to be held responsible for the outcome of any game.

I knew how Jack felt. If I were to break either of those rules to myself I'd feel like a complete failure.

He moved in again, and this time I did nothing to stop him. But when his body came down, I got a glimpse of the clock on the bedside table behind him.

"Oh, crap," I said. "I gotta go. My flight's in a couple of hours and I have to stop back at the Omni and get my stuff."

"You on the two-fifteen flight?" he asked and I nodded. "Me too. Hang on, and I'll go with you to the Omni, then we can go to the airport together." He lifted the sheets off of himself, looked down at my body and groaned with reluctance. "Or we can just skip our flights and take the red-eye back tonight."

I thought about JoJo's stuff that I'd strewn all over my room at the Omni in my rush to get to the poker game.

Just as Jack seemed resigned to miss the flights and reached for me, I slid out from the bed on the other side and started reaching for my clothes. "No. I need to get back this afternoon. Lorelei's probably going crazy watching over the boys. And I want to check on Gus."

"Botz called me last night right before I went to Ralph's. Gus has regained consciousness and was able to see his friends. Your friends."

I turned to him, my earlier discarded clothes held up as a shield to cover my nakedness. I didn't know why I bothered; the man had inspected every inch of me over the last few hours.

The relief across my face at hearing of Gus' well-being must have been obvious.

"I'm sorry I didn't tell you earlier. I couldn't at the game of course, and then afterward…" He motioned to the bed between us, its covers in total disarray, pillows thrown to the floor, condom wrappers on the beside table, traces of the bourbon that he'd licked off my body on the sheets.

Embarrassed, I turned and headed for the bathroom to dress. "It's okay. We were both distracted. I'm just glad Gus is going to be okay."

I left the bathroom door open and started to throw my clothes on. "Was Gus able to tell Detective Botz anything that was helpful?" I asked loudly so Jack could hear me.

"No. It was like the doctor thought, he was shot from behind. Gus never heard or saw anything."

"Still, it's weird that Danny was shot point blank and Gus from far away."

"Yes, it is," was all Jack would give me. I figured cop Jack was due to return any moment now. Even more reason not to let him see my room at the Omni.

Dressed, I stepped out of the bathroom and looked around for my jacket. "So, I'll see you at the airport?" I said, not looking at him.

"This is silly. Give me fifteen minutes to shower and I'll be ready to go with you. Better yet, let's shower together," he said, but I was already headed toward the door.

"No. I want to shower with all my stuff that's at the hotel. I'll just see you at the airport."

He put his hand on my arm, stopping me, turning me toward him. He watched me for a second, then said, "Hmmm."

"Hmmm, what?" I asked, scared that maybe I really did have a tell that only Jack Schiller could see.

He shrugged. "Nothing. I just never took you for the high-maintenance kind. Needing your own products and shit."

Other than deodorant there wasn't one personal product of mine in my room at the Omni. Plenty of JoJo's.

I put my hand to his bare chest. He'd thrown on jeans while I'd been in the bathroom and they hung low on his lean hips, the button fly only half done. My fingers tangled with the rough hair on his chest, and I saw with satisfaction a mark I'd left on him. "You may have done a background check. But there's a lot you don't know about me, Jack Schiller."

He placed a finger on my horseshoe pendant, then slid his hand up and behind my neck, taking my nape in his strong grip. He pulled me close, my ear just below his mouth.

"I don't doubt that for a second," he said softly, then let me loose.

As I entered the lobby of the Omni Hotel, the Louisville basketball team was walking out, making their way over to the Omni Center for their afternoon game with Pitt.

Karl Richardson was trailing the rest of the team, holding what appeared to be an ice pack to his head. His eyes were half closed, and a member of the team was helping to lead him through the lobby. He looked like death warmed over.

No forty points today, Karl.

I started to duck my head as we passed each other, but given the shape he was in, and the difference in my appearance, I just kept walking.

He didn't even notice me.

I found Jack at the gate for our flight. He rose when he saw me, and started walking toward me. "Flight's delayed. They're de-icing the plane. Let's wait it out in the bar." He said this all as he took my carry on from my shoulder, added it to his, swung me around and took my hand to lead me in the direction I'd just come from.

It felt so unusual to have someone else make a decision for me. I hated to admit it, but I kind of liked it. But I didn't want Jack to get the idea he could do it too often, so I was about to balk, when we reached the bar and I saw the Louisville / Pitt game was on the television.

"Sounds good," I said, taking a stool that gave me optimum viewing.

Jack sat with a bourbon in front of him for most of the first half, not touching it. I noticed, but just barely, consumed with the game.

"You got money on this game?" he asked when he saw my interest.

"Some," I said. He nodded, then seemed to retreat into his own staring match with his glass.

I drank several cups of coffee, it feeling like morning to me.

The caffeine had nothing on the rush going through me from the game.

At halftime, Pitt was up by five, a stunning upset in the works. Karl Richardson had only played the first three minutes then went into the lockeroom. The announcers said he wasn't expected back.

"Looking good?" Jack asked me, nodding toward the screen.

"Very good," I said, and my body relaxed some.

He seemed to be waiting for that, because he turned to me then. "So, do we need to have the morning after talk?" he asked.

I took a deep breath, let it out. So, this was it. The "it was fun, but"...talk. I'd had it before, been on the giving and receiving end. I just didn't want to have it with Jack Schiller. "It's okay," I said trying to head him off. "I'm cool."

"Cool with what exactly?" he asked, studying me.

"With what happened last night." I shrugged my shoulders—no big deal—and took another gulp of coffee.

"You're...*cool*...with it?" He raised a brow at me.

"Yes," I answered.

"Johanna, that room looked like a fucking cyclone went through it when we were done. I came three times. And you –"

I held a hand up, perfectly aware of what my body had gone through—I was still having after-shocks. "So, what are you saying, Jack?"

"That I want to see you again. I mean, with my schedule and yours it's going to take some doing, but..."

"Oh," I said, surprised.

"You seem surprised," he said. "Do you have nights like that a lot?"

"No," I said quickly—too quickly I realized as I saw his grin.

"It seems stupid to walk away from something like that."

"So, what? You're talking a relationship? Or a friends with

benefits situation?"

He looked away from me. His hand traced the outside of his still-full glass of booze. "I'm not sure. I'm no prize in the relationship sweepstakes." He tapped his glass, bringing my attention to it. I didn't know if that was his intention or just his subconscious. He looked back at me, puzzlement in his eyes, as if he wasn't sure what he was asking of me.

Asking of himself.

"I'm not perfect, either," I said, motioning to the television where the second-half of the game was just starting.

He took his hand off of his glass, put it on the bar, slid it toward mine, but stopped just short. "Listen, I don't want to cure you. I don't want to save you. Your demons are your issue. I like you just fine the way you are. Let your iceberg of vices stay afloat until Al Gore can save it."

"You're okay with my issues? Really?" I asked

"Hey, as long as they're legal, and gambling is in Vegas, why should I care? You're not breaking the law, right?"

I looked down at my carry-on resting on the floor between us, JoJo's clothes buried inside. "Well, not homicide, anyway," I said and laughed.

My laugh sounded nervous, forced, even to me. He looked at me just a moment too long and then chuckled also. He turned to his drink, lifting it to his lips, apparently content with our decision—vague as it was.

But I had a feeling nothing I did fooled Jack Schiller.

An hour later I sat at the stool, my gut churning as Louisville's point guard was having the game of his life. Having previously been only an assist-maker for Karl Richardson, he was getting his time to shine, hitting one three-pointer after another.

With two minutes left, Louisville was up by seven. I was

still clear as long as Pitt didn't—

"Looks like Pitt's going to have to start fouling to save the clock," the announcer said on the television as Pitt did just that.

Jack got up from his seat. "I'm hitting the john," he said. "Then I'm going to give Frank a call and see if there's any news." He put his hand on my back, and I bristled.

He looked at me, his eyes slid to my hands, which held my coffee cup in a death grip. He didn't question me. Or assume it had anything to do with him. Jack Schiller had the good sense to look up at the television. He looked at the score, nodded, gave my shoulder a squeeze then left.

Maybe there was hope for something with him after all.

The last five minutes of the game took thirty, with Pitt fouling every time Louisville got the ball. Louisville made every free throw. And what was worse, Pitt missed every shot they took.

With five seconds left and Louisville up by fifteen, I looked out through the wall of windows from the bar to the hallway where Jack was on his phone, presumably with Detective Botz.

I wondered if I slid off the barstool, changed my flight to Puerto Rico and just disappeared if he'd notice?

If he'd come after me?

I knew Vince would, which is why I stayed in my seat. Or, if Vince didn't come after me, he'd go after Ben and Lorelei—which was so much worse.

Jack met my eye. He pointed to the television set, gave a thumbs up and then a thumbs down, silently asking me how I'd done.

I almost gave him a thumbs up, but knew better than that. He'd know I was lying, and I figured between his drinking and my gambling there'd be plenty of half-truths in our future. Starting off whatever this was going to be with a lie didn't seem the way to go.

I raised my thumb neutrally, like Caesar pronouncing

judgment, and then turned it down. He mouthed the word "sorry" and I shrugged, like it happened everyday.

The truth was, this had never happened to me before. Every game JoJo had been…involved with…had gone the way it was supposed to. That's why the need to involve players—and more of a chance of being caught—had never been necessary.

Jack started talking again, turning his body away from me. I wondered if he liked chicks with limps.

Jack had two bourbons during our flight. I had three. I wanted to be totally numb for what was to come, but instead I fell into a deep sleep and had to be shaken awake by Jack.

We got to the huge luggage pick-up area, though we both had only carry-ons.

"I'll go get a patrol car to take you home."

"My car's in the parking deck," I said. "I'll give you a ride home."

He shook his head. "Botz is going to pick me up. We're heading to the station."

So, this was our first goodbye. Would we kiss? Hug? Instead we were saved by Jack's cell phone—at least momentarily. He took the call, then made a motion for me to stay where I was while he walked to a private alcove, out of my line of vision.

I stepped out of the way of a few people jostling for luggage retrieval position. I looked around, and saw Paulie enter the huge room on the same end that I stood.

My nerves must have been giving off a neon glow, because he saw me right away and started hustling toward me.

Every muscle in my body wanted to run, but I knew that was useless. I had ties here. A home. Ben. Lorelei. Gus, Jimmy and Saul. I couldn't run. That's what people like Vince counted on.

"Anna," Paulie said, disgust in his voice. "You need to come with me."

My eyes flew to the alcove that Jack would be appearing from any minute. "I know Paulie but now isn't the best time. Tell Vince I'll –"

Paulie grabbed my upper arm, squeezing hard. "I ain't telling Vince nothing. You can tell him whatever lame excuse you came up with. Right now."

He started pulling me, but I held firm. With all the craziness that was going on, I didn't want Jack thinking I'd disappeared. But I didn't want him seeing Paulie either.

"Listen, Paulie," I started, my voice going to plead mode. "I'll come with you. I will. But you have to give me a couple of minutes here. I'll meet you–"

"Jesus Christ, Anna, do you think I'm an idiot?"

I pulled on my arm, trying to get loose, but Paulie didn't budge.

"Excuse me," I heard Jack's voice from behind me. "Is there a problem here?"

Paulie kept hold of my arm, but pulled me close to him. "No problem. Just having a tiff with the girlfriend."

Jack looked at me, no expression on his face. "Are you okay, ma'am?"

My voice cracked, but I managed to croak out, "Yes. Thank you, everything's fine."

He nodded, his eyes boring into mine, trying to see any hint of distress, but I only looked guilty. The guilt, I was sure, was all over my face. Not the guilt Jack would think—that I was involved with someone else when I'd slept with him—but guilt just the same.

But I needed to set that aside for now. I did not want Jack and Paulie to become better acquainted. "Really. It's okay. But thanks for your concern."

"You know how it is," Paulie said to Jack, mano-a-mano

style. "We got into a tiff, she goes away with out telling me. But she's back now, and we'll go talk it through. Isn't that right, baby?"

Jack looked at me hard. I needed to get him out of here. I put my arm around Paulie's waist. I looked Jack square in his beautiful brown eyes. "That's right. We really should get going."

Paulie nodded at Jack who nodded back without looking at me again. He held his hands up, almost hold-up style, then dropped them. "My mistake," he said, then turned and walked out of the airport.

Sixteen
❖❖

"MY CAR'S PARKED HERE," I told Paulie, but he just herded me toward his, which sat at one of the meters in the short-term lot.

"I'll bring you back for it," he said and I clung to that. It meant I'd be driving again after my meeting with Vince. "If you're able to drive," he added and my stomach clenched.

"How'd you know what flight I was on?" I asked. He just looked at me like I'd insulted his intelligence. Of course Vince would have ways to find that out. And Lorelei had booked the flight in my real name.

The drive to meet Vince took a half hour during which I'd worked myself up into a full-blown panic. The thirty thousand I owed Vince wasn't killing debt. It *was* bodily harm debt. But I had no idea how much of his own money Vince had bet on the Pitt game—he could be out some major change for which he'd hold me responsible.

Shit, he'd probably taken the under, too, to piss him off even more.

I've got to tell you, the idea of Paulie pounding on me, of that excruciating pop as my foot broke; I had to roll down the window to keep from hyperventilating.

But to have this happen now, when Ben and the boys needed me around—the shame overcame my fear, which was beyond potent.

Thoughts of Jack whistled past me, too. He knew I had baggage and seemed accepting of that, but even if he got over—or beyond—that scene with Paulie at the airport, me showing up with bruises and broken bones might be more than he signed on for.

I wouldn't be able to tell him anything. He wouldn't be able to help in any way, and that would probably drive him crazy. He'd said he didn't want to save me, but he was a cop after all.

And a man.

During the interminable drive Paulie gave me no words of encouragement. He said nothing the entire ride. Once I even saw him wipe a bead of sweat off his upper lip. I knew he didn't want to beat me up—but he would if Vince gave the word.

He didn't take me to a casino. Instead we pulled up to a no tell-motel dive in one of the seedier sections of town.

No cars were parked out front, but Paulie knew exactly what room to park at. He pointed to the room in front of us and released the locks on my car door.

I let myself out of the car and slowly walked to the motel room door. I looked back at Paulie, but he couldn't meet my eye. I turned to the door and knocked.

"Come in," Vince answered and I did.

He sat in a chair at a little round table in the room. There was no chair for me I noticed. No book with Vince. No coffee cup. It was if he'd just transported into that chair. Nothing of any personal nature anywhere in the room.

Because he didn't want to leave any evidence at a crime scene?

"Vince, I…" I stopped as he held up a hand. I didn't really know what I'd say anyway.

"Don't, Anna," he said. He looked at me, turned his head from one side to the other, as if measuring me.

I just hoped it wasn't for trunk size.

"You've always been a good customer, Anna," he said. I didn't say anything, waiting for him to go on. My hands were shaking by now and I clasped them behind my back.

This was different than controlling your emotions in a poker game. That was money, and money could sometimes feel like life or death, but this truly was life or death—or at the very least really horrible pain.

"Other than that one unfortunate incident ten years ago, we've done very well together."

My foot ached as he mentioned my "incident". I vaguely wondered if Paulie would break the same one, or if I'd have a matching set of fractures?

"So, you can imagine my predicament. I've made lots of money off of the games you've… worked… for me." I liked his choice of euphemism. Like I was one of the timekeepers or refs or something.

"Because of that, I'm giving you a choice," he said.

My eyes grew wide with surprise, then narrowed with suspicion. "What's the choice?" I asked, hoping it wasn't just between my left foot or right.

"You can either owe me the original thirty with the interest still running and one week to pay." That was unbelievable to me and I was about to jump at it when he added, "Taking, of course, the requisite physical punishment."

Which is what I'd expected, a hospital stay, pissing blood, rehab and still owing Vince money I didn't have.

"Or?" I asked.

"Or your tab goes to one hundred large which is your thirty and what I lost today."

"No…physical punishment?" I said, and my heart started beating again.

"No. Same terms apply. You have one week to pay it back."

"Can I pay it off with a different game?" I asked.

He thought on that. He must have known it was the best

chance to see his money again, but I didn't blame him for being gun-shy after my screw up today. "I'll take thirty k off for services rendered. You're on your own for the other seventy."

"What if you took the money line, and it was a long shot?" I asked. "Would that be worth a hundred grand to you?"

When betting a game, you usually bet the point spread—such as in the Louisville / Pitt game, the point spread was 10, with Louisville the favorite. So, if you wanted to bet Pitt, you had the same relative chance of winning getting ten points as you would if you bet Louisville giving ten points. And the payouts would be the same, or nearly so.

The money line didn't take point spreads into account—you bet on who you thought would win the game, so the odds were much higher for the underdog to win outright, and thus the payout higher.

The kicker was, to get a really high payout for a money line, it would have to be a big time underdog winning in a huge upset. Those didn't happen every day.

But one would have to happen soon, with JoJo's help.

"You'd have to have some buy-in if you went for a moneyline game," Vince pointed out the conclusion I'd reluctantly just come to. "You can't just have a high-scorer out with a roofie hang-over."

I nodded, not surprised that he'd deduced JoJo's methods. And waited.

"One week. The money line has to be at least +500." With that, Vince could bet ten thousand—a fraction of what I owed him—and walk away with winnings of $50,000.

I nodded, started to feel a shimmer of hope that I was going to get out of here with all my limbs intact.

"And, Anna," Vince said. "You know what will happen if this doesn't work." I nodded again, still unable to trust my voice. He motioned to the door, dismissing me. "I want to know the game within two days," he said.

I nodded once more. "Thanks, Vince," I managed to croak out and quickly headed for the door.

"Send Paulie in here," Vince said. I did, and sat in the car waiting for Paulie to get the benign—and surely puzzling—instructions to take me back to the airport and my car, not off into the desert and then to the hospital.

"Gin!" I heard Lorelei declare from the foyer as I entered the house. I plopped my carry-on down on the tile, then thought better of it and quickly carried it to the back of the house and my bedroom, stowing it in the back of my closet and shutting the door.

I then made my way back into the main part of the house, following the noise to the dining room where Lorelei, Jimmy, Ben and Saul were playing cards.

"Hannah, dear, come and join us," Ben said as if I'd only been away a few hours rather than two days.

Ben was no dummy; he knew he was setting the tone. Nobody would ask where I'd been if he didn't. Jimmy did flash me a questioning look and I gave him a slight nod. He seemed satisfied with that.

Lorelei saw that and then gave me a questioning look of her own—about the money I deduced. I shook my head this time and she leaned back in her chair with a soft sigh.

I went to the sideboard where Lorelei had set up a coffee pot and some snacks, and filled myself a mug. I took a piece of one of the sub sandwiches she had provided and put it on a plate. I took it all to the table and sat down. "Who's winning?" I asked.

Lorelei beamed. "Me! Can you believe it?"

"That's great," I said. Then in between bites I managed to get out, "Thanks for the sandwiches, this really hits the spot." I reached across the table, grabbed her hand as she was reaching for her just-dealt cards. "Thank you for everything you do, Lor. I couldn't make it without you."

She waved my thanks away, but I could tell she was touched. She kept her head down as she looked at her cards, and let her red mane fall to shield herself.

"Christ, what happened to you while you were gone? Getting all touchy-feely on us?" Jimmy asked, earning a scowl from Ben and Lorelei.

I put my cup down after a satisfying gulp of the hot liquid. I couldn't tell them that I was relieved to be alive—or at least upright—after my meeting with Vince. I couldn't tell them that I was saddened by the thought of my burgeoning whatever it was with Jack Schiller was now doomed thanks to Paulie.

Thanks to me, I corrected myself—the root of it all came back to me. Always came back to me.

And gambling.

What I did say, and I meant it, was, "I think the things that have happened lately can only make you stop and take stock of your life. Remind you what you're grateful for."

Ben and Saul nodded, never looking up from their cards. Jimmy snorted. Lorelei leaned over and squeezed my hand, then returned her gaze to her cards.

"Has there been any break in the case? No more... attempts...have been made on any of you, have they?"

I, of course, knew there hadn't been or Jack would have told me. But they didn't know I'd had my own personal police escort up until a couple of hours ago.

"No news from the police," Ben said. "And nothing strange has happened to any of us."

"And you're all being careful? Sticking close to each other?" I asked them all, but I looked at Jimmy, who only shrugged as Ben and Saul nodded.

"How's Gus?" I asked.

"Much better," Saul answered. "Much better. This morning when we went he had his barber in giving him a trim and a darling girl doing his nails."

"Sounds like Gus," I said with relief, and a little awe.

"He'll be able to leave tomorrow," Saul continued.

"He's not going back to his apartment is he?"

"I wanted to talk to you about that, dear," Ben said, placing his cards down on the table, earning a huff from Jimmy that the card game had come to a stop.

"Absolutely he can stay here. The other guest room is okay, isn't it Lorelei?"

When we bought the house, Lorelei insisted there'd be times when we'd want five bedrooms. Because of Ben, we'd only looked at ranch-style houses, and to have all we—we as in Lorelei—wanted, it had to be a sprawling house, and it was. U-shaped, with the main living areas, one guest room and the office in the base and each extension containing two bedrooms.

In normal circumstances, Lorelei and Ben shared one wing, so that Lorelei could hear Ben in the night while I was out. I had the other wing with the empty guestroom, which I assumed held either Saul, or was soon to house Gus.

Other than helping Ben at times in his bedroom, and looking for Lorelei in hers, I don't think I've stepped foot in the guest rooms since the last time my parents had come for a visit.

"The guest room is fine, all set," Lorelei said to nobody's surprise. "Although we wouldn't have room for both Gus and all his clothes." We all chuckled, thinking of Gus having to wear comfy clothes like pajamas or sweats for a while instead of his dapper suits. "We'll put Gus in the one in the main part of the house so that people are around him more."

I nodded, then looked at Jimmy. "The offer still stands, you know. There's plenty of room." I could easily bunk with Lorelei or take a couch or the fold-out in the office, I'd certainly crashed there many times after a long night and not even making it to the back and my room.

Jimmy just raised a brow at me. I was surrounded by men who had perfected that look of derision. Though I didn't really expect to see Jack again—not in anything other than an official capacity anyway.

"We gonna play cards, or what?" Jimmy said in answer to my offer.

"Shuffle up and deal," I motioned to them, and got up to refill my plate.

Lorelei had pushed the framed photos that usually took center-stage of the sideboard to the back to make room for the food and coffee. One in particular held my gaze. Ben, Saul and Rachael, Saul's deceased wife. I'd seen the picture hundreds of times as I'd walked by, but I looked at it this time—really looked at it.

It was taken in the late sixties, in black and white. The three of them stood together, arm in arm, Rachael in the middle. Behind them was the door to Ben's office at the casino he'd worked at.

Saul and Ben both had crew-cuts, though they'd been out of their army stint during WWII for years by then. They wore identical white (or at least light-colored in the black and white photo) short-sleeve work shirts and black, plain ties.

Rachael, her dark hair in a Jackie Kennedy knock-off do, wore a sleeveless shift with a crazy print that made me glad I couldn't see what was bound to be bright colors.

She was a beautiful woman. She'd followed Saul out to Vegas from New York after the boys got back from the war. I'd seen her picture tons of times, and yet today there was something about her that made me look closer.

Something somehow familiar, but I couldn't place it.

I took the picture and my full plate back to the table and sat down. I put the picture down flat on the table and looked at it while I ate.

"What's up?" Jimmy said, nodding toward the picture between hands while he shuffled the cards. Ben and Saul turned their heads, taking in my studying of the picture of the three close friends in happier times.

"Nothing. I just…" I didn't know what it was that captured my attention. "Saul? Rachael was from New York, right? Like you and Ben? She didn't have any family around here?" I was thinking about how familiar her face seemed to me, but Saul took my introduction of the subject of his dead wife as a means to reminisce. Which I knew I'd infinitely enjoy, as I always did when the boys let the memories flow.

"Yes," he said, in a small voice and I felt a twinge of guilt about bringing up something that still seemed so painful to him even decades later. "We fell in love in high school, but she wouldn't come out here when Ben and I did. We stayed in touch though. Even then I knew she was the one for me, that there'd never be any other woman.

"So, I waited. I waited for three years, and then the war broke out and Ben and I went. I wrote her a letter every week while I was overseas. She wrote back, but never told me how she felt. But…I knew…I knew," he tapped his head, as if Rachael's love was at the tip of his head.

"When we got back, we came through New York and the first place I went—even before seeing my own mother—was to see Rachael."

I leaned forward, this was one story I'd never heard. Saul always seemed too pained to talk about Rachael. Maybe Danny's death and Gus' shooting had made him take stock, too.

I noticed Ben's hands had gone still, his cards leaning forward—which Jimmy took advantage of and snuck a peek. Ben's face seemed to fall right before my eyes. Of course Rachael had been one of his best friends. From what I'd heard, the three of them had been inseparable.

"That night she agreed to be my wife. I was the proudest

man in all of Brooklyn, isn't that right, Ben," Saul said and looked at his best friend.

Ben's eyes grew misty, he nodded. "That's right, Saul," he said quietly.

Saul pointed to the picture my hands still traced. "Remember the day that was taken, Ben?"

Ben looked at the picture, his face pained. "Yes, Saul, I remember."

"Rachael had gone back to New York for several months. Her mother was dying and she went to look after her and then help her father adjust after the funeral. That was my Rachael, always thinking of others."

Ben nodded again still looking at the three of them, frozen in time.

"She got back the night before. And that very next morning we went to see Ben at the casino. She wanted us to all be together again. The three of us."

Saul placed his cards down on the table. Jimmy gave up all hope of the game ever resuming and threw his cards into the middle of the table.

"To have my Rachael back. To be the three of us again. It was a good day." His voice was nearly a whisper at the end. He pushed back his chair, making a shrill sound that ran a chill down my spine. "If you'll excuse me, I think I'll call it a night."

"It's still early," Jimmy pleaded, wanting the car game to continue.

"I'm sorry, Saul. I didn't mean to bring up painful memories."

"Ah, no, Hannah darling. Talking about Rachael just makes my heart *plotz*, that's all. I'll be good as new in the morning," he said. He walked past me, patted my cheek, squeezed Ben's shoulder as he walked by him and left the room.

"You sure know how to kill a card game," Jimmy said with an accusing glance my way.

"And I was actually winning," Lorelei said, though no accusation was in her voice.

"Sorry," I said.

Ben patted my hand. "There are more important things than card games."

Jimmy raised a brow at me and I couldn't help but smile.

Ben sighed. "Well, to *most* of us there are more important things than a card game."

Jimmy said his goodbyes soon after and Lorelei cleared the sideboard with my help and then shooed me out of the kitchen when I tried to help with cleanup.

"Go back and talk to Ben," she said. "He seemed so sad when Saul was talking about the old days."

I brought Ben a refill of coffee and sat in the chair next to him. The picture of him, Saul and Rachael was right in front of him, he'd obviously moved it while I was helping Lorelei.

"You never know how it will turn out, do you Hannah, dear?" he asked quietly.

"No, Ben, you don't," I said thinking of the three people in the picture. If I had my dates correct, Rachael would be dead a few years after that picture was taken.

"Danny had a good marriage to a woman he loved. Saul found the love of his life at sixteen but lost her early. Jimmy married a woman who could never love him for what he was and they were miserable. Gus…ah Gus…he had a love of his life every three or four years."

A small smile crossed my face. "And you, Ben? Did you ever find love?"

He'd never talked about a woman in those terms before. I'd met some "lady friends" of his past since I'd known Ben, but not one seemed like it was ever anything more than…well, what Jeffrey and I had, I supposed.

He patted my hand, left his warm, wrinkled one on top of mine. "I did. I did. But I was young and I was a fool."

I turned my hand palm up, clasped his in mine. "We're all fools about love when we're young, Ben."

"I thought there was plenty of time. I thought…" his voice croaked, he cleared his throat. "I always thought there'd be more. That we'd be together eventually. That we'd have children. Lots of them."

His hand trembled in mine as he continued, "That I'd be surrounded in my old age by family that loved me and wanted to take care of me."

I leaned over, putting my arm around his bony shoulders, kissing his wrinkled face. "You are, Ben, you are."

Ben let me help him to his room where he decided Saul had the right idea about using sleep to chase away the demons. I only wished I could hit the hay early too, but I had to come up with a game for Vince.

After seeing Ben to his room, I went back to the main house intending to head to the office and start doing some research for JoJo's next crusade when the doorbell rang. Jimmy had just left. Ben, Saul and Lorelei were in their rooms.

Strangers at the door had been very bad news of late.

As I opened the door to Jack Schiller and his dour cop face, my only thought was that the streak seemed to be continuing.

"Is something wrong?" I asked, stepping back for him to enter, but he stayed in the doorway.

"There's been no change in the case. Gus is still fine. We're tracking down information on the Pittsburgh guys."

I exhaled a huge sigh of relief, my body relaxing until Jack reached out and grasped my wrist.

"But yes. *Baby*," he said in a perfect imitation of Paulie calling me baby at the airport. "Something is definitely wrong."

Seventeen
❖❖

"YOU DON'T REALLY THINK THAT PAULIE AND I—" My voice cut off at Jack's incredulous expression.

"Please," he said with exasperation. He walked past me, still holding on to my wrist, checked out the living room, which was empty, and led me to the couch where we plunked down side by side. Only then did he let go of me. A part of me wished he hadn't let go. After this conversation I wasn't sure Jack would want to touch me ever again.

"Although I'm not sure what bothers me more, that you could be involved with that low-life romantically, or that you aren't —" I tried to set the record straight, but Jack held his hand up for me to stop and continued. "Which would mean you're involved with him for gambling reasons."

"It's what I do, Jack. You know I'm a professional gambler."

He waved that explanation away like it was an unwelcome house fly buzzing around our heads. "Bullshit. There's nothing professional about Paulie Gonads," he said, surprising me that he knew Paulie's nickname. Jack worked homicide in a huge city, so I'd assumed he wouldn't know a lowly loan shark enforcer. But Jack surprised me yet again.

I sat back on the couch, crossed my arms over my chest. Universal body language for back the hell off.

"Are you in deep?" he asked softly, reading my temperament.

"Nothing I can't handle," I said.

He looked at me for a long time. I met his gaze, held it, tried to convey sincerity while secretly praying I wasn't struck by lightning.

He shook his head. "If you had been in that dive motel room for one more minute—"

"You followed me?"

"You really think I was going to let you walk away with that scumbag and not make sure you were all right?"

Ben and Lorelei care about me. Deeply. My family back in Wisconsin love me. I know this. But I don't remember the last time somebody looked out for me that way. "Jack…I…" I had no idea what to say.

He leaned forward. "Johanna," he whispered as his mouth met mine. It had only been hours ago that we'd been together in Pittsburgh, but he kissed me like it'd been years.

Thoughts of Saul and Rachael meeting again after years and a war flew through my mind. And then to lose each other too soon. How fleeting it all can be.

I moaned and wrapped my arms around Jack, pulling him into me. He tasted of coffee and bourbon, a taste I figured I'd come to recognize if I was lucky enough to have him kissing me after tonight.

We sank back into the couch and I silently blessed Lorelei for her choice in soft, cushy, plush couches when I heard her clearing her throat from the doorway.

"I…I'm sorry…I thought I heard Detective Schiller's voice and I thought there might be some news." She was clearly embarrassed, but in true Lorelei fashion, she regrouped quickly.

"No news," Jack said, straightening up away from me. I still lay sprawled on the couch, too content to get up.

"Jo, I need to run out and get a few things," Lorelei said to me. I didn't know if she really did or if she was making a point of leaving because of Jack.

"Okay," I said, finally sitting back up. "I'm here for the duration, so take your time. You must need a break, Lor, you've been with the boys nonstop since Gus was shot."

She shrugged, like that was all part of the gig. And it was, but that was supposed to be *my* part of the gig. I told myself I went to Pittsburgh to get information, and that's probably what Lorelei—and maybe even Jimmy—believed. But I knew I'd have never left Ben's side if I weren't into Vince for money.

Lorelei grabbed her purse and keys from the foyer table and one of her many tablets of paper. "By the way, Ben couldn't sleep. I heard him rustling around in his room, so he might be on his way out here. Just in case you guys…" She made smooching sounds and then laughed her girlish giggle. "You'll have to tell me later how this…*case*…developed."

I tossed a pillow from the couch at her. "Thanks, Lor." She nodded, still giggling, and left. I turned back to Jack, ready to get a couple more kisses before Ben made his way out here. A make out session on the couch. Man, it must have been high school since I'd had one of those.

But Jack's cop face was back in place and he was reaching into his jacket pocket. He pulled out an envelope. One I recognized.

"Here's your money back," he said and tossed the envelope of cash Lorelei had left for me in my desk two days earlier.

"Same envelope," I said.

He just shrugged. "It was what that guy at Ralph's house gave it to me in."

"Mr. Lee," I said.

"Whatever. You started with twenty k, right?" I nodded. "That's in there. I took what I started out with out, there was a few hundred left. I'm going to donate it to Danny O'Hern's family."

The cash stared at me accusingly. "I can't take this. You won it. I can't stand that you did. But you won it."

"Yes you can. Pay Vince back and be done with it."

Oh. Jack thought I'd borrowed money from Vince to get into that game to help Ben. Why, that almost sounded... noble. My heart sank a little as I came to the realization that I wasn't going to set him straight. If he wanted to see me in such a favorable light, I'd damn well let him.

Twenty thousand wasn't going to get me out of my troubles with Vince...but it might pacify him long enough to work something else out.

JoJo enlisting a player to throw a game was a line I did not want to cross if I could help it. One of the two rules I lived by. Rules I clung to. A sense of morality I could wrap around myself when dealing with people like Vince.

"Besides," Jack said. "If you borrowed from Vince Santini to get in that game in Pittsburgh so that you could help with an investigation? Well, that's like the money the police department gave me to do the same thing."

That made me wonder. I guess I never thought about how Jack came up with the buy-in money for that game. I'm frequently around people who can easily come up with that kind of money for a poker game. "The Las Vegas police department gave you that kind of money? To play in a game you might lose?"

He shrugged. "Well not exactly. Not all of it."

"How much of it?"

"Plane fare and hotel."

"How'd you get the...you know what. Never mind. It's none of my business."

"My savings. And Botz's."

"What if you'd lost?"

"I'm a better cop than I am a poker player. I knew I'd find a way to get some names to check out before I lost too much of it. Then I'd bow out. Turns out I didn't lose after all."

I tried to raise one brow at his jab, but he just laughed at my attempt.

I wanted to take the money and run out the door, straight to see Vince, but instead I gave one last half-hearted attempt to be the person Jack saw somewhere in me. "Really. Jack, I can't. You won this. Totally up and up."

He sighed heavily. "I'm a cop. I was on duty playing in an illegal card game. There's no way I can keep that money."

Well…when he put it that way, it was really my civic duty. I took the envelope.

Another thought went through my suspicious mind. "You didn't just give that back to me because we slept together did you?"

He snorted. "Johanna. It was good. Damn good. But you aren't worth twenty thousand."

"Or…because you want to sleep with me again?"

He put his finger on my horseshoe pendant. My pulse picked up and I swear he felt it, because a smug smile crept up his face. "I don't need a show of goodwill to get you back in bed."

"Oh, no?" I said with challenge in my voice even though he was dead right.

"No," he whispered, then leaned in to kiss me. Just as he was grazing my lips a dinging went off. "What was that?"

"Ben's sliding glass door. I put a little bell on it so I could hear when Ben went outside. I have this irrational fear of him tripping his walker and falling into the pool and not being able to get his footing. So Lorelei installed it. Crazy I know, but –"

"So, he's going outside?"

"Yes."

He was already off the couch and headed out the door of the living room. "I thought I was clear about going outside."

"I thought—we thought—you meant, like going out."

He shot a look over his shoulder at me.

I rose and followed Jack out of the living room. "Down the hall and out the back," I said to Jack's back as he followed my instructions.

I started after him, but froze in my tracks as I heard a gunshot.

Eighteen
❖

JACK WAS KNEELING OVER BEN who lay sprawled on the patio stones.

A low groan escaped my lips. "Ben," I shouted and started forward but Jack's outstretched arm stopped me.

"He's fine. He just fell. The bullet didn't hit him. Stay in the house. Get away from the windows!"

"Like hell," I said and ran out the sliding glass door to Ben, keeping my head low like they do in the movies. Holy shit, had it come to this? Dodging bullets?

But there were no more shots.

"Jesus, what are you doing?" Jack said to me, moving his body as I knelt over Ben so he shielded not only Ben but me too. He reached into his jacket and pulled out a gun. Not that a gunshot and Ben laying on the ground wasn't enough to make this all too real to me, but Jack holding a gun and looking around the back of the yard sure did.

"Ben? Are you okay?" I asked.

He looked at me, fear in his brown eyes. "I'm fine, Hannah, go back inside."

"Not without you," I said which prompted a sound of disgust from Jack.

"Ben, are you hurt?" Jack asked while still scanning the landscape beyond our pool area.

The U shape of the house surrounded our patio and pool area which had a low fence along the back end. Beyond that was maybe twenty yards of lawn before the tree line that separated our subdivision from an elementary school playground.

It was late on Sunday night so—thankfully—no kids would have been on the playground. The tree line that ran along the back of our property was dark and still, but Jack's eyes continued to scan over it, looking for movement.

"I'm fine," Ben said weakly. "Just shaken from falling. Help me up, Hannah."

Jack looked at Ben hard, assessing what he'd said. He nodded his head, as if assuring himself that Ben was indeed okay. He looked at me. "Help him inside. Call 911, tell them officer needs assistance." Then he turned and ran to the back of the pool area, vaulted over the fence in one swift movement, and ran into the tree area.

My breath caught as I watched him run into the area where the shot had surely come from. Ben started to move and I quickly focused my attention onto getting him into the house and calling for backup for Jack.

It was slow going. Ben was sore and we were trying to stay as low as possible although I had to believe that whoever was out there had started running the minute Jack came out onto the patio.

Finally we got back into Ben's room—the closest room that had access to the house—and I eased him into a chair and then hurried to the phone. I made the call—and suggested they contact Detective Frank Botz as well.

I went back to the sliding doors. And peered out into the darkness.

"Hannah, darling, come away from the window," Ben said, but I stayed where I could see.

A moment later an out of breath Saul came rushing into Ben's room from the hallway. "Was that gunshot? I was sleeping, and thought maybe I'd dreamed it. Then I heard commotion and came running." It would have been a jaunt for poor Saul, going around the whole house. It would have been shorter to cut through the patio area, but I'm glad he hadn't thought of that. One old man as target practice was enough.

Saul looked from me to Ben, looking so small in his chair, his hands shaking, his eyes wide with shock. Saul seemed startled to see his friend in such a state. It was startling to me as well. "Ben? You're…you're…you're all right?" he finally got out, crossing the room to his best friend.

Ben nodded slowly. He took Saul's hand. I grabbed a blanket from the bed and wrapped it around his scrawny frame, which seemed even frailer than it had two days ago.

"Where's Jimmy?" Saul asked.

"He left," I said.

"And Lorelei?"

"She's out," I said.

Saul looked at me pointedly. "How long ago did Jimmy leave?"

I shrugged. "I don't know. Right after you went to your room, I guess."

"And Lorelei?"

"Not too long before…before somebody shot at Ben," I said quietly, not sure where Saul was going, if he was going anywhere.

"How long exactly?"

"I don't know. Not long. Only a couple of minutes."

Saul looked out the glass door of Ben's room, looking across the back yard to the tree line where Jack was emerging.

We all watched in silence as Jack made a sweep of the yard and then came in through the door, shutting it and closing the blinds.

"Did you find anything?" Saul asked before I could.

Jack shook his head. "It's too dark to see anything. And

whoever was there is long gone. We'll cordon the area off and search it tomorrow in the daylight. It doesn't look like rain, so nothing should disturb any signs our shooter left." He looked at me. "Did you call 911?"

I nodded. "They're on the way. I had them contact Botz too."

"Good. That's good," Jack said distractedly and I could tell he was already thinking about shell casings and trajectories and all that other stuff cops think about. "You okay, Ben?" he asked softly and then knelt in front of Ben, taking his shaking hand in his own steady one.

The compassionate sight warmed me and it must have been too much for Saul as well, because he reached for the other side chair in the room and lowered himself heavily into it. He couldn't take his eyes off of Jack and Ben. I walked over to him and placed a hand on his shoulder. He shook his head and lowered it to his hands, resting his elbows on his knees, covering his face. "Too close," he whispered. "Too close."

"I'm fine," Ben said after Jack asked him again. "I just turned too quickly. My walker leg got caught on one of the chairs and I slipped. If I hadn't fallen…" He didn't finish the thought no one wanted to finish.

I squeezed Saul's shoulder once more then crossed to Ben. I knelt next to Jack and placed my hand on both of theirs. "It's okay, Ben. You're okay."

He only nodded, still in some form of shock I suppose.

"Maybe we should take him to the hospital and have him looked over," I said quietly to Jack.

"No," Ben said with more force than I thought his stunned body had in it. "No more hospitals. Gus leaves tomorrow. And that will be all of hospitals for us. Right, Saul?"

Saul got out of his chair, came across the room, sat on the bed next to our little group. "Right, Ben, no more hospitals."

I heard the sirens coming down the street.

Four hours later I sat with Jack and Frank Botz at the dining room table. Saul and Ben had finally gone to bed. Lorelei, after initially freaking out when she'd gotten home, had calmed herself with true Lorelei behavior—putting together an impromptu buffet for the police officers. The patrolmen had appreciated it, too, after taping off the area and doing as much work as they could do in the dark with portable lights.

A Terrible Towel with a Pittsburgh Steelers logo was found in the woods and was taken away as evidence. I wasn't sure if you could get fingerprints or DNA or anything like that from a towel. Fibers of some kind, I guessed.

But it confirmed to Jack and Frank that the attempts on Ben's and Gus' lives and Danny's death were all connected.

Not that any of us had any thought that somebody else was just randomly shooting at Ben outside his own home. But still, it seemed to give the detectives a small pleasure that the shooter had left his calling card.

Jimmy had been notified, but had been told to stay put. A patrol car was going to stay outside of his home for the rest of the night. I didn't think Jimmy would stay there unless he'd talked to Ben, so I'd brought the phone to Ben who reassured Jimmy that he was okay.

I refilled Jack and Frank's coffee cups while they both talked to various people on their phones. It was a way of being able to hear them, although after Pittsburgh, I assumed that Jack would keep me in the loop—as much as he was able to—about the case.

And not because we'd slept together. Because I put it together the same way he had and showed up at the same game he did. I think my investigative skills stock soared with him for that one.

They both got off their phones at the same time, and

continued writing notes in the their notebooks. After a few moments, they both looked up at each other, then Jack turned to me.

"First off, you need to tell me if any of this can in any way have a connection to you and Paulie Gonads."

I shook my head. "No. Not possible."

"You're sure? I'm only trying to help. This is your business, but if it's…"

"It's not," I said. "If this was about me, they'd come after me."

That seemed to jive with what Jack must have already thought, because after looking at me closely for longer than felt comfortable, he nodded and turned to Botz. "What do you have?"

Botz cast a glance in my direction. Jack looked at me but didn't say anything. He had to know I'd put up a holy stink about being kept in the dark, and he looked pretty tired. Not up to a holy stink tonight. He looked back at Botz, raised a brow.

Botz shrugged. "Uniforms stopped by the homes of Ralph Stankowski, Leonard Martin and Charles Godwin. They were all there, all were woken up by the officers."

It was late here, it would be even later in Pittsburgh.

Jack nodded. "It would have been cutting it pretty close for them to get out here, and set up so quickly when I just saw them last night."

"We made it back," I said, and then regretted it. Jack might not have told Frank about me being in Pittsburgh.

"True," Jack said. "By the way, I told Frank about you being at the game."

I looked at Frank. "Good piece of detective work, there, Anna," he said. I noticed he'd dropped the Ms. Dawson and I wondered if Jack had told him about the entire trip.

"I also told him about…well…that we're together," Jack confirmed. This time I couldn't look at Frank, only nodded in his general direction.

"Good piece of—"

"All right. All right," Jack said, cutting Frank off which only gained him a chuckle from his partner. "What else did you find out?" Jack asked. He looked at me and shrugged, his silent apology for his partner, I guessed.

Frank looked back at his notes, I looked at Frank's Fred Flintstone tie.

"Not much else. The three names you came back from Pittsburgh with all check out for tonight at least. Locals there are going to question them about the O'Hern and Morgan shooting dates tomorrow." He looked at his notes again. "We're checking on Terrible Towels and where they can be purchased here in Vegas, but with online shopping…who knows," he said with a shrug. "If that doesn't lead anywhere, then we'll have the Pittsburgh PD start with the Towels…but that's going to be pretty common in that town."

It made me wonder if the internet and internet shopping had put a severe disadvantage on good old fashioned detective work. In some ways, it probably helped. Like if you had a suspect, and then got their home computer and the site for Steelers memorabilia was bookmarked—that would certainly be incriminating. But, probably gone were the days when detectives would count on a clerk at a—in this case—a sports memorabilia place be able to help detectives with a description.

It was mid-February, well past football season. The purchase of several—or at least five—Terrible Towels in Las Vegas would probably be something a clerk would remember. But not if they were bought online.

Or if they were bought in Pittsburgh and brought here.

"Jimmy says he was at home and Lorelei was running errands at the time of the shooting, neither of which are confirmed," Jack read from his notes, not willing to meet my eye. Smart man.

Still, thinking my friends could somehow be involved in this didn't sit well with me and I tried to make the Pittsburgh slant more feasible.

"I'm not surprised all of those guys in Pittsburgh were home. Those bigwigs aren't going to do their own dirty work," I said. Although, I could kind of see Ralph Stankowski taking the responsibility on himself. He seemed like a "out of the way, I'll do it myself" kind of guy.

But not a murderer kind of guy, if I had to guess.

"But that's the fun of the revenge motive," Frank said. "Doing it yourself. Seeing the one who caused you pain getting his."

I waved that away. "So how are all the hit men in the world making livings? Some of those have to be revenge crimes."

"We're not thinking these jobs were professionally done," Jack said and Frank nodded his agreement. "With the possible exception of Danny."

"Right. But even that isn't consistent with the other two shootings. That was close range, back of the head, assassination-style."

"Exactly," Jack said. "Gus and Ben were not shot by a professional."

"How can you be so sure?" I asked.

"Because they'd be dead."

Jack crawled into my bed at six a.m. "Should you be in here?" I asked, though I was happy to curl my body around his big, warm, male one.

He'd decided to stay at the house over night. I don't know if it was to make me feel better, or for his sense of duty, but I was glad to have him in the house. I'd offered to share my bed, he opted for the couch.

"The patrol car's outside," he said as he started divesting me of my sleepwear. "I'm officially off duty until—well, until we're finished."

I chuckled. "I love the way you keep hours."

"Me too."

"And I'm more attractive to you than a bourbon? For the few minutes you're off duty?" I asked, hoping he heard the tease in my voice. No way was I going to get on his case about his drinking when I knew I had a visit with Vince ahead of me today.

"This time," he said, and rolled me over.

"What's on your schedule today?" he asked later as he dressed.

I didn't think there'd ever come a day when I'd tire of looking at a naked Jack Schiller. I might get sick of that damned raised brow, but not the whole, gloriously naked package.

I pointed to the envelope with the twenty thousand dollars in it that sat on my bedside table. "I need to take care of that today."

He slipped his pants on. "Good."

"And whenever Gus is ready to be discharged I'll take the boys to get him."

"No."

"No?"

"The boys aren't going anywhere. I'll get Gus and bring him here."

"That might freak him out, not to have us there. Just a cop coming to get him, not even taking him home."

He sighed, scrubbed his face with his hands. "Okay. Call me when you know what time that is. I'll meet you, and only you, at the hospital and escort you both back here. How's that?"

"He's going to want to stop at his apartment and gather up some clothes."

"Can't he wear something of Ben's? Or we'll just pick him

up some sweats or something."

"Oh, Jack," I said like I was talking to a three year old. "You haven't really met Gus, have you?"

He sighed again, started buttoning his shirt. "I didn't know you'd be such a package deal."

"Yes you did," I said. The man was a detective for Pete's sake. "Besides," I added, slipping from the sheets, kneeling on the bed and pulling him toward me by his belt loop. "I'm worth it."

He raised a brow at me as he came even closer, but his actions said he agreed.

"What am I supposed to do with this?" Vince asked, tossing the envelope of money into my lap.

"Put it toward my tab," I said, but it sounded more like a question, because of course, Vince was calling the shots.

"I thought your tab was going to be paid with other arrangements." Not even a hint of question on his end.

"That was before I had this money."

"What if I've been making plans based on our previous agreement? It's not really fair to change your payment plan now."

Payment plan. Like he held my mortgage or something.

Vince had probably started shifting funds around—sending Paulie to collect from some poor souls—so that he had a huge chunk to plunk down on the game JoJo would be working.

The long shot underdog that *had* to have an upset.

The extra pressure at the thought of Vince putting so much money on one game made my stomach churn.

"I'm sorry if that's the case," I said. I took it from my lap and pushed the envelope toward him across the little wrought-iron table at the gelato stand in the Bellagio.

He ignored it. "There's not a hundred k in there. I'd say twenty."

"My debt is for thirty. This is a start."

"The choice was thirty and a…physical penalty. Or one hundred."

"I know, Vince," I said, disgusted with myself at the pleading in my voice. "But this is what I have. I can't leave Ben right now to fix a game."

My level of desperation was so high I actually uttered the words that I never had before…fix a game.

"You're not going to do Ben any good sitting in a hospital," Vince said pointedly.

"So, those are my choices?"

He shrugged, took a bite of his ice. "Those were your choices yesterday. You were thanking me then."

"That was before Ben was shot at," I said. Vince didn't seem surprised.

"Yeah, I heard. That's too bad," he said. I didn't ask how he'd heard so soon. I didn't really want to know how far-reaching Vince's network was. "But the offer stands. And it's a damn generous one at that, Anna."

"I know," I said quietly, trying to desperately think of a way out.

"I want an answer now, and I'm holding you to that. I don't want you taking a few days and trying to play that twenty k into a hundred."

He'd just read my mind. "Why not? You'd get your money."

He took another bite of his ice, wiped his mouth with a napkin. "Yes. But I could make a killing with this game."

My mind whirled, but I came up with nothing that would pay back Vince, keep me in town for the duration, and keep me out of the hospital. Even if I could bear the shame—and I wasn't sure I could—of asking Ben or Lorelei for it, and the slush fund was healthy, it probably wasn't a hundred thousand healthy after the Lexus and the twenty thousand that now sat staring at me.

"This is business, Anna," he said.

I nodded. "I know, Vince." I sighed, cornered. "I'll have the game to you in a couple of days," I said and started to leave, taking the envelope from the table. It would have to be my seed money to make JoJo's plans grow.

"Tomorrow. By five," he said, and I knew better than to argue.

"Tomorrow," I agreed.

"And the game is played by Sunday."

"By Sunday," I said, wondering how the hell I was going to leave the boys in the next few days to take care of this.

And what Jack would say about me suddenly going out of town?

Nineteen
◆◆

"SO, JACK, HOW IS IT THAT YOU ENDED UP IN LAS VEGAS?" Ben asked that night as we sat around the dining room table playing cards. Jimmy and I'd suggested poker—for cash of course—but Lorelei had insisted on gin rummy so that she could play too.

She'd lived with me for years and yet she still didn't know if a straight or flush was the higher hand.

"How do you know I'm not from Vegas originally?" Jack asked Ben as he discarded a three of clubs.

"Nobody's from Vegas originally," Jimmy said. I looked around the table. It was true of all of us. But gambling—and dancing in Lor's case—had brought all of us here. I didn't see police work as something that would necessarily drive someone to Vegas.

Of course, there'd be no shortage of cases.

"I've been on the force here for just about a year. I was in the Portland area for fifteen years. But I was raised in the Bay area."

Huh. So he had stuck to the truth in his cover in Pittsburgh. Except for his name.

He leaned over to me, touching my shoulder with his. "Always stick as close to the truth as possible," he whispered. "That way you have less rope to tangle in."

"I'll remember that, Danny Lowenstein," I said. He chuckled, and leant into me, bumping shoulders. I held my hand of cards closer to my chest like he was going to sneak a peek, which only made him chuckle louder.

Ben and Saul looked at us and gave each other knowing smiles which made me blush. As much as I can blush at a card table.

"Were you on the police force in Portland, too?" Ben asked, studying his cards.

"Yes, sir. First vice then homicide."

At the mention of vice, Jimmy gave me an amused look. "Bet you dealt with a lot of degenerate gamblers in vice," Jimmy said. I scowled back at him.

"Not as many as I've dealt with here," Jack answered.

"Here, Vegas? Or here, at this table?" Ben said earning laughter from everyone. Except Jimmy and I.

"Both," Jack answered to more laughter.

"Gus, how are you feeling? Can I get you anything?" I asked.

Gus had come home with Jack and me unwillingly at first, but more easily once we'd swung by his apartment and picked up some of his things. When we got here, Jack not only pulled Gus' things out of his car trunk, but a duffel bag of his own.

I hadn't said a word, but gave Jack's arm a squeeze, letting him know he was welcome—whether he was on duty or not.

After Gus had rested for a while, he insisted on playing cards with us, so we had his leg propped up on another chair. He wore silk pajamas and a robe. Very Hugh Hefner.

"I'm fine, Anna. All I need is better cards. Can you do something about that?"

"If I could, we'd all be wearing diamonds," I said.

"We do just fine," Ben said sternly to me. "Nobody here needs diamonds."

I looked at him. I knew he was scared, and freaked out,

and probably sore as hell from falling yesterday. But this was the first time that anything even close to censure about my gambling came out of him.

"I know, Ben," I said softly.

He looked around the table, saw the game had pretty much come to a stop and everyone was looking at him. His brown eyes grew soft. "Hannah, I…"

"Well, nobody *needs* diamonds," Lorelei jumped in, saving the day. "But I sure wouldn't turn 'em down."

"Next big win, get yourself some, Lor," I said.

"I'm going to hold you to that," she said.

"Good. You deserve them."

"Every pretty girl deserves to wear diamonds," Gus said, winking at Lorelei.

She gave him a girlish giggle that earned a groan from Jimmy "Guess that bullet didn't do too much damage," he said, as the hand came to an end. He headed to the sideboard that Lorelei had once again prepared with a great spread.

A ding went off and I saw Jack start to rise. I put a hand on his arm. "Oven," I said, knowing he thought it was Ben's door being opened. A door that with all the others—and windows—had been locked up tight. And then double-checked by Jack.

He sat back down, semi-embarrassed. "They sound a lot a like," I said.

Lorelei started to rise but I motioned for her to sit. "I got it, Lor," I said.

"Really?" she said with disbelief.

Now I was semi-embarrassed in front of Jack. "Just take whatever's in the oven out and turn it off, right? How hard can that be?"

She opened her mouth, no doubt to give me oodles of directions, but saw me glance to the back of Jack's head, and just said, "Thanks, Jo," and returned to her cards.

I headed to the kitchen wondering why I cared that Jack

not think I was an idiot in the kitchen.

Okay, I'll admit it. It took me some time to find where Lorelei kept the oven mitts. When I had the incredible smelling dish that Lorelei had prepared out, I tried to figure out how to turn the oven off. In my defense, it's state-of-the-art and completely digital.

Finally managing it, I was just about to head back to the dining room and turn it all back over to Lorelei when Jimmy came with a plate in his hand and said, "Lorelei said the ziti was done."

I looked back in the baking dish. Baked ziti. "Looks done to me," I said as Jimmy leaned over my shoulder and took a peek.

"Nah, the cheese on top needs to be browned a little. Put it back in and turn it to broil for a couple of minutes."

When he saw my look of helplessness, he sighed and pushed me out of the way, handing me his empty plate to hold while he took the mitts and the pan and placed it back in the oven. To my delight, he took a couple of minutes to figure out the settings on the stove himself, but eventually it clicked on and he stepped back and leaned against the counter facing me.

I placed his plate on the counter behind me.

"What's on your mind?" he asked.

He was prickly as all get out, but Jimmy Mancino was one shrewd Italian.

"The guy you used for Big Ten information when you were making odds?"

"Yeah?"

"He still living?"

"Yeah."

"How about the guy from the Big East?"

"Nope, he's been dead ten years now."

I nodded, JoJo's decision made. "You still in touch with the Big Ten guy?"

He shrugged. "Enough."

"Enough to give me his number? And he wouldn't hang up on me if I used your name?"

"He wouldn't tell you nothing. Even if you used my name."

I let out a sigh of defeat.

"What do you need to know? I'll call him," Jimmy said.

I almost hugged him, but I knew that might kill the deal. "This is just between us, right?"

"Please," he said, like he was offended I'd ask.

"Thanks, Jimmy, I owe you one," I said.

"Have Lorelei make me a pan of this ziti once and a while and we're even," he said as he pulled the pan from the oven and I started to tell him the information I'd need from his "guy".

"What do you feel when you place a bet?" Jack asked as he ran a finger down my naked spine, inching the sheet down with him.

I turned my head to the side, to see him.

He was studying my back, but when I turned to him, his gaze came to my face. He tapped his finger at the base of my spine. "Really. I want to know."

I looked forward, to the headboard, rested my hands on my chin. "When you place a bet, you know you're going to win—that's why you do it. And yet…"

He tapped a finger again, higher up, near my shoulder blades this time. His touch had been so light I hadn't realized it had moved. "And yet?" he prompted.

"And yet, a part of you knows there's no sure thing. You've lost enough to know that. So there's these two parts waging war inside of you. It's such an odd feeling.

"When I place a bet, at that moment of jump-ball, or face-off, or kick-off, I feel this tremendous rush." I turned my head to him once more and realized he'd been watching my face, not my body. "It's the most alive I've ever felt." He nodded, seeming to get it. "That's why I do it."

He looked beyond me, toward the wall, but I suspected to some place else altogether.

I knew we'd decided not to poke at each other's demons, but he'd started it, so I asked, "Why do you drink?"

He had to know it was coming; he was already nodding. He looked back at me, his brown eyes boring deep into mine. "When I drink, I feel nothing. Absolutely nothing." He rolled on to his back, folded his arms underneath his head, and stared at the ceiling. "That's why I do it."

"I need to go to the station for a few hours," Jack said around nine two nights later. He stood in the entranceway of the foyer to the living room, his jacket on, keys in hand. I was sitting on the couch in the living room reading the latest *Sports Illustrated*. It probably looked like a relaxing evening at home to him, but it was business to me. "You okay here alone?"

"Hardly alone," I pointed out. "But, yeah, I'm fine." He nodded, but seemed reluctant to leave. "Really, Jack. Go, do what you have to do. In fact, with that patrol car outside, don't even feel you have to come back. I'll make sure none of the boys go outside. They're about to pack it in anyways. Gus is already asleep."

Jack leaving for a while helped me out a lot. Having him not come back at all tonight—or perhaps for forty-eight hours—would put me totally in the clear with the plan I had in mind.

Just finding an hour yesterday to meet with Vince and tell him the game I'd picked (no way would he take information like that over the phone, even cell phones) had been a major juggling act. I'd also needed a favor from Paulie—or from someone Paulie knew of, and had managed to squeeze that in and get back with a few groceries that I let on took me much longer to get than it had.

Plus, Jack hadn't had a drink since Pittsburgh. At least not that I knew of, and he'd been here most of the time that he wasn't at the station working on the case. I'd offered him one several times while we'd been playing cards in the evenings, but apparently he still considered himself on duty even then. He had to be dying for one.

I knew I was dying to place a bet.

"You trying to get rid of me?" He said, raising a brow at me.

That's exactly what I was trying to do, but he didn't need to know that. I tried to raise a brow back of course failed and he chuckled at me. "Of course not. But I figured this all had to be a whole lot of togetherness for a guy who lives by himself. That you might need some alone time." A thought struck me. "You do live alone don't you?" I guess it was a little late to be asking if he was married or involved with anybody, but it hadn't occurred to me. I inherently knew Jack was the kind of person who wouldn't start something with me if he had any lines still dangling.

He snorted. "Fine time to be fishing for whether I'm attached or not."

"I was just thinking the same thing."

"Do you really think I'd be with you if I was with anyone else?"

"No," I said. "No, not for a minute would I think that. That's why it never occurred to me before this to ask."

He moved out of the entranceway, came and sat down on the couch beside me. He took the magazine out of my hand and tossed it on the table. "Okay. Here's the abridged version of Jack Schiller. Married wife number one when I was eighteen—"

I put my hand on his chest to stop him. "There's more than

one wife in this story?"

He sighed and nodded. "You want me to go on? Because it's not really stuff that affects you and me. It's all ancient history."

He wasn't just asking if I wanted him to go on. The unasked question here was where were we going? What were we going to be?

If this was all it was going to be—poker with the boys, sliding into each other's beds in the wee hours—there was really no need to bring our pasts into it. Our current issues—his drinking, my gambling, someone wanting to kill my best friends—were more than enough to deal with for something casual. If we brought our pasts into it, we were saying to each other that this was going to be something more.

I swallowed. There was a very good chance that in two days Jack would never want to see me again. But that would be his choice, not mine. "Go on," I whispered.

He bent his head and placed the softest kiss on my forehead. He leaned away from me. "So, wife number one."

It wasn't as bad as I thought. And really, was I anyone to throw stones about anybody's past? If I hadn't met Ben at that hospital, I have no doubt I'd either be turning tricks today to pay for my next bet. Or dead.

As it was, I wasn't exactly living my life by the letter of the law—both legally and ethically.

Jack's parents had had a nasty break up when he was seven. He didn't see his dad much and his mom seemed to emotionally check out. When he was sixteen he started dating someone with a big, loving family that took Jack under their wing. "I think I really just wanted to be a part of that family," he said. "Not necessarily a husband to Chas."

"Chas?"

"Chastity."

"You're kidding?"

He shrugged. "It was The Bay. They were left-over hippies."

"So what happened?"

He leaned back into the soft cushions of the couch. "Oh, nothing really. We grew up. We knew the mistake we'd made. I wanted to go to college, she wanted to have babies. It only lasted a couple of years. Thank God we didn't have any children."

"So, you don't have kids?" The thought of a little boy out there with Jack's—albeit rare—smile and that raised brow made me feel…I don't know how it made me feel. Jealous of that boy's mother, I guess.

"Well, that brings us to wife number two."

The pang that went through my heart surprised me. There was someone out there—maybe more than one someones—that had Jack's DNA.

He met Lisa—thank God the mother of his child (children?) had a normal name—his first month in Portland. It sounded like a normal relationship. Dated for a year. Married. Baby boy a couple of years after that.

"So?" I asked after his pause seemed to last too long. "Why are you here in Vegas and not in Portland with Lisa and your son?"

"The reasons I'm not with Lisa? The job. My drinking. Her cheating. Pick one and the others evolve from it. A classic chicken and the egg situation."

"And why aren't you in Portland?"

"Lisa married my partner about three weeks after our divorce was final. I…didn't handle it well. I had to get out of there. It took me a while to come to terms with it."

"And your son?"

His sigh was heavy, defeated. "Lisa's a good mother. I know that. And as much as I hate the fact that they're together, Brett—my ex-partner—is probably a better father than I could be to Casey. At least right now."

"But you're his father, Jack."

He scrubbed his hands across his face. He looked about

five years older than he had ten minutes ago. A look of complete despair crossed his face. "I know," he barely whispered. He cleared his throat and spoke again. "I finally—finally—had a family of my own. A whole, complete, family and totally fucked it up."

"There's still time to build a relationship with Casey. He's young, you're his dad. You can still make yourself a part of his life."

He nodded. "I know. We've started. I've gone to Portland once a month for the past four months. Lisa's open to me having him here for a week at Easter."

"That's good. That's a start."

He swallowed, his Adam's apple moving slowly down his strong neck.

"Families come in all packages. The idea you wanted when you were a little boy might not be what you get. But that doesn't mean you won't be a part of a family. Hell, look at how you just spent the evening. Playing cards with four octogenarians, a showgirl and a gambler. That's family, too, Jack."

He put his warm hand on my knee, I leaned over to him, wrapped my arms around his neck. "We can make it up as we go along," I said and he nodded agreement.

I prayed he'd still be in agreement two days from now.

Twenty

I MOVED QUICKLY. Minutes after Jack left I knocked on Ben's door. Saul was in with him and they were playing backgammon at the table in the sitting area of his spacious room.

"Oh good, you're both together."

"Do you need something, Hannah, darling?" Ben asked.

I pulled out a chair and joined them at the table. "Sort of." At the tone of my voice both Ben and Saul put down their dice holders and turned their attention to me. "I need to go away for a couple of days," I said. I tried to sound decided, forceful, but it came out dripping with the guilt that I felt.

"Now? You're leaving me now?" Ben said with disbelief which only shoved the knife in deeper.

"You know I wouldn't leave now if I absolutely didn't have to." There was pleading in my voice that I hoped Ben would hear, and understand.

But he didn't. I didn't blame him. He'd been shot at. His friend had been killed, another one wounded and it seemed to him like I was abandoning him in his time of need. He stared at me with hurt in his eyes that nearly killed me.

But it was either this hurt or him visiting me in the hospital. And then he'd be having to look after me.

"Ben, please…"

He turned away from me like a pouting child, his arms

across his chest and the cut sliced deeper.

Saul placed a hand on mine. "Go, Hannah. We know you wouldn't even think of leaving now if it wasn't absolutely necessary. You go take care of what you have to, dear."

"Ben…" But he still wouldn't look at me.

"It's okay, Hannah. We'll be fine, and Ben will realize what a putz he's being."

Ben huffed, but didn't look at me.

"I'll be back as soon as I can," I said and rose from the chair, deciding to leave Ben to Saul. Nobody handled Ben better than his oldest friend. I headed toward the door.

"Will that detective be here, or is he going with you," Ben said.

I turned around, but Ben wouldn't look at me. "Jack will be back in a couple of hours. His phone numbers are by the phone in the kitchen if you need him before that. Lorelei is here, too."

"Does he know you won't be here when he gets back?" Saul asked knowingly.

"No," I said.

"So, he might not stay then, like he has been?"

I thought about Jack. How furious and hurt he'd be when he'd learn that I'd left with no notice, no information on where I'd be. And then I thought about Jack the cop.

"He'll stay here as long as he's needed," I said and walked out the door, praying nothing would happen to my boys while I was gone.

I wouldn't be able to bear anything happening to them anytime, but the guilt of it happening while I was cleaning up a mess of my own making would put me over the edge.

"What am I supposed to tell Jack when he comes back?" Lorelei asked me in my bedroom as I packed a carry-on bag.

None of JoJo's usual clothes had to come this time, so I was able to pack in front of Lorelei after I'd dropped my bomb on her.

"Tell him you don't know where I went, but that I'll be back in a couple of days. It's the truth."

"How can he get in touch with you?"

I pulled my iphone out of my jacket pocket and placed it on my bedside table. "He can't."

"How can I get in touch with you…if something… happens."

I thought about it for a minute. It was a chance I'd have to take—telling Lorelei about my old phone. She needed to be able to get me if something happened to one of the boys.

"Do you still know the number to my old phone?"

She narrowed her green, cat-like eyes, but only nodded.

"Don't tell anyone else I still have that phone and only call it if there's an emergency."

She gulped. "Cripes, Jo, you're starting to scare me."

I was scared shitless myself, but I tried to brush off her concern. "It's fine, it's fine."

"It's not fine, or you wouldn't be leaving the boys right now."

"They're in good hands with you and Jack, and the police car outside. Anybody would think twice about trying anything."

"I don't know. Whoever this is seems pretty determined. Jack and Frank still have no leads?"

I shook my head. "They don't tell me a lot. But I think they're still checking into the Pittsburgh guys. Probably banking records, stuff like that, to see if any of them made big withdrawls recently." At Lorelei's puzzled look I added, "To pay for a hit man."

"Jesus," she said under her breath.

"I know, this is so crazy. To think someone could want revenge so deeply, for so long that they'd try to kill five old men…" I shook my head, unable to finish.

I went into my bathroom, grabbed some necessities, and threw them into my bag, and zipped it up.

"Jack's a detective, you know. Do you really think he's not going to look for you?"

"I thought of that," I said. My look cut off her follow-up questions. "I have to go."

"Jo…"

"Please, Lor, this is hard enough. I can't take a lecture right now."

She sighed, threw up her hands in defeat. "All right. Do what you have to. Come back as soon as you can. I'll look after the boys."

I hugged her quickly then stepped away, afraid that I'd never let go if she hugged back. "I know you will. I can't thank you enough for everything you do. You're a life saver."

"I'll be expecting diamonds your next win," she teased.

"You got it," I answered as I started to leave the room, hoping I'd have working opposable thumbs able to play cards with after this was all over.

"But Jo," she said, and I turned from the doorway to face her. "If nothing else makes you take a look at your life…leaving the people you love when they need you most…"

I nodded, totally agreeing with her, but not wanting to deal with it right now.

Hell, not wanting to deal with it. Period.

I called Jimmy on my way to his house. "You still up?"

"Yeah."

"Can I come over?"

"Where are you?"

"About a block away."

"There's a cop car out front. You need me to shake 'em and

meet you somewhere?"

I didn't even want to guess at what Jimmy thought I might be involved in, but I was touched at his willingness to forgo his own protection to help me out.

"I've been wanting to test the balls of those two young shits for a couple a days now," Jimmy added, wiping away his points.

"No. Not necessary. They can know I was there." I didn't want Jimmy leaving the house if it wasn't necessary. I knew he might have to leave for me in the next day and that was enough.

"They'll probably call Jack," he said, but I'd already thought of that.

"I won't be there long enough for it to matter," I said and hung up.

I parked in Jimmy's driveway. I crossed to the patrol car and they rolled down their windows. "Hey, guys," I said. They were two that had rotated with the ones in front of our house, so they knew me. I knew them, too, but couldn't remember their names.

"I'm just bringing Jimmy some of Lorelei's dinner tonight." They nodded. I handed them one of my two grocery bags. "She made a lot. Here you go." There were two containers, plastic utensils, napkins and a couple of Cokes. Lorelei had fixed it for me, so I knew she'd have thought of everything.

"Wow, thanks, Ms. Dawson," the blond one said and the other one nodded.

"No problem, I'm just the delivery person. Lorelei did all the work."

"We'll thank her next time we're at your place," the dark-haired one said and they both got a glassy look in their eyes, thinking of Lorelei and her spectacular dancer's body and flowing red hair.

I made my way to Jimmy's front door hoping the food - and thoughts of Lorelei—might delay them in wondering if they should call someone and let them know I was at Jimmy's house.

I only needed ten minutes.

Jimmy let me in, took the grocery bag out of my hand and led me to his kitchen. Jimmy still lived in Henderson in the cute little bungalow-style house that Ben said Jimmy had shared with his wife forty years ago.

He'd taken care of it. It still had all the original wood and fixtures. He could probably get twenty times what he'd paid for it now, but Jimmy seemed content to stay where he was—in his comfort zone.

Who could blame him?

"What do you need?" Jimmy asked as he put the bag in his refrigerator.

I pulled the envelope of money out of my jacket pocket. I had taken an empty envelope from my desk. I took two thousand out and put it in the empty envelope. I put that one back in my jacket. I put the other envelope on the table. "I might call you tomorrow and ask you to place a bet for me."

"Might?"

"Might."

"What will determine if you make that call?"

"There's two things, neither of which might happen. So, it might not happen at all. But I need to know you can get to a casino, make the bet and still keep yourself safe."

He snorted. "That's not a problem."

"You don't have to elude the cops, Jimmy. Take them with you. You're just placing a bet, perfectly legal."

"Do you really want them to know what game I'm betting on? Or to see how much I'm betting?" He nodded at the envelope of money on the table.

"If you can place the bet without that information getting out, that would be better…but…it's not as important as you not being in danger."

He shrugged. "If you and I are the only ones that know about it, there's no way that this fucker that's shooting at us would be aware of it ahead of time, be able to plan for it."

"Right. That's what I was thinking. You just let the cops know you need to run an errand and that they should come along—better yet, ask them to drive you."

I could see he didn't like that—he really wanted to show he could best the young cops and lose his tail. But Jimmy wasn't stupid. "Yeah. Yeah, that's what I'll do."

"And Jimmy, if things don't feel right, or if anything else happens in the meantime, don't do it. Don't leave the house to make the bet."

He thought for a moment before speaking. "If it comes to that, I can have somebody stop by, get the money and make the bet for me."

"You have somebody you trust enough to hand thousands over to and hope he makes your bet?" I said, having just done exactly that. But that was the point…I trusted Jimmy to do this for me.

He shrugged. "I know a guy."

My last stop before the airport was to meet Paulie in the Bellagio parking deck. He handed me an envelope. I looked inside. A license with the name Marie VanSipe on it and the picture Paulie had taken of me yesterday when I'd come to him with my request—and my money.

There were two credit cards also in the envelope both in Marie's name. Stolen account numbers no doubt, but I'd only use them for extra identification and at the hotel when I registered. I'd pay for everything with cash.

I was about to break a whole bunch of laws, but I wasn't a thief.

Twenty-One
❖

I SAT IN THE PARKING LOT *at the apartment complex in Dubuque, waiting for Raymond Joseph's roommate to leave for class.*

I looked at my notes, sitting next to me on the passenger seat of the rental car. The roommate had a ten-fifteen on the other side of campus, so he'd have to get going pretty soon.

I thought of my own attendance at Friday morning classes years ago and hoped this kid was a little bit better student.

I grabbed the other sheets of paper from the passenger seat. Stats. Names of people and places in Chicago. All things I might need and should be able to rattle off like I knew what I was doing.

When I placed them back on the seat I noticed that my hand was shaking.

Five minutes later the roommate emerged and headed to the parking lot. I waited until he got in his car and drove out of the complex lot before looking around to make sure the lot was deserted, which it was.

I got out of the car and quickly walked to the apartment door. I knocked loudly enough to be heard by the boy inside, but not so loud that others in the building would hear and perhaps look out their peepholes at me.

I heard the shuffling of feet coming to the door, then the door was swung wide and a half-dressed Raymond Joseph stood in front of me. He had sweats on but his ebony chest was bare. I had either interrupted his getting dressed or this is what he slept in. It didn't matter.

I pushed past him and into the apartment just like I had at the motel in Minnesota only a few weeks earlier.

"We need to talk, Raymond," I said. I then put on the JoJo twang and added, "Or should I say Mr. Smith?" I saw the recognition quickly come to his eyes.

He shut the door behind him, then followed me into the living room of the apartment. "How much money did you make off of that Minnesota game?"

"None," I said.

"Bullshit," he said.

"None. It was a fee-based transaction."

He studied me, then nodded. "Go on," he said

I knew right away I'd made the right choice. Raymond Joseph was a very smart kid. And savvy. And he'd need both of those qualities for what I had in mind.

It was just a shame that I was really starting to like him.

I pointed to the kitchen. "Is that coffee I smell?"

"Probably," Raymond said. "My roommate always has a couple of cups before class."

"Any left?"

"Why, you gonna slip something in it?"

"It's not that kind of visit, Raymond."

"No? What kind is it?" He made his way into the tiny kitchen. I sat at the kitchen table and waited for him to pour himself and me a cup and sit down across the table from me.

He was keeping his cool, waiting to hear me out, which only reconfirmed that Raymond was the one for the job.

"Did Lurch ever put together what happened in Minnesota like you did?"

He shook his head. "No."

"Did you tell him?" He shook his head again.

"Did you tell anyone?" Another shake as he took a gulp of

coffee. So did I as we studied each other.

"Why not?" I asked.

He shrugged. "Dunno."

"I think you do know, Raymond."

"You tell me, then, JoJo."

"Instinct. Instinct told you not to tell anyone about my visit. That there might be a reason not to. It's what makes you a great basketball player, Raymond. Instinct."

He stared at me, not giving anything away. He'd make a good poker player.

"I bet you're not entirely surprised to see me on your doorstep, are you?"

There was just a hint of a smile and I knew I was right.

Maybe he wouldn't make that great of a poker player after all.

It had been between Raymond Joseph at CIU or Karl Richardson at Louisville. In some ways, Richardson would have been the easier mark. He was greedy and he didn't really care about his team the way Raymond Joseph did. He made up eighty percent of Louisville's points.

But Karl Richardson didn't have Raymond Joseph's instincts. He probably hadn't—still hadn't - put together my visit and his horrible game the following day.

Or what that could possibly mean in the gambling world.

But here sat Raymond, and he knew the score. And that would save me valuable time.

"What's the spread on tomorrow's game?" he asked.

Yes. Definitely the right choice.

"The spread doesn't matter," I said. "Penn State has to win."

The look on his face was why I had made never knowingly involving a player a rule to live by.

Disbelief. Anger. He started shaking his head. "There's no way we'd lose to Penn State. They've only won three games in the conference."

"It's about to be four."

"No. Somebody would know something was up."

I took a sip of coffee. "Upsets happen every day. Every week in the Big Ten. There's a lot of parity in the conference this year."

"Not between us and Penn State," he said indignantly.

"Northwestern beat Wisconsin last week," I pointed out. "Upsets happen all the time."

"I can't guarantee a loss," he said, pain in his voice. I wasn't sure if he meant that he couldn't do it in practical terms or in moral ones, but it didn't matter.

"You're the point guard, you control the game."

"So what, I throw three wild passes and coach benches me. Then I'm no help."

I shook my head. "You don't fix games on offense. That's what everyone thinks, that you pull your shots, or make bad passes. But that's not it."

He leaned forward, elbows on the table. So did I. "You fix a game on defense. You give your guy an extra step on his dribble. You take a step back when he's in three-point range. It looks like he's having the game of his life, nobody even notices you."

"Coach will," he said.

"Maybe, but is he really going to take you out if you're having trouble guarding a hot shooter? Your replacement—the kid has what, ten minutes total playing time this year?—is he going to do any better? No, he'll keep you in there."

"No," he said. "I won't throw a game. How much to cover the spread?"

"That offer's not on the table."

"That's the only offer I'm willing to talk about."

Underneath the table my legs shook. I summoned up all my bluffing skills, honed through hours and hours at the poker table.

I stood up. "Then we have nothing more to discuss." I started toward the door, waiting for him to stop me. When he didn't, my admiration for him went up. As did my distaste for what I was about to do.

I still had an ace up my sleeve.

At the door I turned around. He'd followed me as far as the living room where he now stood.

"How's your little sister doing, Raymond?"

I hated myself for the pain that washed across his face. "What do you know about my sister?"

More than Raymond himself probably knew, I thought, knowing how thorough Jimmy's guys were. "I know she needs help."

He let out a sound—something between a moan and whimper.

I stepped back into the living room, but didn't touch him. He wouldn't want comfort from me. I didn't blame him. I hated myself right now, too.

"I know you're the man of the family. That your mother has worked two jobs for years to keep you and your sister fed and safe. But it wasn't enough Raymond. Not this time."

He walked backward until his shins hit a chair—a beat up la-z-boy—and he dropped into it. He leaned forward, his elbows on his thighs. I waited for him to look up at me. When he finally did, I continued.

"She needs to go to a good rehab, Raymond. If she stays in that neighborhood, she's going to die. Your mother's doing all she can. You're doing all you can. But you're miles away and she needs professional help."

I felt horrible about the guilt he probably felt, but it was nothing to compare to mine, so I went on. "Coach Wayne is known for running a clean program here. I know there's no alumni slipping you money at gatherings. No cushy jobs in the summer. No cars in your mother's name suddenly appearing."

"That's why my momma wanted me to come here. She liked Coach Wayne. Heard good things about him," *Raymond said softly.*

"And she was right. He's a good man. But there're lots of players out there, at other schools, who play the same game you do and aren't struggling the way you are. Their families aren't hurting like yours is."

He nodded. He knew this, had obviously come to terms with it at some point. And still he'd chosen CIU over one of those schools. It only made my estimation of him rise even more.

"I've got the name of a great rehab center in Chicago. One that your mom could get to easily enough when she'd be allowed to visit but one far enough away from the neighborhood."

"We know about that one. Momma's insurance won't cover it, she already checked."

"I know," I said.

"It costs twenty thousand dollars just for the two-week detox program."

"I know that too."

"We don't have that kind of money," he said, knowing what I would say.

"You would on Monday."

He said nothing for so long I almost started to move, but my poker playing senses kicked in and I did nothing, said nothing.

"Penn State. Fuck," he finally said.

I had him.

And I felt like shit.

We moved back to the kitchen table, I poured us both more coffee.

"So, how does it work? The money I mean."

I sat down at the table, handed him his cup, took a sip from my own. "You get two thousand today, the other eighteen after the game."

"Why not half and half?"

"Ten thousand dollars is a lot of money to a kid like you. What assurance do I have that you'd fulfill your part of the bargain?"

"But you know I need twenty thousand."

"And you'll have it. After the game."

"How do I know I can trust you?"

"You don't."

He snorted at that. "So, I get two thousand. You go and bet

the farm on the game, I do all the dirty work, and I never see you again."

"That won't happen."

"How do I know that?"

"First of all, it's in my best interest to make sure you're satisfied, so that you don't go to the authorities."

He nodded, that made sense to him.

"Second, there may come a time when we want to do business again."

"No. No fucking way. This is a one-time deal. To help my sister."

"If that's the way you want it."

He stared at me, hatred in his eyes for what I'd driven him to. I held his gaze, not flinching. I'd faced hatred across a table before. And with more money on the line.

I pulled out an envelope from my jacket pocket. I wrote down the phone number of my old phone on it and slid it across the table. "Here's the two thousand. And a number where you can reach me to arrange pick-up of the rest. After the game."

"Where are you going to be?"

"I'm staying here. I'll be at the game. I can meet you right afterward with the rest of the money if that's what you want."

"What're the odds on Penn State winning?" he asked. I was glad I'd thought ahead. I wanted this kid to get more for his sacrifice.

"Five to one when I last looked. I don't think they'd change this late."

"So, if you bet my entire twenty thousand, I'd have a hundred," he said.

"I won't bet that much for you. That kind of money showing up all at once would raise a lot of questions."

"I'm not stupid. I wouldn't spend it all at once. Besides, if my sister makes it through the detox, the rest of the program is going to cost some major change."

"I know you're not stupid, but I'm not going to hand that

much money to a kid. I'll bet half for you. You'll win fifty k, with your twenty for the work, you'll walk away with seventy. You can keep your sister in rehab for the whole program. If people question it, tell them the insurance company came through. I'll let you figure out what to tell your mother."

Raymond nodded. He'd been the man of the family since his father had been shot in front of him during a drive-by when Raymond was ten, according to Jimmy's source.

I pulled out my phone. "Let me make sure that your bet can be placed, first."

"You're kidding," he said.

I shrugged. "My contact is having some…issues…right now. I want to make sure he'll be able to place the bet before promising it to you."

He stood up. He took off his simple gold cross from around his neck, and the diamond stud from his ear and placed them on the table. "I'm taking a shower," he said and left the room.

Jimmy answered on the third ring. "It's me," I said.

"Yeah?"

"Any news?"

"Just a pissed-off detective. But no, no news on the shootings."

"Did he come there?"

"Yeah. He made a lot of noise about you being gone didn't look good. That it could make you a suspect. That he just wanted to help with whatever kind of trouble you were in. We both knew he was pissing up a tree if he thought I was going to give him anything."

"Sorry. And thanks."

"It's okay. You need a bet placed?"

"Yeah, if you think you can still do it."

"I can do it. I'm dying to get out of here for a couple of hours anyway. I'll hit the casino and then head over to your place and see the boys."

"Thanks, Jimmy," I said.

"How much on who?"

"Ten thousand on Penn State over Central Iowa."

"Getting, what? Fifteen? Sixteen."

"Not the points. The money line."

"Really?"

"Really."

"Penn State, a sixteen point underdog that hasn't won a Big Ten game on the road is going to come to fourth in the nation Central Iowa and beat 'em straight up?"

"Yes."

There was silence for a moment, then, "Mind if I piggy-back on this bet?"

"Not at all, I was going to suggest it."

"You getting in on it beyond…beyond…"

"No."

"You want to? I could lend—"

"No. No," I said a little forcefully.

"Okay, okay. Sheesh, I was just asking."

"I know, sorry. Thanks, but I'm good. Just the ten thousand."

"Okay. Consider it done. So, I'm assuming you won't be back in town before this game or you'd place the bet yourself."

"Right. But, it looks like now I'm going to have to fly back, collect the bet and then get back on a flight to…" I didn't finish the sentence. Jimmy had to know where I was, but I wasn't going to put in the position of knowingly lying about my whereabouts to Jack.

To anybody.

"Let me know. I can collect the bet and meet you at the airport if you want."

"It'll depend on flights. I want to have this done and get home to Ben as soon as I can, so I may take you up on that."

"Hey, for what I'm going to make on this game, that's the least I can do."

I smiled, it took a little of the sting out of it. I was just about to sign off when the diamond of Raymond's earring hit the light and reflected at me. I picked it up and held it to he light, twirling it. It

was fake, but it gave me an idea. "Jimmy, wait."
"Yeah?"
"Bet it all. Bet the whole eightteen thousand I left with you."
"You sure?"
"Yeah."
"Okay. Done. Stay safe."
"Thanks, I'll be in touch," I said as I hung up.

I set the phone down on the table, placed my palms down on the formica and took a deep breath.

I told myself that it didn't count. That betting on the game wasn't for my gain. Was for something else entirely, so it wasn't really breaking my rule.

I didn't buy it.

In the space of an hour I'd just broken the only two rules I lived by.

And it was only eleven-thirty in the morning.

Twenty-Two
❖❖

"I GOT ONE. I GOT ONE," the scalper yelled outside—well outside—the arena the next day.

"Where's it at?" I asked. CIU was having a championship season and tickets were sold out for all home games. Doubles in anywhere but nose-bleed sections were hard to come by, but singles sometimes were available in pretty good sections.

"Lower bowl. Seven rows behind the team. Primo seating."

I half-heartedly haggled, then paid for the ticket. I didn't really care about the price, but Ben and Saul had taught me the value of good bartering.

Thinking of Ben and Saul made my heart hurt so I pushed the thoughts aside, put on my poker face, tapped my horseshoe pendant three times and walked into the arena.

Raymond had listened to JoJo, that was apparent from the way he played. Nobody would ever have guessed that he was responsible for the kid from Penn State being hot as a pistol. Raymond would put a hand up, look like he was defending the perimeter, but only the most watchful eye would notice that the hand went up a second or two too late. The kid had plenty of time to get set for his shot.

It helped that Lurch was cold today. I wondered if Raymond had had anything to do with that, but decided not to ask him.

At half time, CIU was up, but only by five, when normally

they'd probably be up by at least ten.

In the second half, the entire CIU team seemed sluggish, a step slower than normal. It took me a minute to realize that not only did he control the game, but Raymond Joseph set the tone for his entire team.

I silently congratulated JoJo on her choice.

With three minutes left, the game was tied and my throat was so clogged with fear I could barely swallow. If one team got a couple of baskets up, the remainder of the game would be spent fouling and at the free-throw line.

Exactly what had killed me in the Louisville / Pitt game.

I held on to my pendant as Raymond took the ball inbounds and started down the court. Even I could see Lurch was open at the far end, under the basket. Raymond threw a laser pass that I knew was going to end up in a slam dunk and my admittance into Las Vegas General when out of nowhere, the Penn State point guard swooped in and intercepted the pass, went the length of the court, made a juke move on Raymond, and went in for the easy lay-up.

CIU called time out. As the team made their way to the bench, Raymond looked to the crowd and met my eye. I hadn't even realized he knew I was sitting near the team. He gave the tiniest of nods to me, and I took my hand from my pendant.

I didn't need it.

I had Raymond Joseph on my side.

Midnight at the Vegas airport on a Saturday night. Two a.m. Iowa time. Way too late Anna time.

Normally my night would just be gearing up now, but these were no longer normal times.

As we'd discussed when I'd called him after looking at flights, Jimmy met me in the arrivals area, not too far from where Jack and I had met up with Paulie only six days ago.

Six long days ago.

"Jesus, Christ, I almost had a heart attack watching that game," Jimmy said by way of greeting.

"Me too," I said.

"It was a thing of beauty, Anna. I'm still not sure who you had in your pocket, and I was watching for it."

I nodded. Raymond was that good, he sure deserved the praise, but I kept his name to myself.

"Anything new? No…developments?"

He shook his head. "Nope. Not a peep."

"That's good. Right?"

"I used to figure every day I woke up was a good day. Now, I figure everyday I wake up and don't get no bullet shot at me is a good day."

"Jesus, Jimmy."

He shrugged.

"It was okay to place the bet? And to come here?"

He nodded. "Yeah, me and those young punks have an understanding." He nodded over his shoulder and I saw the two young police officers that I'd given Lorelei's food to the other night. I waved. They nodded back.

"Plus, I get great parking. Right to the door."

I chuckled. "That's good, Jimmy. Keep them close. We can't lose you." I patted his rotund belly. He looked embarrassed.

I was about to say more, but he handed me an envelope. "Here you go."

"Can you hang on a minute?" I asked and he nodded.

I ducked into a women's room, into a stall. I took my money belt out from under my shirt. I counted out Raymond's money from the envelope, put it in my money belt and tucked it back under my shirt. I kept the rest of the money in the envelope, put it in my jacket pocket and walked back out into the huge luggage claim room.

I handed the envelope back to Jimmy. "Can you hang on to this for me?"

He nodded. "Yeah sure."

"Better yet," I said. "You know a guy who knows their way around diamonds?"

He shrugged. "Course."

Of course he did. He even seemed hurt that I'd ask. "Would he come to you?" Jimmy nodded. "Okay. Take that money and buy the nicest diamonds you can with it. Something that could be worn everyday, though, no tiaras or anything." Although the idea of Lorelei's flaming red hair held back by diamonds was tempting.

"The whole wad on diamonds?" Jimmy asked.

"The whole wad."

Jimmy looked at my unadorned ears, my cheap watch. My plain silver horseshoe pendant. He shrugged. "Well, her ziti's pretty damn good."

I laughed. "Exactly," I said. It took a little of the sting out of how far I'd fallen.

Just a little.

"That all?"

"Yep. Thanks, Jimmy. For everything. You're a life saver." I didn't need to add "literally". Jimmy's been around, he knew the score.

He waved my thanks away. "I'll see you when you get back," he said and turned and walked away.

I stood watching him until I heard a familiar, deep, and angry voice behind me say, "And just when exactly will that be?"

I had expected the uniforms that were with Jimmy would report back to Jack, even down to seeing Jimmy hand me an envelope and me hand it back after a quick trip to the ladies room. That was fine; nothing Jimmy and I were doing was illegal. He was placing a bet for a friend and paying her off.

It was fine in Vegas…but…what happened in Dubuque stayed in Dubuque.

I hadn't expected Jack to move as soon as he heard that Jimmy had headed to the airport, but I guess I shouldn't have been surprised.

In a sick way, even after leaving the way I had, I was happy to see him.

But Jack Schiller did not look at all happy as he took my hand and led me back toward the main terminal. "You have time for coffee before you fly off to God knows where?"

"You're just going to let me go?"

"I can't really stop you, can I?"

"No," I said.

"So, time for coffee?"

I looked at my watch. My flight back to Dubuque didn't leave for three hours. "A couple of minutes," I said.

He raised a brow, but didn't say a word, just walked toward the Starbucks stand.

He brought me a huge cup, himself a small one. We sat at a table, taking small sips. Him staring at me, me not meeting his eye.

After a while he let out a huge sigh. "You going to tell me where you were since Thursday night when I left your house?"

I shook my head. He nodded, like he'd expected that answer. "No Johanna Dawson has been on any flight manifest in the last forty-eight hours. But you know that. And you knew I'd check, too, right?"

I said nothing.

"Can you at least tell me if this has anything to do with the shootings? Is there anything about the case I should know?"

"I don't know anything new about the case," I said, not really answering his question, but telling him all I could.

"Jesus, Johanna," he whispered. He leaned forward, took my hand. "How deep are you in? Let me help you."

"That's not how the game's played, Jack," I said. "I can't get my cop boyfriend to bail me out. You play the cards you're dealt."

He sat back, scrubbed his hands across his face. He looked tired. He'd probably had as much sleep as I had since Thursday night—which was none.

I wanted to reach out, to smooth away some of that tension. To let him know it was going to be okay. That it was over.

I kept my hands around my coffee cup instead. I knew myself, and I couldn't swear this type of thing would never happen again. So far, I hadn't outright lied to Jack, and I didn't want to start now.

I had the sneaking suspicion that it didn't matter.

"I don't think I can do this, Johanna," he said, confirming my worst fears. He was going to bail. I didn't blame him, but it hurt nonetheless.

God, it hurt.

Not like with Jeffrey where it was my pride that stung. This hurt on a deeper level.

It ached. My pride should have kicked in. I should have just agreed—in a way I did—wished him the best and walked away. But where I could do that with Jeffrey, I couldn't with Jack.

Not without trying.

"What about not touching each other's issues, Jack? What about letting our icebergs float?" I tried to keep my voice level, to not let him hear the fear in my voice.

"Christ, Johanna, this isn't about me showing up drunk on your doorstep some night. Your 'issues' are going to get you killed. I can't just sit back and watch that happen."

"But—"

He put a hand up, cutting me off. "And yeah, I know drinking's going to kill me too—but I never drive when I'm drinking, so it's going to be a slow death. You? Not at the rate you're going." He took a deep breath, let it out. "It's more than I can handle."

"So you're going to run? To bail? Like you did on your marriage? Like you did to your kid?" I saw the wince of pain on his face, but I kept on. "It's never going to be perfect, Jack. Not the perfect family you've been searching for your whole life. But you keep trying. It's messy, real life."

"You don't think I know that," he said, he voice low and deadly. He leaned across the table, his hand grabbing my wrist. "You don't think I see the horrible things families do to each other? Things people do to people they supposedly love? I see it every God damn, day, Johanna. And there's usually a chalk outline around it."

I sat back, tried to free my arm, but he held tight. "That's why I need more from you. I'm not going to get a call some day and have to see your body in that chalk outline. Or if I do, at least I'm not going to have been in your bed the night before."

I understood. I really did. And I would have made the same choice if I were him. But I gave it one more shot. "I'm surprised, Jack. I didn't think you'd back down from this."

He looked at me, his brown eyes turned from anger to pain. He leaned back, let go of my hand. "Neither did I," he said so quietly I almost missed it.

He got up, and walked away from me, never looking back.

I know, because I watched until he was out of sight.

I should have been able to sleep on the flight back to Dubuque, but the pain in Jack's eyes kept me awake.

When Jeffrey dumped me, my pride had stung. But this was different.

Jack was different.

As of today, I'd be out of debt with Vince. I could go to Jack, tell him it was over, that I'd stop betting on games. That poker in casinos—games I'd have to have the money up front for—were all I'd play from now on.

He might take me back. He'd *probably* take me back.

But I'd be lying to him.

I tried to think back to what number lying to loved ones was on the list of signs for compulsive gambling that Lorelei had pulled out at her most recent intervention.

It didn't come to me.

I called first to make sure the roommate was out of the apartment as agreed upon. When Raymond gave the all clear, I left the rental car and made my way to the apartment that I'd left forty-eight hours ago.

"You did really well," I said as I entered the apartment.

"You got my money?" Was all he said.

"Yes, of course."

He made a motion with his hands. "Give it."

I pulled an envelope out of my inside jacket pocket. "Sixty-eight thousand. The remaining eighteen thousand for the game, and fifty thousand winnings on your bet."

Emotions ran across Raymond's face. Relief, that was one I knew well. Disgust—I knew that one too. And finally resignation.

Yep, I'd pretty much created Raymond Joseph in JoJo's image.

"Don't do anything stupid. Or flashy. Get the money to the place for your sister's rehab. Tell people the insurance came through. Put the rest of it away, but not in the bank or anywhere else that has a paper trail. I didn't spend ten hours on flights so there'd be no paper trail of the money just so you could turn around and pay cash for an Escalade."

He snorted. "I'm not stupid, you know."

"I know," I said. "That's why I chose you."

His eyes were cold. "Lucky me."

I turned to leave.

"Lose my number. Lose my address. Forget you ever met me, or someone's going to hear about you," he said.

I looked back at him, nodded. "Fair enough."

I walked to the door, opened it, but turned one more time. "But if you ever want to do business again, I know someone who would pay very well for what you did yesterday."

He walked toward me. When he reached me, he put his hand on my chest, just over my horseshoe necklace and gently, but firmly, pushed so that I stepped back, outside the door jamb. He stared at me, but did not say a word as he shut the door in my face.

I thought about Jack on the flight home until it hurt so badly that I had to think about something else. But thinking about Ben and the boys and who was trying to hurt them scared me, so my thoughts went back to Raymond Joseph and how his sister would be getting the help she needed.

At least somebody would be benefiting in this whole shitty mess.

And Lorelei would be getting some much-deserved diamonds.

I, however, had sunk to a new level.

And what damage would this do to Raymond? He, who when JoJo had first met him in Minnesota had bragged about his team with such joy and pride. Was that all gone now? Would he forever be cynical?

Welcome to the real world, Raymond.

An hour into the flight I asked for a bourbon and downed it in one swallow, a silent toast for what was not to be. It, along with nearly two days without sleep, did me in and I finally dozed.

My dreams were hazy, fueled by exhaustion, bourbon, remorse and guilt.

Mostly guilt.

I dreamed of Vince sitting in a motel room, a gun on the table next to him. I looked behind me to the parking lot but instead of Paulie being in the car it was my mom and dad and it was Wisconsin. When I looked back, it was no longer Vince and a motel room but Jimmy sitting in the book room of the Bellagio, eating directly from a pan of ziti, a smile of pure delight on his face.

Then the scene switched to the hallway at the morgue where we went the night Danny was killed. But this time the hallway was so much longer, never ending. And in the distance was a shadow or a person, and I tried to make them out but I couldn't. I tried to run in that direction, but hands held me back. When I turned I saw it was Jack and Frank Botz, only Jack was wearing a crazy tie and Botz had on Jack's leather jacket and a chambray shirt. They both had unlit cigarettes dangling from their mouths.

I opened the door to one of the rooms and Lorelei, in a leotard, was doing dance movements at a barré along the mirrored walls. Gus, in his hospital gown was at the barré, too, but he couldn't lift his wounded leg and he screamed at me to get out.

I looked at Lorelei as I closed the door and she had changed from her leotard to a doctor's white lab coat, her hair up in a tidy bun. She started walking toward me, writing something on a clipboard and laughing and I turned to leave the room.

My hand was grabbed and I was pulled down to my bed. I knew it was my bed, but it looked like the motel room that I'd met Vince in. Jack's body began moving over mine, a languid feeling coming over me, soon replaced with fear as I heard the gunshot and was running down the hallway to Ben's room.

I entered the room to see Ben and Saul playing cribbage,

but it was in Saul's room, not Ben's. Jack came in the sliding glass doors, holding a gun and Saul pulled out a chair for him to join their game like he'd been expecting him. The game then turned into poker and that kid that I'd lost to with my fake tell, Jason, came in and played with them. Nobody seemed surprised that Jason was playing with them, even though I was the only one that knew him.

I jolted awake, startling the man sitting next to me. My mind went back over a detail in the mish mash of my dream.

And over it again.

Holy, shit. I knew who was trying to kill The Corporation.

Twenty-Three

❖

I COULDN'T BELIEVE IT. I played it over and over in my mind. I wasn't sure, there could be a logical explanation.

And yet...and yet I knew who was behind it all.

And what was worse, I thought I knew why.

But there were parts that didn't add up. Big parts. It wasn't something I could take to authorities. Not yet. There was too big of a gap in my theory. One that I thought I could fill on my own.

If I was right, I was dealing with someone very unstable, and I didn't want that person near anybody else. I really didn't think they'd hurt me, but it was a chance I was willing to take.

For the people that I loved.

I spent the remainder of the flight figuring out how to prove my theory.

"Lor, who's all at the house?" I asked from my phone at the airport as soon as I landed in Vegas. I tried to keep my voice normal sounding but it was hard with the knowledge I'd come to believe I had.

I was expecting a full house at my place. With a long wait in Dubuque and the time change, it was four o'clock on Sunday afternoon.

About the same time Jack and I were getting in from

Pittsburgh last Sunday and had been met by Paulie.

Paulie wouldn't be meeting me today. There was no need. JoJo had delivered.

"Jo?" Lorelei said on the other end of the phone. "Where are you?"

"At the airport."

"What airport?"

"Here, in Vegas,"

"Are you coming home, or flying out?"

"I'm coming home. I have to make one stop and then I'll be home. Who all is there right now?"

"Me, Ben, Saul, Gus and Jack."

"Jack's there?" I said, the surprise apparent in my voice.

"Yes, but," she stopped. I could hear her moving into another room. A door shutting.

"But what?"

"I heard him on the phone with Frank, setting it up so that Frank would come and relieve Jack when…when…"

"Whenever I showed up," I finished for her.

"Yes. What happened?"

"Nothing. Everything. It all caught up with me, Lor. I couldn't keep all the plates in the air."

"Oh, Jo," she said, pity—God, how I hated that—in her voice.

"Lor, I need you to do something. It's really important."

I think the gravity in my voice came through because the pity was gone and she was all business as she said, "What do you need me to do?"

I launched into the story I'd come up with to make sure I'd have enough time to find out what I needed to know.

After she agreed to do what I'd asked, I gave Lorelei my time frame, thanked her again, and then hung up the phone.

As I made my way out of long-term parking in my Porsche, I called Paulie. "Is Vince available?

"When?"

"Now."

"You mean like right now?"

"Right now."

He hung up on me and I took the long way to the strip to buy some time. I didn't need it, Paulie called back in less than ten minutes. "He can see you now."

"Where?"

"The Picasso exhibition at the Bellagio?"

"Really?"

"What? A guy can't look at pretty pictures?"

"No, no, it's just that… Never mind, I'll be there in fifteen minutes."

"He said to look for him around the sculptures."

"Okay, thanks."

"Hey, Anna, you did real good—"

But I cut Paulie off as I hung up the phone, shaking my head. Vince Santini looking at Picasso sculptures on a Sunday.

The Superbowl had already been played, and it was a couple of weeks away from March Madness, so it was just the normal tourist Sunday at the exhibit, which was to say pretty light.

The art gallery exhibitions they got into the Bellagio were big names, and I'd taken Ben to a few, but Vegas was for gambling, and then a far, far second, shows. The attendance in the exhibition rooms reflected that.

Vince was easy to find and when I caught his eye, he nodded toward one of the alcoves with just one lone sculpture where no one else was near.

"I'm sorry to need to meet on such short notice," I said as we met up.

"No problem, I was just heading in here when you called

Paulie."

It was Sunday and he was looking at art, but Vince still had on one of his beautifully cut suits. His hair combed back from his handsome olive face. Impeccable.

In my travel-worn clothes and with airplane hair that not even a good brushing could tame, I felt like a total schlub next to him.

We circled around the sculpture so that our backs were to one of the three walls that made up the small alcove. We'd be able to speak quietly here without anyone being able to hear, and we'd also be able to see if anyone came near.

He stared at the sculpture, leaning his head to see it at the different angles. He looked in his brochure that they gave out at the entrance, read about the sculpture. Studied it again. I waited.

It looked like every Picasso did to me; odd, askew and had me wondering what old Pablo had been smoking.

He took a step away from it, putting him side-by-side with me at the back of the little room. "What can I do for you, Anna?" he said softly, his eyes still on the piece of art.

I took a deep breath. "I just wanted confirmation—from you personally—that we're even. That all slates have been wiped clean."

He tilted his head just slightly in my direction, not really looking at me. "Have I ever given you reason to suspect that I wouldn't uphold my end of a bargain?" There was no hurt in his voice, he knew this wasn't about him.

"No, you haven't."

"So?"

"I just...with all this stuff that's going on with the boys...I don't want to have any loose ends. I need to be available for them completely for a while."

If I was right in my suspicions—and I could prove it—being available would be the least of it. All hell would break loose.

"We're good. Clean slate. You're welcome at a game of mine anytime."

"Thanks, Vince."

"But, Anna," he said turning to me this time. "Don't take it the wrong way if I say I hope you don't show up at any of those games."

I tried to smile, but it probably came out as more of a grimace. "That's not a good business move. You should want me in to you heavy."

He shrugged. "Business will survive. There's always other…"

He was about to say low-life, dead-beat—or worse—gamblers but he stopped himself.

"Yes, there will be," I answered his unfinished thought.

He took a deep breath, looked me over from head to foot. It made me wish I'd tried harder with that brush. "You don't look so good, Anna."

"It's been a long weekend," I said.

"I imagine it was." He turned back to the sculpture. "But a good one."

I thought of Jack turning away from me. Of Raymond Joseph's ideals crashing down around him. Of figuring out who wanted my boys dead.

I also thought of getting out from under Vince. Being free.

"Parts of it," I conceded.

"Let me know if there's anything I can do to help with The Corporation," he said, dismissing me.

"I will. Thanks, Vince."

I started to walk away, but he gently placed his hand on my arm. I looked at him. He had a small smile on his face. "Anna, I would never interfere with the way you do your business…"

"Yes?"

"But, watching the CIU—Penn State game…"

I waited, not sure where he was going. Was he going to

critique JoJo's game fixing techniques?

"It was so smooth, so well done. A thing of beauty. I made a little bet with myself as to who was on the take."

It was twisted, but in a weird way, I was flattered. "Who would you have bet it was?"

"Either the point guard or the big center. But that kid didn't look smart enough for it, so I settled on the point guard."

I looked around, making sure no one had moved near to the alcove. "You'd have won that bet."

He smiled to himself, nodded his head. I started to leave, but he still hung on to my jacket.

"You think he'd be interested in future…transactions?"

"He told me to lose his number," I said, remembering Raymond Joseph pushing me out his door.

"That's not really an answer."

I shrugged. "He's done it and survived. Has a taste. He might find he wants more."

"Is that how it happened to you?"

I looked beyond Vince, into the darkness of the other walls of the exhibition, all draped in black velvet. "Probably, who knows anymore," I said with a sigh.

"If you had to place odds on whether you'd hear from your point guard again, what would you make it?"

"Even," I said sadly, then left Vince amongst his things of beauty.

I walked into the house. My house. Our house.

Lorelei had worked her magic and gotten everyone out. Even Gus, though he was probably thankful to get outdoors for a bit.

There'd still been a patrol car parked out front and I'd waved to the officers, but there was nothing strange about me coming to my own home.

I wondered if they'd call Jack and let him know I was there. I figured I'd better get a move on; find out what I'd come in search of.

I moved to the back of the house, where it split into the U. Gus, Ben and Lorelei's rooms were to my left. Mine, Saul's and the office to my right.

I took a deep breath and moved down one of the halls until I got to the room I wanted. I knocked on the shut door, but didn't expect any answer. When met with silence, I opened the door and entered the room, leaving the door open. I wanted to make sure I heard if Lorelei and the boys came home before I was done. I was pretty sure what I was looking for, but I started carefully searching the room for anything out of the ordinary. If I was totally off base, I'd want no signs that I'd been rummaging around.

I didn't find anything in the bedroom, so I moved to the adjoining bath. I got on my hands and knees and moved everything out of the under-sink area. There wasn't much, but it was creatively arranged to hide a bundle in the back.

My heart sank as I reached as far back as my arms would go and carefully grabbed on to the heavy package. I pulled it out. Whatever it was, it was completely engulfed in a black garbage bag.

It was heavy and shaped like a gun, but the gun was wrapped in something. I peeked inside the garbage bag, careful not to touch the surface of the gun with my hands.

Not a problem, the gun was wrapped in a Pittsburgh Steeler's Terrible Towel.

I wondered about just leaving it and calling Jack, but this was my home, so I was pretty sure that anything I found would be considered admissible in court. It wasn't like I needed a search warrant for my own house.

Admissable in court. God, was that where this was all going

to lead?

My question was answered by a soft throat clearing from behind me.

I whipped around, my hands still holding the package.

"What have you done?" I asked the person in the doorway. Stupid, but that's all that came out.

Then I saw the gun they were holding.

Twenty-Four
❖❖

"OH, SAUL, WHY?" I whispered.

But I knew. I'd learned from Jack.

I thought the word just as Saul said, "Revenge."

He stepped back, out of the doorway. "Come out here, Hannah darling, this is not a conversation for the bathroom."

I eyed the gun he held. Felt the heft of the one in my hands, wrapped in a towel and then plastic garbage bag. Could I move it so that I'd be able to shoot? Could I reach the trigger through the layers?

Was it even loaded?

"No," Saul said as if I'd thought it out loud. "That gun is not loaded. But this one is."

"Where'd you get that one from?"

"My car. I left it there when I came to stay here." He shrugged. "Who knew when an opportunity would present itself?"

I put the garbage bag down on the bathroom floor and raised myself up. Saul could have been bluffing; the gun could have been loaded. But that would have meant I was prepared to shoot Saul.

I wasn't.

Not yet, anyway. Hopefully it would never come to that.

I moved toward the door. He stayed well out of my reach,

the gun trained on me the entire time. I really didn't think Saul had it in him to hurt me, but until a couple of hours ago I would never have thought he'd kill his friends, either.

I didn't want to underestimate him physically. He was much more agile than Ben. Just thinking about him shooting at Ben and then sneaking in through the side doors in time to come running into Ben's room filled with concern made me realize his capabilities were much more than I'd originally thought.

He waved me over to one of the upholstered leather chairs that sat in the sitting area of the large room. I sat. He looked around as if he was wondering what to do next.

So was I.

"Saul, you know there's no good way out of this," I said.

He sighed. "I know," he said. But it wasn't regret in his voice. It was resignation. That's when I knew that he didn't intend for me to walk out of there.

I cursed myself for having Lorelei keep the boys away for a few hours so I could search the place. Jack would stay with them. I wasn't sure how Saul had made his way back here, but Jack wouldn't have been too concerned due to the patrolmen out front.

Those officers had probably seen Saul come in, but that wouldn't be unusual to them. Saul had been staying here since Gus was shot. They would stay out there unless I could signal them in some way.

Hopefully not by gunshot.

He pulled the other leather chair back a few feet, so there was a good distance between us, and sat down. He let out a weary oomph as he sat.

Time. That was the only thing that was going to help me now. Either that or make a move for Saul, but I didn't see how I could do that without one of us getting hurt.

Even though it seemed that I was right; that Saul had killed Danny and tried to kill Gus and Ben, I still wasn't prepared to do him harm.

He had been like a second—well third, behind my own and Ben—father to me for the past ten years.

Buy time. Wait for Lorelei, Ben and Gus to get back. Though the thought of those three walking into this scared me to death, I knew Jack—or Frank Botz—would be with them. I'd worry about the logistics of getting Jack in here without endangering the others when the time came.

Assuming Saul hadn't shot me by then.

"How did you know?" Saul asked. Good, he wanted to talk. Was probably dying to talk to somebody about this. He and the boys shared every secret, talked for hours everyday at breakfast. Keeping this to himself was probably killing him.

"When Ben was shot…" I started. Saul nodded. "You knew Jack was in the woods."

He went back in time in his thoughts, but came up with nothing.

I wasn't surprised; I didn't catch it at first either. It was only after that crazy dream when my sub-consciousness was so hazy that I'd latched on to it.

"You went to your room. Ben went to his a little later…"

"Yes?"

"Jack came over *after* that."

He nodded for me to continue.

"When Ben was shot, Jack went to him on the patio, then out to the woods, where he disappeared because of the trees and darkness. *Then* you came into Ben's room."

"Yes?"

"You wouldn't have—shouldn't have—known Jack was even there. You would have been surprised to see him, asked where he'd come from… something… at the very least not known he was in the woods." I leaned forward. Even though we were too far apart for me to touch him, Saul leaned back. "But you knew he was there, because you'd seen him come out to

Ben's side from where you were hiding. Somewhere in the trees."

"And that was it? That knowing Jack was there was enough for you to believe I'd done these things?" He chuckled, looked at the gun he was holding.

I shrugged. "We're here, aren't we?"

His eyes narrowed at me.

"But there were other things, too," I said, stalling for time. "Things that didn't add up."

"Nothing added up," he said, his anger dissipating, pride taking its place. "That was the beauty of it."

I shrugged again, waited.

"Such as?" he asked, impatience tingeing his voice.

"Such as the guys from Pittsburgh. The *Sports Illustrated* article."

He hooted—actually hooted—with laughter. For the first time I realized that this was not the Saul that had taught me Pai Gow. I didn't know this man in front of me.

Something had snapped in Saul.

And now that I knew about his secrets, there was even less of a chance he'd just let me go. I eyed his gun again, knowing now that it would probably be him or me.

He leaned his head back, then seemed to remember he was on guard duty and snapped back to attention. "Oy, that was a sight to behold. Everybody chasing their tails over some big shooters in Pittsburgh."

"So, there was no big loser in Pittsburgh from the Superbowl?" I thought about Chuck and Ralph's emotions when that game had been mentioned. They had both lost big in that game, I'd bet on it.

"Oh, there was a loser all right, or at least the betting went that way. Probably more than one with the kind of money that came in. You might even have met them when you took your little field trip to Pittsburgh, Hannah."

The surprise showed on my face.

"What? You think I didn't know where you were? Jimmy's not the only one who can get information you know."

I started to ask how, but it didn't really matter. Saul had wanted us distracted by the Pittsburgh crew and we were.

"The day that article came out." He tapped his head. "I knew. I knew I finally had the smoke screen I needed.

"What if I hadn't thought of the Pittsburgh connection?"

"Somebody would have figured it out eventually. Those detectives wouldn't have been able to keep the information about the Towels out of it for too much longer. They knew there was a Pittsburgh connection." He stopped, smiled, and tapped his forehead again. "They *thought* there was a Pittsburgh connection. They would have had to outright ask us about what we knew about the Steelers soon, and somebody would have made the connection."

"I just sped up the process," I said.

"Yes, Hannah, darling, you did."

"Planting those Terrible Towels at the scenes was just a way to get the red herring of the Pittsburgh gamblers started."

"That's why you're such a good card player, Hannah…your ability to think like your opponent."

"You're not my opponent, Saul," I tried. "You're my friend. And I love you."

"I love you too, dear," he said, but I could tell I hadn't gotten through. He was going to kill me. He wouldn't want to, but he'd feel he'd have to.

"Danny was shot point blank, and yet you only shot Gus in the leg. You missed Ben outright. Why?"

He leaned back. "Another anomaly that left the police scratching their heads. The truth is Hannah, only one member of The Corporation was supposed to die. Only one *deserved* to die."

He leaned forward, his eyes boring into mine.

"Can you guess which one, Hannah?"

Twenty-Five
❖

"Only one member deserved to die you said?"

Saul nodded.

"And you mentioned revenge already."

He nodded again, motioning for me to go on. Unwrap his riddle. He was enjoying this. Yes, the Saul I'd loved was gone.

"On Ben I take it," I said.

He leaned forward, waiting for more.

"For Rachael."

He looked satisfied. But then a frown crossed his face. "He told you? He told you about him and my Rachael?" There was fury in his voice and his hand shook. The hand that held a gun pointed right at me.

"No. No, Saul. Ben never said a word. I just put it together the other day."

"The picture?"

"Yes."

He leaned back in his chair. Pointed to the small table near me. "*That* picture."

I noticed a framed photo turned face down on the table, amongst a checkerboard, set up in mid-game, and odds sheets. I turned it over. I hadn't even noticed it was missing from the sideboard, but then, I probably hadn't been back in the dining room since the day that I'd asked Saul about it.

Saul closed his eyes for a moment, as if in pain. I thought about making a move, but he seemed to remember the situation and quickly opened his eyes, sat up straighter.

"I told you about the day that picture was taken, yes?"

I nodded. "Rachael had been away, taking care of her dying mother in New York for a long time. You guys went to see Ben at the casino the day after she got back. The three of you reunited."

He snorted. "Reunited, bah! I was sending Ben a message that day. That Rachael was mine. Would always be mine. That she'd come back to me. For me."

I waited. This is what the last few weeks boiled down to. The fury in his eyes was raging.

"She was away for months, yes. But her mother wasn't ill. That woman lived for another twenty years—outlived Rachael by years."

"Then, where was she for all that time?" I asked, dreading the answer.

"She was having a baby. A bastard."

I sucked in a breath. "Ben's?"

He nodded, tears welling up in his eyes. He bristled, pulled himself together. He was on an emotional roller coaster, and the instability of that alarmed me. "Rachael and I had been married fifteen years. No babies. I suspected that maybe I was sterile. I'd had the mumps as a child. Back then, sometimes…"

I nodded, waited, mesmerized. And scared to death of the gun he held. He was telling me more secrets now. Would it be more reasons not to let me live?

"I should have said something before we got married, I know Rachael wanted lots of babies…but I wanted her so badly…had loved her the moment I met her."

"You couldn't have been sure, Saul. Surely they didn't have the tests to know that kind of stuff back then." Despite everything he'd done, and that he probably would try to kill me before this was over, Saul was my friend, and he was in pain.

He shrugged. "If they did, we didn't know about them. If you didn't have children back then, it was just God's way."

"But then Rachael got pregnant," I led for him.

A look of bliss came over him. "Oh, that was a joyous day. We'd waited so long, thought it was not going to happen. Oh, how we celebrated."

"And then?"

The bliss left, replaced by sorrow. "I started thinking about it too much." He sighed. "Oh Hannah, if I could go back, that is the one thing I would change. I would have kept my mouth shut, raised and loved that baby. So many lives would be different today if I only had."

"So, you asked Rachael about it? That must have gone over well."

"All I had to say was how blessed we were that after all theses years a miracle had happened. She broke out sobbing. Sobbing, Hannah. My beautiful Rachael in so much pain. I could have cut out my tongue.

"She confessed that she and Ben had been lovers. Not long, not often, she said. And she'd ended it. But there was no doubt that the baby was his."

"Oh, Saul, I'm so sorry," I said, and I meant it. I was sorry for Saul. And Rachael, because I believe she probably loved two men. And for Ben who was in love with his best friend's wife. Nobody could win.

And everybody had lost.

"The rage…the rage that overcame me, Hannah. I'm not proud of the way I handled it," he said softly.

As opposed to how he was handling things now? I kept still.

"I wanted her to get rid of it. She said she'd leave me first…that she'd go away and I'd never see her again. I couldn't bear that. But I couldn't raise Ben's child either. Knowing every time I looked at the child that I'd be reminded of their betrayal."

I didn't offer up the option of Rachael leaving Saul for Ben. Either it wasn't discussed, or it was, but Saul wasn't going to tell me about it. Apparently she'd loved Saul, had wanted to stay with him.

Only questions a woman long since dead could answer.

"So, we compromised. She'd have the baby, but give it up for adoption. We were able to find a place that would allow us to know about the baby. Where he lived, how he was doing, even pictures every now and then. This was before open adoptions, so Rachael felt fortunate."

"But she gave up the baby she wanted so badly?"

He sighed. "I used her guilt over her affair with Ben. It was…I was…I believe that's what killed her so early. The guilt. First from being with Ben, and then from giving up the baby. She died not too long after the baby turned five. Heart disease the doctors said. *Broken* heart, I said."

"And Ben never knew? She never told him?"

A small smile played across his face. "No. That was part of our deal. I would agree to her keeping in touch about the baby if she swore never to tell Ben. That was what kept me going. Ben had loved my wife, but I knew about his child, something he would never know about."

"Jesus, Saul," I whispered.

"Yes, Hannah, that is why Ben must die—to avenge my Rachael."

"Saul, that had to be close to forty years ago."

"And I thought about it every day of those forty years," he said with what seemed like validation in his voice. "And then about a year ago…when I learned…" His voice trailed off.

I briefly wondered if Saul had entered into some kind of dementia? He seemed sharp as a tack, but for something to come to such a boil after forty-years…

I eyed the gun again.

"You know what they say, Hannah."

"What, Saul?"

"Revenge is a dish best served cold."

"But Danny, Saul. Danny." My voice cracked thinking of poor Danny dying at the hand of his friend. For the only reason of deflecting guilt off of him and trying to make it look like the entire Corporation was targeted. "You shot him point blank. You'd do that to set up a ruse?"

Saul's shoulders sagged. "Ah, Danny. What you don't know, Hannah darling, what nobody knows is that Danny was already a dead man."

"What?"

He took a deep breath, preparing for a painful story, I could tell. "Danny came to me a few days before that day at the Sourdough…the day Jimmy brought the magazine?"

I nodded, remembering the day. I'd been so proud of my boys.

"Danny came to me and told me he was dying. Brain cancer. Doctors told him he only had a few months. And it wasn't going to be pretty. Painful. But he was willing to deal with the pain, Danny was. But he didn't want that burden for Moira."

My hands came to my face, startling Saul, but he relaxed when he saw it was just emotion driving me. "Oh, poor Danny."

"He told me he wanted to kill himself. Have it done with. Clean, neat. No lingering. But he didn't want Moira to know he'd killed himself. And of course there was the insurance to consider…"

"He asked you to kill him."

He nodded. "I told him no, of course. I could never do that to someone I loved like Danny."

I scoffed at that. "Danny had never lain with my wife," he retorted. "Anyway, he begged me. Told me he'd hire someone to do it if I didn't, but wanted someone he trusted to handle it."

"And so much cheaper," I added, the disgust in my voice.

"Don't judge, Hannah. Moira was the light of Danny's life. They were happy together for over fifty years. He wanted to spare her, and make sure she was provided for."

"I know," I said. And I did know how much Danny doted on Moira. How it would kill a proud man like Danny to deteriorate in front of the woman he loved, to have to be nursed by her for God knew how long. Given the same circumstances, I'm not sure I wouldn't take the same route Danny had chosen.

"So, you changed your mind, obviously."

"The day that article came out I started thinking. That one quote kept jumping out at me and I thought about how miffed the person in Pittsburgh would be when he read that and I felt bad that I'd even said anything. But it stayed with me…"

"And became your false motive."

He nodded. "Danny would die first. It would be as he wished. I went to him and we worked it all out; the deserted parking lot, only one car, point blank so there'd be no mistakes." His voice cracked. "Oh Hannah, it was awful. But it was what he wanted. And he was my friend."

I waited while he pulled himself together. I wanted to buy time, and I also wanted to hear this story as Saul let it unfold.

"But it got me to thinking about endings. I'm eighty-two years old. How much longer do I have? Could I go to my grave with never having hurt Ben the way he hurt Rachael and I?

"So, if I had to do something so horrible to my friend, I said to myself, then I was going to get something out of it too."

"Finishing it with Ben."

He nodded. "Yes."

"But that first night, the police suspected you guys, brought you all in."

"That's why another member had to be a target quickly, to shake suspicion off of us before they got as far as following us or getting warrants." He nodded his head toward the bathroom where the garbage bag sat. "I couldn't have them finding the Terrible Towels or the gun that killed Danny, but I still needed them."

"So, you shot Gus? Jesus, Saul, he could have died."

He shook his head. "I shot *at* Gus. I had no intention of hitting him. I was going to shoot near him, leave the Towel in the bush where I shot from and let the police think I'd missed." He looked over my head, lost in his own thoughts. "Ben would be next, and I wouldn't miss then."

"But you did shoot Gus," I pointed out.

"He moved at the last minute. He'd gotten his mail and dropped a letter. He was just entering his door and I was shooting low, to the flowerpots next to the door, when he realized he'd dropped some of his mail. He moved, and…"

"And you shot his leg."

He nodded. "Even then I didn't think it was so bad. It added weight to the whole thing, that this guy from Pittsburgh wasn't going to stop with just one member of The Corporation.

I didn't know until that doctor talked to us in the hospital how close it had been, that the bullet had almost hit an artery."

I remembered Saul being overcome with emotion when the doctor had told us that Gus was going to be all right. I thought at the time that it was just the same relief that all of us were feeling. And it was relief, but mixed with shock and grief over how close he'd coming to killing a friend.

One that wasn't dying of brain cancer.

"So, you shot Gus, left another Terrible Towel, and the investigation turned to the big loser—or losers—in Pittsburgh."

"It was supposed to, but I had a feeling your detective wouldn't leave it at that."

I didn't bother pointing out that Jack wasn't *my* detective any more—if he ever was. Saul was right though; Jack had never completely given up on the possibility that the shooter was someone closer. A theory that had infuriated me at the time.

A theory I should have paid closer attention to.

"So," Saul continued. "I knew I'd have to move quickly. You asking me to stay here, under the same roof as Ben, was a Godsend."

"Glad to be of help."

He snorted, then a look of anger washed over him. "And it was perfect. That day. I was in my room." He pointed to the sliding glass door that faced the outside—not the patio side. There was one on the other side of the bedroom as well, that faced the patio. "I went around the side, the patrol car couldn't see me from that angle, and of course it was dark. I went to the woods, I was going to wait until Ben went to sleep and slip into his room—I'd unlocked his patio door earlier in the day.

"I would tell Ben about the baby—his baby. One that had lived a life never knowing his father. And then I'd end it.

"But then he came out onto the patio, turned on the outside lights. It wasn't exactly what I wanted—I wanted him to hurt—but it had been so hard to find an opportunity that I knew I had to do it while I had the chance" he whispered with reverence, and again I wondered about Saul's stability.

Then his voice turned harsh. "And then he had to go and trip and fall."

"Thank God for crowded patio furniture and walkers," I said earning a glower. Not what you want from a man holding a gun on you.

His anger was rising and I tried to turn him back to his mastermind plan—he seemed happy to talk about that.

"How was this all going to end, Saul? If I hadn't come back here tonight what was the plan?"

He shrugged. "I wasn't going to stop until it was finished, but it was getting harder to find opportunities since Jack moved in here. It was important to keep the threat real. I was going to stage an attempt on me this evening."

"And then?"

"Sooner or later there'd be a time to get to Ben alone."

"And after that? When you had…hurt…Ben? It just stops?"

"It stops. The police make of that what they want."

"And the fact that Jimmy was never targeted? Doesn't that make him look like a suspect? Or was that the whole idea?"

"It wasn't the original intention, but if it worked out that way…"

"Oh, Saul."

"What? They wouldn't be able to prove anything. He didn't *do* anything."

"So, this is all about timing? You've been seeking revenge on Ben for forty years, and all the stars just aligned for you now?"

He nodded, even chuckled a little. "Yes, it's as simple as that. And that's how I thought of it too; all the stars aligning. Danny finding out he was dying. The article in that magazine. It was finally time for Ben to pay for what he did to Rachael. To me."

The perfect storm of murder.

"Hannah, darling, I never wanted you hurt. But I'm also not going to let you stop my plans. Ben will pay. For my Rachael."

He started to stand, to get on with whatever he'd decided to do when we both heard noises from the front of the house.

Somebody was coming home

Twenty-Six
❖❖

IT WAS TOO FAR AWAY TO MAKE OUT whose voice was whose, but it was definitely human sounds. Opening and closing of doors. A low voice and then a higher one.

I looked at my watch. "It's Lorelei and Ben and Gus. I told her to stay away until now."

Saul looked around the room, looking for a plan, I assumed.

"How did you get away from Lorelei? Why aren't you with them anyway?" I asked the question that had been bothering me since Saul had walked in on me.

"I knew something wasn't kosher, she was too jittery, too anxious to get us out of here. Telling us that you needed us to come and get you. That you could be in danger." He shook his head. "That girl will never make a good poker player."

"So what did you tell her? The house was empty when I got here."

"I told her I needed to go over to Jimmy's. To make sure he was okay. I took my own car. She seemed to be okay with that. That's when it was obvious she just wanted us out of the house. She didn't care that we were together. That's when I knew I needed to get back here. Plus, if everything was kosher here, it would allow me to set up the fake attempt on me."

"Was Jack here earlier? Did he go with them?" I was thinking if Saul had seen through Lorelei, surely Jack had as well. Although he might have made the same assumptions Lorelei probably had.

If he hadn't been glad he'd washed his hands of me before, I'm sure he was now.

"He didn't want to. I think he suspected Lorelei was up to something too, but," He lifted his hands. "What could he do? He had to go with them. For protection."

"What about your protection?"

He shrugged. "He had officers follow me to Jimmy's. So I went there, but I only stayed a moment and then came back. Officers followed me home, too. And of course there are the officers outside." Humor dripped from him as he said, "Protecting us."

"My car's in the driveway. Whoever came in, they'll know I'm home."

"Mine too," Saul said, his mind working furiously. I'm sure this was a far cry from the ending he'd had in mind to his vendetta against Ben.

"Push your chair to the table. Pretend we're playing checkers." Now he was the one buying time.

But whereas I'd been buying time to try and find a way out of this all, I knew Saul was trying to buy time to finish the job.

To tell Ben about the baby. To hurt him as Saul had been hurt.

And then kill him.

I did as Saul told me. We quickly settled in at the table, Saul's back to the door, blocking anyone's view of the gun he had trained on my gut.

"Okay, Hannah, darling, let's see that famous poker face."

"I won't say anything, Saul. We can get rid of whoever's out there and then leave out the side door. I have my keys in my pocket. We can go somewhere and…work this all out."

He let out a bark of laughter. "Yes, dear. Let's do that. But remember, if you send some kind of signal, say something off, not only will it harm you, but it will cost the lives of anyone else you drag into this. Jack. Lorelei. Gus."

A sadness came over his face. "I've killed one of dearest friends, Hannah. I'm an old man. There's nothing left for me now. All I want is to have my revenge on Ben. To avenge my sweet Rachael." I saw the subtle movement as he fidgeted with his gun hand under the table. "It really doesn't matter what else happens from there."

Which means he wouldn't hesitate to kill Jack or Lorelei or me if we tried to stop him.

It would be best to do as I'd said, get rid of whoever was heading down the hallway. No matter who came to that door, I wouldn't be able to send any kind of sign.

I jumped—as did Saul—at the loud knock on the door.

"Saul?" Jack's deep voice asked.

"Remember," Saul whispered. "No signs of any kind. Or it all ends now."

I had thought—on some level—that I might be able to talk Saul out of hurting anybody else. I had given up hope of trying to talk him out of hurting Ben—another reason to get Saul out of the house calmly and without attention.

I nodded to Saul's warning. I wasn't going to do anything. I truly believed that getting rid of Jack and getting Saul out of here by myself was now our best bet.

The best bet of saving Ben and making sure Lorelei and Gus were safe.

And Jack.

"Yes, Jack," Saul called. "Come in."

"Saul, have you seen—" Jack's voice stopped when he saw me playing checkers with Saul. "Oh, you're in here. I saw your car out front."

"Hi, Jack," I said. Any tension I was feeling about Saul having a gun pointed at me could be construed as awkwardness over seeing Jack for the first time since he'd dumped me.

"You're back," he stated the obvious.

"Yep," I said and moved one of my checkers.

"Are you all back, Jack?" Saul asked. He'd turned his head to look at Jack, his body, and the gun, stayed pointed at me. "Or are Lorelei and Gus and Ben still out?"

"We're all back," Jack said. "Or were back. Lorelei has taken Gus back to his apartment to get some more clothes. The patrol car went with them."

Saul laughed and turned back to me, a glint in his eye, knowing that Ben was alone out in the front and that the patrol car was gone. "That sounds like Gus, needing more clothes." He used his non-gun hand to move a checker, then put the hand back down in his lap, under the table. "Jimmy was fine, and a little cranky, so I came back here," Saul explained to Jack even though he hadn't asked.

Jack was looking only at me, with those soft brown eyes tracking every move I made.

God, he looked so good standing there in his chambray shirt and khakis, his tie totally wrecked. He looked tired, but then he had since I'd met him. The familiarity of him flowed over me.

As did regret.

I calmed my emotions, pretended I was at a poker table playing the top dogs instead of checkers with an octogenarian.

An octogenarian with a gun trained on me.

"Jimmy cranky? That's a new one," I said and chuckled. Saul laughed with me. Just two pals playing checkers, talking trash about a buddy.

Nothing to see here, folks, move along, I silently begged.

Jack never cracked a smile.

"Can I talk to you privately?" Jack asked me.

I looked at him. With our relationship in the state it was, it would make perfect sense for me to say, "I think we've said all there is to say, Jack." Which is exactly what I did.

He looked at me for a moment. I expected the brow raise, but he didn't offer it up.

That, more than anything else, told me it was definitely over with Jack.

He sighed. "Yeah, you're right. I just wanted to make sure…"

I looked at him, waiting for him.

He raised his hands, then dropped them. In defeat? Resignation? "You're right. It's nothing. I'm just glad you're back and that you're…okay."

"I am," I said, making another move on the checkerboard.

"Okay, then. Well, Frank is here now, so I'm going to take off."

"Are you coming back?" Saul asked what I desperately wanted to know.

"I'll be available while the investigation is ongoing," he said, his cop voice, and face, firmly in place. "But Detective Botz will be here most of the time."

"Oy, what'd you do this time, Hannah," Saul teased me.

I wanted to throw the checkerboard in his face. Ah, but that pesky revolver.

"Just the usual, Saul."

Saul chuckled, like men tossed me aside all the time. They didn't, even though it sure felt like it recently.

Jack looked around the room, crossed to both sliding glass doors, checked the locks. Closed the horizontal blinds up tight, making sure there were no big gaps, even though they'd already been closed. Saul's movements were subtle, but he kept the gun out of Jack's sight the entire time. He even put both hands up on top of the table once while Jack was looking in his direction, but it wasn't enough time for me to do anything.

Not that I would have with Jack still in the room.

Finally, apparently satisfied that the room was safe from all outside threats, Jack walked back to the door.

"I'm glad you're back, Ms. Dawson," Jack said, pushing a knife into me. Back to Ms. Dawson.

"I'm back, and have no plans to leave anytime soon... Detective," I said.

"Saul," Jack said as he departed.

"Goodbye, Jack," Saul said, his back to the door, to a retreating Jack.

Saul was out of his chair seconds after Jack had shut the door. It reminded me how spry the old man was. I'd be wise not to think of Ben's infirmity when dealing with Saul.

Saul locked the door then looked around the room. "You're right. We need to leave here, Hannah. We'll work this out somewhere else. I'll come back for..."

He didn't finish his sentence, but he didn't need to. I knew that the only thing driving Saul now was killing Ben. His life had come down to this burning, ferocious need to kill his best friend.

Nothing—and no one—was going to get in his way.

"Right, Saul." I said, but I knew then that he had no intention of working anything out, his blood lust for Ben was too high.

And I was to be another casualty. Just as Danny had been. As Gus had almost been.

"We'll wait for a few minutes, then leave through the door." He pointed toward the glass door that opened to the side yard.

"Okay, Saul, that's what we'll do."

He'd get me out of here, kill me, dump me somewhere, then come back for Ben.

I thought furiously for options. I figured it would still be safest to get him away from the house. Maybe not safest for me, but definitely for Ben.

Besides, maybe I could overpower him when the time came. He was agile and strong, but he was still in his eighties.

The minutes passed, Saul looking at the door to the side, me watching him. "Okay," he finally said. "Let's go. Slowly, Hannah."

I pushed the chair away from the table and stood. Saul was facing the door leading to the side of the house. I faced the door that led to the patio.

And then I saw it. The barrel of a gun, slipping through a tiny gap in the vertical blinds, coming in through the patio door. A door that Jack had just checked the locks on a moment ago.

It moved in a little more, so slowly, so quietly. I could see a little bit more of the hand, then the wrist.

Wearing a chambray shirt.

Twenty-Seven
❖

"SAUL, WHY DON'T YOU PUT THE GUN DOWN NOW? I said I'd leave with you. You're right, let's just go out the side door now," I said, hopefully tipping Jack off that I knew of his presence—and that Saul had a gun.

Though if Jack was skulking around outside, he must have figured something was up. That's why instead of checking the locks on the door, he'd unlocked it. He had also probably figured out that a gun was most likely involved.

Now he knew for sure.

Saul looked at me like I was crazy, repeating myself, stating the obvious. But Saul knew I wasn't crazy, and he was no dummy.

He started to swing back to the main door, the door Jack had left through, expecting something from that direction.

"Come in, come in, Jack," I yelled. It was enough for Saul to turn fully to the door leading to the hall, and away from Jack.

I dove for the bathroom door, slamming it shut behind me.

I snatched the plastic garbage bag from the floor where I'd left it as I jumped into the bathtub, dropping to the bottom just as Saul shot through the door.

Right where I would have been standing to get the gun.

The enormity that Saul really would kill me rushed through me.

Stupid, I know. He'd told me all his secrets; of course he'd had no intention of me being able to repeat them. But somehow I thought that Saul wouldn't be able to do it.

Not to me.

I fumbled with the bag, trying to right it to get the gun out, praying Saul was only bluffing earlier about it being unloaded.

Who knew? Maybe his last bullet was the one that had missed Ben.

No. He would have been ready. That was why he'd so easily agreed to come and stay here when I'd suggested it. How fortunate for a hunter to be under the same roof as his prey.

As the bag unwrapped and I could grab the towel and gun out from it, I heard Jack's voice. "Drop the gun, Saul."

I didn't know if Jack had fully entered the room or if he was protecting himself with the glass door and side of the house.

The only thing I heard was the harsh sound of my breathing. Had Saul surrendered to Jack? Was he even now being handcuffed?

I slid out of the bathtub, staying low to the ground, inching my way to the door.

"Stay in the bathroom, Johanna," Jack called out. I stayed.

"I mean it, Saul. I don't want to hurt you. Just drop the gun."

"No, Jack," Saul said, determination in his voice. "I can't."

"I know you don't want to hurt Hannah, Saul."

"I didn't Jack. I never intended for her to be involved in this."

I noticed he didn't say he wouldn't kill me now, though. Now that I knew everything. But Saul had to know that the jig was up. No way was he going to be able to go through both Jack and me, both armed, to get to Ben.

I heard the moment he figured it out, his loud sigh carrying through the door to the bathroom. "I'll tell you what, Jack," Saul said.

"No, Saul, I'll tell you—" Something must have happened

to stop Jack. I was at the door now, and I opened it a crack. Saul had lifted the gun to his own head.

"Don't do it, Saul. It's not that bad. We can figure this out."

Saul's move didn't sit right with me. I knew he would have killed me in order to carry out his warped mission of vengeance. And he loved me.

Killing himself before he was able to tell Ben about his lost child and avenge Rachael was not in his game plan.

"He's bluffing," I said. I started to rise. As I did the Terrible Towel finally fell away from the gun that had in most likelihood killed Danny. I aimed it at Saul.

A look of resolve crossed Saul's face.

Jack kept his gun on Saul, but his eyes quickly moved to me, took in the Towel, the gun and my fierce determination.

"Put the gun down, Johanna," Jack said.

"He's bluffing, Jack."

"It doesn't matter. Put the gun down." There was a steeliness in his voice that I had never heard before.

"I'm going to do it, Jack," Saul said, ignoring me and the gun I had aimed at him. "I killed Danny. I have nothing to live for. I can't live out the rest of my days in a prison."

Both Jack and I didn't move our guns, both still aimed at Saul.

"Give me one last request, Jack."

"Put the gun down, Saul, and we'll talk about it."

"Let me tell Ben I'm sorry that I shot at him. Let me seek forgiveness from my friends."

"No," I said sharply.

"Put the gun down, Saul, and then we can talk about it. You know I can't let Ben in here with you holding a gun."

"But you won't bring him in without it, either, will you?" He kept the gun to his head.

It was a classic Mexican stand-off, and we could have stood that way forever. And then I heard the unmistakable sound of

Ben's walker coming down the hallway. Of course he would have heard the shot from Saul.

"Hannah, darling, are you here? Are you all right?" Ben called from down the hallway. The squeak of the metal along the ceramic tile sending shivers down my spine.

"Ben, stay away. Go back. I'm fine."

"Ben," Saul called. "Ben. I need you."

"Stay back, Ben. Don't come in here," I yelled, raising my gun at Saul. "Shut up, Saul."

"Put the gun down, Johanna," Jack said his own gun never leaving Saul. "Go back into the bathroom."

"Like hell," I said.

"Ben, hurry, Ben," Saul cried out, his eyes dancing with vengeance. He looked at me, a smile crept up his face. A face so distorted with hatred I barely recognized it. "Hannah needs you, Ben."

Ben's walker was closer now, nearly to the door. Ben would never believe Saul was who killed Danny, not without proof, so yelling that out wasn't going to stop him. "No, Ben, please, go away." I tried to control my voice, but the fear in it came through and I heard Ben's shuffle speed up so that he was outside the door.

Jack had moved closer to the door that Ben was approaching. "Saul, drop the gun or I'll shoot," he said. But I knew he wouldn't, at least not while Saul still had the gun pointed to his own head. He was only an imminent threat to himself.

But I knew something Jack didn't. That nothing in this world was going to stop Saul from killing Ben.

"Ben, please," I whispered, my throat going closed as I saw the doorknob start to turn.

I looked at Jack who had not taken his eyes off of Saul. He tightened his hand on the trigger of the gun.

I looked at Saul, who began to smile as he saw the doorknob slowly turn. He moved so quickly, his gun coming away from his

head and toward the door.
A gunshot rang out.

Twenty-Eight
❖❖

JACK MOVED QUICKLY TO ME, took the gun out of my hand.

The gun with which I'd shot Saul.

"Stay out, Ben," Jack said. He'd already moved to the door, shutting it just as Ben was opening it. He kicked the gun Saul had held away from Saul's fallen body, across the room. "Everything's okay. Hannah's okay. I need you to call 911. Can you do that?"

"Saul? Hannah?" Ben cried out from behind the door.

I started to go to him, but would have had to step over Saul's body. Jack's hand up stopped me as well. "I'm fine, Ben," I called out. "Jack's right. It's okay. Just go call 911." I heard the shuffling of his walker retreating down the hallway.

There was a phone on Saul's bedside table. My cell was in my pocket. And I assumed Jack probably had a phone on him or some kind of police radio. But calling 911, getting him away from this room, was what would be best for Ben.

He didn't need to see Saul's body. And then the body moved. Groaned.

Dear God, I hadn't killed him.

I wasn't sure if that was a good thing or a bad thing.

Jack moved to Saul's side, knelt down, pushed Saul's shirt back, inspecting the wound. He turned to me and gave a small shake of his head. Saul wasn't going to last.

"Ben," Saul croaked out.

Even now, as the man lay dying, my protective instincts for Ben held fast.

"Don't let Ben in here. Don't let him anywhere near Saul," I said to Jack. I didn't really think Jack would lead a parade of people back here, but I knew Ben would try to see his friend after calling 911, and that could not happen.

Yes, Saul was disarmed, and dying, but his words to Ben could be, would be, well…mightier than the sword.

"I won't," Jack said. He looked around the room, started to scrub his hand across his face then realized he was holding a gun in each one. "Jesus, Johanna. Why the hell didn't you just go back into the bathroom?" He moved to where he'd kicked Saul's gun. He picked it up carefully and put it, and the one I'd shot Saul with down on the bed on the other side of the room. He hung on to his own.

"What a fucking mess," he said looking at me, and then Saul's body. "I wasn't going to let him hurt Ben," he said. "You should have let me handle it."

I shrugged. On some level I knew that. But I'd been taking care of Ben for a long time, and it seemed only fitting that I be the one to take care of him now.

"But you didn't trust that I would, right?" Jack said.

"No, it's not that, it's just that—"

"Just like you won't trust me to help you with whatever trouble your gambling got you into."

"Jack, I…" But what could I say. There was some truth to his words.

Saul groaned again and I moved to him, dropped to my knees. Emotions warred inside me. I'd loved this man and he was in pain. Pain I had caused him.

But he was obviously not the same man who had been my friend for the past ten years.

I cradled Saul's head in my lap. "I'm sorry, Saul," I said.

And I was. Not sorry that I'd shot him, not if it meant saving Ben. But sorry that it had come to that.

"Hannah," Saul whispered. "Ben?"

"He's out in the front of the house calling for an ambulance for you Saul. Just hold on," I said, though I knew an ambulance wouldn't be able to help Saul.

"So," he said, his voice holding more New York than normal. "He won't pay for what he did to my Rachael."

"He paid, Saul," I said. "You all paid. You. Rachael. Ben. You all made mistakes. And you all paid."

"Not enough," he said his strength draining from him, but the fury still in his voice. A gurgle of blood came up as he coughed. I wiped it away with my sleeve.

"Stop, Saul. Save your strength."

Jack stepped over to us then. Saul looked up, his eyes focusing on Jack. He smiled at Jack, but the effort it took cost him. He coughed again, his whole body wracking with a shudder. "Ah, but I won in the end," Saul said still looking at Jack.

He slowly turned his head from Jack, reluctantly, as if he didn't want to take his eyes off him, who was surely no threat to Saul now.

He craned his neck to look up at me. "I won, Hannah. Because Ben will never know his child. He took my Rachael, but I took away his child."

"Oh, Saul," I said. I was trying to think of what else to say, what would ease his tortured soul when the light went out of his eyes.

Moments later it seemed, although I'm not sure how long I actually sat there holding Saul's limp head in my lap, Detective Botz eased me away.

The room was filling with policemen. I was handed over to

a uniformed officer. Detective Botz turned to Jack.

"What the hell happened?"

Jack shrugged. "It was Saul all along. All of it. Some kind of vendetta but I don't have all the details yet. Ms. Dawson was alone with him for quite a while, so I'm assuming she has the entire story."

I nodded.

"And you had to shoot him?" Frank Botz said to his partner.

I prepared myself. At least Ben was safe. Lorelei would look after him if I had to go in for questioning, or was charged with killing Saul. The slush fund would have to be raided to afford a high-priced lawyer, but I'd probably walk. It just might take a while.

"Ms. Dawson shot him." Jack said and the policemen all turned to me. The patrolman assigned to me, slowly reached out and put his hand around my upper arm.

Jack took a deep breath, let it out. "Saul had turned his gun on her," Jack lied. "It was an act of self defense."

The patrolman let go of my arm, motioned for me to leave the room. As I passed Jack, I stopped. Jack nodded for the patrolman to go ahead and he did. Frank turned his back on us and walked to the other side of the room.

"That's not exactly how it happened," I whispered.

He looked back at me, his brown eyes warm. "No, but if I explained how it went down there'd be a lot more questions and reports than there's already going to be. You were right. Sometimes you need to bend the rules."

I nodded and started to leave the room—now the crime scene—anxious to get to Ben, who must have been going crazy out in the living room where some other policemen were waiting with him.

But something occurred to me, and I turned back to Jack.

"How did you know? How did you know to come back? I was so careful. I didn't want to put anybody else in danger."

He raised a brow at me and a feeling of…hope?…rushed through me. "I told you in Pittsburgh, Johanna…you have a tell."

Twenty-Nine
❖

THREE DAYS LATER—three very long days—I got dressed for Saul's funeral.

I put on one of my stylish black suits that normally only came out of my closet for final table television appearances.

They were getting entirely too much use in the last month with first Danny's funeral and now Saul's.

Lorelei and I debated holding a funeral for Saul. He had no family left, we were the only ones that would have done it. I didn't want to, still pissed at Saul, but Lorelei felt it would be good closure for all of us. Especially for Ben, who had nearly fallen apart when he learned about Saul's motives.

We talked to the rabbi, found out Saul would not be allowed to be buried in the Jewish cemetery. So in the end, we decided to have Saul cremated and planned a memorial service of sorts. It wouldn't be at the Jewish funeral home, but a non-denominational one.

But we would be there. To say goodbye.

I'd spent a fair amount of time in the last three days talking with the police, though Jack and I had never been alone together…probably by choice on his part.

I'd told them what Saul had told me about Danny dying. And that had been confirmed first by the coroner and then by Danny's physician that he'd told Danny that he was indeed dying. The dates matched up with Saul's story.

I told them about Saul not meaning to hit Gus. Gus remembered dropping the mail, moving at the last minute. He seemed to hang on to that like a lifeline, allowing himself to come to terms with his best friend targeting him.

I told them about the whole plan being about revenge on Ben for his affair with Rachael years earlier.

I didn't tell them about Ben's child being given away. Who would that serve? Not knowing who Saul had dealt with nearly forty years ago, there was probably no way to find that child now. A child who would be grown, probably with kids of their own.

And it would have broken Ben's heart to know that he and Rachael had had a child together. One that she had given up as her penance for being with Ben.

Jack had heard Saul mention Ben's child, but had never brought it up, either in front of me or in any kind of report that I had seen. Botz hadn't asked me about it, so I assumed Jack hadn't even mentioned it to his partner.

If I were ever able to speak to him alone again, I'd be sure to thank him for that.

I checked my appearance one final time in the mirror and started to leave my room but was stopped by my phone going off. I started to reach for the iphone on my dresser but realized the sound was coming from my bedside table. It was my old cell phone.

A feeling of dread ran through me. I didn't know who was calling, but knew it was probably someone I didn't want to talk to.

I should have just left, just walked out of the room, but I didn't. I walked to the stand, sat on the bed, smoothing my skirt across my lap and picked up the phone.

"Hello?" I said.

"JoJo?" Raymond Joseph said.

My shoulders sagged. Somehow I knew he'd make this call, that he wouldn't be able to resist. I'd just hoped that maybe I was wrong, or at the very least I wouldn't be getting this call so soon.

"Yes."

"You know who this is?" he said, not wanting to say his name over the phone. I looked at the caller ID on my phone. Unknown caller. He was probably at a phone booth. He was a smart kid, Raymond, that's why he'd been chosen.

"I know who this is," I said.

"What's the line for the Michigan State game?"

"I have no idea," I said truthfully.

He snorted on the other end, not believing me. "Come on, don't shit me."

"I've been out of circulation for a few days. I haven't seen any lines." No need to tell him how I'd spent the days since I'd left him in Dubuque.

"USA Today has it at eleven," he said. He'd done his homework. He was so promising, it broke my heart thinking about what he would become.

Me.

"That's probably what it is…" I almost said here but caught myself, though I probably wasn't fooling him. "In Vegas."

"Would you pay for a guarantee that Michigan State would lose by ten or less?"

"No," I said. I heard a hiss in his voice. "But I know someone who would," I added.

"And would that someone pay me part up front? And would you be able to bet that part for me?"

I sighed. I had fed a hungry dog, and he'd followed me home. It seemed I now owned him. "Yes, I believe he would. And yes, I would do that for you."

There was a pause on the line and then he said, "Fuck." I didn't know if it was out of relief, dread, happiness or something else all together. Raymond had just had experienced a hummer.

Or a cock squeeze as Jimmy called it. Either way, he was hooked.

"When can you make arrangements? So I know for sure. How much do you think we're looking at?"

"Well, you're unknown to my…associate…he has no reason to trust you, so probably no more than five thousand."

"Unknown? I…"

"He doesn't know you were involved," I said.

"Five? What the fuck? You paid me twen—" he cut himself off. Smart.

"We're talking playing the spread here right? Not an outright loss?"

"Right."

"Well, that would pay a lot less."

I waited for Raymond to absorb this. Praying he wouldn't ask what the money would be for a loss. I'd damaged this kid enough.

"Okay. Go on," he said.

"After this, and you're…proven…I would imagine your fee could go up."

I didn't like speaking for Vince. And Vince probably didn't like me speaking for him, but I knew he wouldn't want an opportunity like this to slip away, either.

"All right. Five. But get as much up front as you can, bet it all."

"Fine."

"When can you call me back?"

I looked down at my black suit, pantyhose and pumps. The funeral wouldn't last long—who was going to get up and talk about Saul for hours? I'd have to get Ben and Gus home and stay here for a bit, but then I could probably meet Vince later tonight. "I have to be somewhere right now, but I think I can probably get back to you really late tonight. Or tomorrow morning."

"Tomorrow would be better. I'll call you at eleven. My

time." Very smart.

I hung up and left to go bury another friend. Or a man who had once been my friend.

There were more people than I'd expected at the funeral home. Saul had known tons of people of course working in the casinos for years, but after the news of Saul's guilt had been in the papers I figured people would stay away.

Maybe they hadn't seen the papers or heard the news. Or maybe they were attending out of a fascination, a disbelief that Saul was capable of murder and plotting more murder.

Or maybe, like us, they chose to remember a man who at one time had been a good friend and to say goodbye to *that* man.

We were brought to the front and there we sat. Gus, Lorelei, Jimmy, Ben and me. I could tell the room was filling up behind us, but I kept my eyes forward, my hand in Ben's.

Saul's ashes sat in an urn on top of a table in the front.

The service was mercifully short. At one point I saw a tear stream down Ben's face, but his demeanor never changed. He sat stoically by my side.

I couldn't imagine the thoughts that must have been playing havoc in his mind.

Gus and Lorelei seemed to be comforting each other. I put my hand on Jimmy's arm for a moment and he let it stay there and he brought his other hand up and squeezed mine.

There'd be no recession with pall bearers at this service, so when the funeral director motioned to us, we got up and started down the aisle.

It was then that I saw Jack and Frank Botz sitting near the back. They both wore suits and ties, and it pained me somehow to see Frank in a plain blue-striped tie instead of his regular cartoon characters.

They both nodded to Ben and me as we walked by. I could feel Jack's eyes staying on me, almost burning a hole in my back.

A few rows later I saw Vince. He must have seen my surprise, but he only nodded to me. I nodded back. Ben ignored him, but Jimmy and Gus both nodded at him.

The funeral director asked me into his office where I settled up with him. Lorelei and I had both agreed that we would pay for Saul's funeral expenses. We didn't tell Ben. He didn't ask.

He handed me the urn with Saul's ashes. I was surprised at how light it felt in my hands. It seemed like the older one lived, the heavier your urn should be, but I knew that was ridiculous.

By the time I got outside, the parking lot had turned into an informal meet and greet as will happen at funerals, especially one that didn't have a burial planned or an after-service reception of some kind to go to. Some of these people hadn't seen each other in a while, a lot of them casino retirees, and they wanted to catch up with each other.

I just wanted to go home.

Gus was still staying with us. He hadn't mentioned going back to his place and Lorelei seemed to like fussing over him.

I turned to Jimmy. "You want to come over for a while?"

He shrugged. "You having people over?"

I shook my head. "Not people. Just us."

He nodded. "I'll be there."

I tried to find Vince in the crowd. If I could talk with him now, privately, then I wouldn't have to leave the house later.

I found him as he was nearing what I assumed was his car. I'd always met him at places, had never seen him arrive or depart. He drove an understated sedan, but a high-end one. Not flashy, but expensive. Kind of like Vince himself.

"Vince," I said and he turned to face me. "Thanks for coming," I said as I neared him.

"Saul was well-respected. He was a pioneer of the sports book industry."

I nodded, appreciating Vince leaving it at that.

"Do you have a second? There's something I'd like to discuss with you."

He gave me a look that I swear held pity. He thought I wanted to borrow money again? All ready? "It's not about me. Well, not directly."

His eyes narrowed now. "Sure, Anna." He looked around at the people milling around, some coming this way to their cars. "Let's get in the car." He walked around, leading the way and opened the passenger side door for me. I got in and settled the urn on my lap. He shut the door and returned to the driver's side where he joined me in the car.

It took only a few minutes to lay out Raymond's intentions to Vince. The idea of a sure thing, one that was only a junior—who had many more games in him, elated Vince.

I assumed it elated Vince, he showed the same amount of emotion he always did, which was to say none.

Our business completed, I stepped out of Vince's car and scanned the parking lot to see Ben, who happened to be standing next to Jack.

Who happened to be watching me. Leave Vince's car.

A look of sadness came over Jack's face and I knew whatever hope I felt that maybe Jack would be able to see past my gambling—and its involvement with people like Vince—came crashing down.

I straightened my shoulders, gave a small shrug; a this is who I am kind of directive.

Jack gave me a small, sad smile and nodded at me, then moved to help Ben toward our car.

He walked slowly beside Ben and something about their movements....so similar. Somebody said something to Ben and both he and Jack turned to address that person, their profiles at the same angle, and my knees nearly gave way.

I knew what had happened a year ago that started this

whole chain of events. What had made Saul snap.

Jack Schiller had moved to town.

A sudden rush came over me of voices and images from the past few weeks.

Something about seeing Jack that first time outside the municipal building when neither of us would go in, noticing his eyes, how they twinkled like Ben's. How something about him seemed so familiar to me.

I thought of the how the picture of Rachael—one I had seen thousands of time—had suddenly seemed different, as if I knew her, recognized her. Enough to ask Saul if she'd been from around the Las Vegas area, thinking maybe she still had family here.

She did, it seemed.

And right now, he was helping Ben into my car.

Jack helped his father get in the Lexus, folded up his walker and placed it in the rear storage area. He shut the door, moved back to the front, leaned into the open window and said something to Ben.

His father, Ben.

Ben must have answered him because Jack was nodding. Then he patted Ben's arm and stood up, stepped back and looked right at me.

He gave another small nod and turned to walk away.

I started to call out to him but stopped as Lorelei and Gus made their way over to the car. "We're ready to go, Jo," Lorelei called out to me, her new diamond stud earrings catching the light.

I walked to the Lexus, still watching Jack's retreating back. He was still within hearing range, but I said nothing, just waited as Lorelei helped Gus into the back seat and then got in herself.

I handed the urn to her, and shut her door. I crossed to the driver's side and got in. Jack had reached his car, turned one last time and looked at us. Then he got in his car and pulled away.

I started the Lexus and drove my family home.

Acknowledgments

A big thank you to Holli Bertram and Colleen Gleason, who gave great feedback on this story, even though they didn't know a thing about sports gambling. (they do, now!)

A shout out to my besties, Kelly Campbell and Amy Pellizzaro, who have been incredibly supportive as I made my way through these uncharted waters. And who bore with me in Vegas.

Ted Kearly gave me a peek into the world of professional poker, and Tom Kearly told me about Black Sunday. Thank you, both.

And a special thank you to my agent, Jodi Reamer, whose belief in this book never wavered.

The Anna Dawson's Vegas series continues with

AGAINST THE SPREAD
ANNA DAWSON'S VEGAS, BOOK 2

Try Mara Jacobs's *New York Times* bestselling Worth series

Worth The Weight
Worth The Drive
Worth The Fall
Worth The Effort
Totally Worth Christmas

Find out more at
www.MaraJacobs.com

Mara Jacobs is the *New York Times* and *USA Today* bestselling author of The Worth Series

After graduating from Michigan State University with a degree in advertising, Mara spent several years working at daily newspapers in Advertising sales and production. This certainly prepared her for the world of deadlines!

Mara writes mysteries with romance, thrillers with romance, and romances with…well, you get it.

Forever a Yooper (someone who hails from Michigan's glorious Upper Peninsula), Mara now resides in the East Lansing, Michigan, area where she is better able to root on her beloved Spartans.

You can find out more about her books at **www.marajacobs.com**

Made in the USA
Lexington, KY
02 December 2014